Dear Reader,

Harlequin is celebrating its sixtieth anniversary in 2009 with an entire year's worth of special programs showcasing the talent and variety that have made us the world's leading romance publisher.

With this collection of vintage novels, we are thrilled to be able to journey with you to the roots of our success: six books that hark back to the very earliest days of our history, when the fare was decidedly adventurous, often mysterious and full of passion—1950s-style!

It is such fun to be able to present these works with their original text and cover art, which we hope both current readers and collectors of popular fiction will find entertaining.

Thank you for helping us to achieve and celebrate this milestone!

Warmly,

[signature]

Donna Hayes,
Publisher and CEO

D1559253

The Harlequin Story

To millions of readers around the world, Harlequin and romance fiction are synonymous. With a publishing record of 120 titles a month in 29 languages in 107 international markets on 6 continents, there is no question of Harlequin's success.

But like all good stories, Harlequin's has had some twists and turns.

In 1949, Harlequin was founded in Winnipeg, Canada. In the beginning, the company published a wide range of books—including the likes of Agatha Christie, Sir Arthur Conan Doyle, James Hadley Chase and Somerset Maugham—all for the low price of twenty-five cents.

By the mid 1950s, Richard Bonnycastle was in complete control of the company, and at the urging of his wife—and chief editor—began publishing the romances of British firm Mills & Boon. The books sold so well that Harlequin eventually bought Mills & Boon outright in 1971.

In 1970, Harlequin expanded its distribution into the U.S. and contracted its first American author so that it could offer the first truly American romances. By 1980, that concept became a full-fledged series called Harlequin Superromance, the first romance line to originate outside the U.K.

The 1980s saw continued growth into global markets as well as the purchase of American publisher, Silhouette Books. By 1992, Harlequin dominated the genre, and ten years later was publishing more than half of all romances released in North America.

Now in our sixtieth anniversary year, Harlequin remains true to its history of being *the* romance publisher, while constantly creating innovative ways to deliver variety in what women want to read. And as we forge ahead into other types of fiction nonfiction, we are always mindful of the hallmark of our s over the past six decades—guaranteed entertainment!

YOU
NEVER KNOW
with WOMEN

JAMES HADLEY CHASE

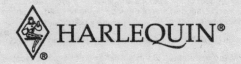
HARLEQUIN®

TORONTO • NEW YORK • LONDON
AMSTERDAM • PARIS • SYDNEY • HAMBURG
STOCKHOLM • ATHENS • TOKYO • MILAN • MADRID
PRAGUE • WARSAW • BUDAPEST • AUCKLAND

Recycling programs
for this product may
not exist in your area.

ISBN-13: 978-0-373-83749-6

YOU NEVER KNOW WITH WOMEN

Copyright © 1949 by Hervey Raymond

This edition published by arrangement with Harlequin Books S.A.

® and TM are trademarks of the publisher. Trademarks indicated with
® are registered in the United States Patent and Trademark Office, the
Canadian Trade Marks Office and in other countries.

www.eHarlequin.com

Printed in U.S.A.

JAMES HADLEY CHASE

was a pseudonym for Rene Brabazon Raymond. Born in England on Christmas Eve 1906, Chase left home at the age of eighteen and worked at a number of different jobs before he settled on being a writer. With a map and a slang dictionary, Chase wrote his first book, *No Orchids for Miss Blandish*, in six weeks. It was published in 1939 and became one of the bestselling books of the decade. It was later made into a stage play in London and then into a film in 1948, which was later remade in 1971 by Robert Aldrich as *The Grissom Gang*. Chase went on to write more than eighty mysteries before his death on February 6, 1985.

were shot for the premiere of Jesse around six
and stayed that way until one the following morning

CHAPTER ONE

THE RAT HOLE THEY RENTED me for an office was on the sixth floor of a dilapidated building in the dead-end section of San Luis Beach. From sunrise to dusk the noise of the out-town traffic and the kids yelling at one another in the low-rent tenement strip across the way came through the open window in a continuous blast. As a place to concentrate in, it ranked lower than the mind of a third-rate hoofer in a tank-town vaudeville act.

That was why I did most of my headwork at night, and for the past five nights I had been alone in the office flexing my brain muscles while I tried to find a way out of the jam. But I was licked and I knew it. There was no way out of this jam. Even at that it took me a couple of brain sessions to reach this conclusion before I decided to cut my losses and quit.

I arrived at the decision at ten minutes after eleven o'clock on a hot July night exactly eighteen months after I had first come to San Luis Beach. The decision, now it was made, called for a drink, and I was holding up the office bottle in the light to convince myself it was as empty as my trouser pockets when I heard footsteps on the stairs.

The other offices on my floor and on the floors below were shut for the night. They closed around six o'clock and stayed that way until nine the following morning. I and the office mice had popped into our holes as the footsteps creaked up the stairs. The only visitors I'd had in the past month were the cops. It didn't seem likely that Lieutenant of the Police Redfern would call at this hour, but you never knew. Redfern did odd things, and he might have thought up an idea of getting rid of me. He liked me no more than he liked a rattlesnake—perhaps even a little less—and if he could run me out of town even at eleven o'clock at night it would be all right with him.

The footsteps came along the passage. They were in no hurry: slow, measured steps with a lot of weight in them.

I felt in my vest pocket for a butt, struck a match and lit up. It was my last butt, and I had been saving it up for an occasion like this.

There was a light in the passage, and it reflected on the frosted panel of my door. The desk lamp made a pool of light on the blotter, but the rest of the rat hole was dark. The panel of light facing me picked up a shadow as big feet came to rest outside my door. The shadow was immense. The shoulders overflowed the lighted panel; on the pumpkinlike head was the kind of hat the cloak-and-dagger boys used to wear when I was knee-high to a grasshopper.

Fingernails tapped on the panel, the doorknob turned, the door swung open as I shifted the desk lamp.

The man who stood in the doorway looked as big as a two-ton truck. He was as thick as he was broad, and had a ball-round face, skin tight with hard, pink fat. A black hairline mustache sat below a nose like the beak of an octopus, and little black eyes peered at me over two ridges of fat, like sloes in sugar icing. He might have been fifty, not more. There was the usual breathlessness about him that goes with fat people. The crown of his wide black hat touched the top of the door, and he had to turn his gross body an inch or so to enter the office. An astra-khan collar set off his long, tight-fitting black coat and his feet were encased in immaculately polished shoes, the welts of which seemed a good inch and a half thick.

"Mr. Jackson?" His voice was hoarse and scratchy and thin. Not the kind of voice you'd expect to come out of the barrel of a body he carried around on legs that must have been as thick as young trees to support it.

I nodded.

"Mr. Floyd Jackson?"

I nodded again.

"Ah!" The exclamation came out on a little puff of breath. He moved farther into the room, pushed the door shut without turning. "My card, Mr. Jackson." He dropped a card on the blotter. He and I and the desk filled up the office to capacity, and the air in the room began to fight for its breath.

I looked at the card without moving. It didn't tell me anything but his name. No address, nothing to say who he was. Just two words: *Cornelius Gorman*.

While I looked at the card, he pulled up the office chair to the desk. It was a good strong chair, built to last, but it flinched as he lowered his bulk onto it. Now he had sat down there seemed a little more space in the room—not much, but enough to let the air circulate again.

He folded his fat hands on the top of his stick. A diamond, a shade smaller than a doorknob, flashed like a beacon from his little finger. Cornelius Gorman might be a phoney, but he had money. I could smell it, and I have a very sensitive nose when it comes to smelling money.

"I've been making enquiries about you, Mr. Jackson," he said, and his small eyes searched my face. "I hear you are quite a character."

The last time he called, Lieutenant of the Police

Redfern had said more or less the same thing, only he had used a coarser expression.

I didn't say anything, but waited, and wondered just how much he had found out about me.

"They tell me you're smart and tricky—very, very tricky and smooth," the fat man went on in his scratchy voice. "You have brains, they say, and you're not over-honest. You're a reckless character, Mr. Jackson, but you have courage and nerve and you're tough." He looked at me from over the top of his diamond and smiled. For no reason at all the office seemed suddenly very far from the ground and the night seemed still and empty. I found myself thinking of a cobra coiled up in a bush—a fat cobra, sleek but dangerous.

"They tell me you have been in San Luis Beach for eighteen months," he continued breathlessly. "Before that you worked for the Central Bonding Agency, New York, as one of their detectives. A detective who works for a bonding company, they tell me, has excellent opportunities for blackmail. Perhaps that was why they asked you to resign. No accusations were made, but they found you were living at a scale far beyond the salary you were paid. That made them think, Mr. Jackson. A bonding agency can't be too careful."

He paused and his little eyes probed inquisitively at my face, but that didn't get him anywhere. "You resigned," he went on after a pause, "and soon after you became an investigator with the Hotel Protection Association. Later, one of the hotel managers complained. It seems you collected dues from certain hotels without giving the company's receipt. But it was your word against his, and the company reluctantly decided the evidence was too flimsy to prosecute, but you were asked to resign. After that you lived on a young woman with whom you were friendly—one of the many young women, they tell me. But she soon tired of giving you money to spend on other young women, and you parted.

"Some months later you decided to set up on your own as a private investigator. You obtained a licence from the State Attorney on a forged affidavit of character, and you came to San Luis Beach because it was a wealthy town and the competition was negligible. You specialized in divorce work, and for a time you prospered. But there are also opportunities for blackmail, so I understand, even in divorce work. Someone complained to the police, and there was an investigation. But you are very tricky, Mr. Jackson, and you kept out of serious trouble. Now the police want to run you out of town. They are making things difficult for you. They have revoked your licence, and to all intents and purposes they have put you out of business—at least, that's what they think, but you and I know better."

I leaned forward to stub out my butt and that brought me close to the diamond. It was worth five grand, probably more. Smarter guys than Fatso Gorman have had their fingers cut off for rocks half that value. I began to get ideas about that diamond.

"Although you are still trying to operate as a private investigator, you can't advertise, nor can you put your name on your door. The police are watching you, and if they find you are still taking commissions they'll prosecute you. Up to now, although you have passed the word around amongst your saloon-keeper friends that you'll accept a client without asking questions, no one has hired you, and you're down to your last nickel. For the past five nights you have been trying to make up your mind whether to stay or quit. You have decided to quit. Am I right, Mr. Jackson?"

"Check," I said, and eased myself farther back in my chair.

I was curious. There was something about Fatso Gorman that got me. Maybe he was a phoney; maybe he was flashing the diamond to impress me, but there was a lot more to him than a cloak-and-dagger hat and a five-grand diamond. His little black eyes warned me he was geared for quick thinking. The shape of his mouth gave him away. Turn a sheet of paper edgeways on and that'll give you an idea of how thick his lips were. I could picture him sitting in the sun at a bullfight. He'd be happy when the horse took the horn. That was the kind of guy he was. A horse with its belly ripped open would be his idea of fun. Although he was fat, he was immensely strong, and I had a feeling if ever he got his hand around my throat, he could squeeze blood out of my ears.

"Don't quit, Mr. Jackson," he was saying. "I have a job for you."

The night air, coming in through the open window on to the back of my neck, felt chilly. A moth appeared out of the darkness and fluttered aimlessly around the desk lamp. The diamond continued to make bright patterns on the ceiling. We looked at each other. There was a pause long enough for you to walk down the passage and back.

Then I said, "What kind of a job?"

"A tricky job, Mr. Jackson. It should suit you."

I chewed that over. Well, he knew what he was buying. He had only himself to blame.

"Why pick on me?"

He touched the hairline mustache with a fat thumb.

"Because it's that kind of a job."

That seemed to take care of that.

"Go ahead and tell me," I said. "I'm up for sale."

Gorman let out a little puff of breath. Probably he

thought he was going to have trouble with me, but he should have known I wouldn't quarrel with a guy who owned a diamond that size.

"Let me tell you a story as I heard it today," he said, "then I'll tell you what I want you to do." He puffed more breath at me, and went on. "I am a theatrical agent."

He'd have to be something like that. No one would wear a cloak-and-dagger hat and an astrakhan collar in this heat for the fun of it.

"I look after the interests of a number of big stars and a host of little ones," he told me. "Among the little stars is a young woman who specializes in stag party entertainments. Her name is Veda Rux. She is what is known in the profession as a stripper. She has a good act, otherwise I wouldn't handle her. It is art in its purest form." He eyed me over the top of the diamond and I tried to look as if I believed him, but I didn't think I convinced him. "Last night Miss Rux performed at a dinner given to a party of businessmen by Mr. Lindsay Brett." The little black eyes suddenly jumped from the diamond to my face. "Perhaps you have heard of him?"

I nodded. I had made it my business to know something about everyone in San Luis Beach who had more than a five-figure income. Brett had a big place a few miles outside the city limits, the last big estate on Ocean Rise where the millionaires hide out. Ocean Rise is a twisting boulevard, lined on either side by palm trees and tropical flowering shrubs, and cut in the foothills that surround the city's outskirts. The houses up there are set back in their own grounds and screened by twelve-foot walls. You needed money to live on that boulevard— plenty of money. Brett had money all right; as much as he could use. He had a yacht, three cars, five gardeners and a yen for fresh young blondes. When he wasn't throwing parties, getting drunk or necking blondes, he was making a pile of jack out of two oil companies and a string of chain stores that stretched from San Francisco to New York.

"After Miss Rux had given her performance, Brett invited her to join the party," Gorman went on. "During the evening, he showed her and his guests some of his valuable antiques. It seems he had recently acquired a Cellini dagger. He opened the wall safe to show it to his guests. Miss Rux was sitting close to the safe, and as he spun the dial operating the lock, she memorized the combination without realizing what she was doing. She has, I may say, a remarkably retentive memory. The dagger made a great impression on her. She tells me it is the most beautiful thing she has ever seen."

So far I wouldn't figure where I came into any of this. I wanted a drink. I wanted to go to bed. But I was broke and stuck with Fatso and had to make the best of it. I began to think about his diamond again.

"Later, when the guests had retired, Brett showed Miss Rux to her room. It had been arranged for her to stop over at Brett's place for the night as the party was expected to go on to the small hours of the morning. Alone with her, Brett reverted to type. He probably thought she would be an easy conquest. She repulsed him."

"Many men think that when a dame entertains in a G-string the writing goes up on the wall."

He ignored the interruption and went on. "Brett became angry and there was a struggle. He lost his temper, and anything might have happened had not two of his guests come in to see what the noise was about. Brett was viciously angry, and threatened Miss Rux. He told her he would get even with her for making him look a fool before his friends. He was in an ugly mood and he frightened her. There was no doubt he meant what he said."

I shifted in my chair.

"When she finally fell asleep she had a dream," Gorman went on, then paused. He pulled out a gold cigarette case, opened it and laid it on the desk. "I see you would like to smoke, Mr. Jackson."

I thanked him. He certainly had his finger on my pulse. If there was one thing I wanted more than a drink it was a smoke.

"Do her dreams figure in this, too?" I asked, dropping the match on the floor to keep the other matches company.

"She dreamed she went downstairs, opened the safe, took the case containing the dagger, and in its place left her powder compact."

A tingle ran up my spine into the roots of my hair. I didn't move. The deadpan expression I had hitched to my face didn't change, but an alarm bell began to ring in my mind.

"She woke immediately after the dream. It was six o'clock. She decided to leave before Brett was up. She packed hurriedly and left. No one saw her leave. It wasn't until late this afternoon when she was unpacking that she found at the bottom of her bag the Cellini dagger."

I ran my fingers through my hair and yearned for a drink. The alarm bell kept ringing in my mind.

"And I bet she couldn't find her compact," I said to show him I was right on his heels.

He regarded me gravely.

"That is correct, Mr. Jackson. She realized immediately what had happened. Whenever she is worried or has something on her mind she walks in her sleep. She took the Cellini dagger in her sleep. The dream wasn't a dream at all. It actually happened."

He had taken a little time to get around to it, but now the body was on the table. We looked at each other. I could have said a number of things, but none of them would have got me anywhere. It was still his party, so I pulled at my nose and grunted. He could make what he liked of that.

"Why didn't she turn the dagger over to the police and tell them what had happened?" I asked. "They would have fixed it with Brett."

"It wasn't as easy as that. Brett had threatened her. He's an unpleasant character when he's angry. Miss Rux felt he might bring a charge against her."

"Not if she handed it over to the police. That'd kick the bottom out of the charge."

Gorman puffed out more breath at me. His thin lips drooped.

"Brett's point might be that after stealing the dagger, Miss Rux had discovered she couldn't sell it. The obvious thing for her to do then would be to hand it over to the police and invent this story of sleepwalking."

"But the compact would support the sleepwalking tale. She wouldn't leave that in his safe unless she was screwy or did walk in her sleep."

"But suppose Brett denied the compact was left in the safe in order to get even with her?"

I stubbed out the cigarette regretfully. It was the best smoke I'd had in days.

"Why couldn't she raise money on the dagger if it's as valuable as you say?"

"For the obvious reason—it is unique. There were only two gold daggers made by Cellini in existence. One of them is in the Uffizi, and the other belongs to Brett. There's not a dealer in the world who doesn't know by now that Brett owns the dagger. It would be impossible to sell it unless Brett personally handled the deal."

"Okay, then let Brett bring a charge. If she flashes her G-string at the jury, she'll beat the rap. It's a cinch they'd never convict her."

He even had an answer for that one.

"Miss Rux can't afford the publicity. If Brett brought a charge it would be impossible to keep the case out of the papers. It would ruin her career."

I gave up.

"So what's happening? Is Brett bringing a charge?"

Gorman smiled.

"Now we come to the point, Mr. Jackson. Brett left for San Francisco early this morning. He returns the day after tomorrow. He thinks the dagger is still in his safe."

I knew what was coming, but I wanted him to tell me. I said, "So what do we do?"

At least, that produced some action. He fished from his inside pocket a roll of money big enough to choke a horse. He peeled off ten one-hundred-dollar bills and laid them fan-shape on the desk. They were new and crisp, and I could almost smell the ink on them. I had already guessed he was in the chips, but I hadn't expected him to be as well-heeled as this. I hitched my chair forward and took a closer look at the notes. There was nothing wrong with them except they were on his side of the desk and not on mine.

"I want to hire your services, Mr. Jackson," he said, lowering his voice. "Would that fee interest you?"

I said it would in a voice I didn't recognize as my own, and ran an unsteady hand over my hair to make sure I hadn't lost the top of my head. The sight of those iron men had sent my blood pressure up like a jet-propelled rocket.

From another pocket he produced a red leather case. He opened it and pushed it toward me. I blinked at the glittering gold dagger that lay on a white satin bed. It was about a foot long, covered with complicated engravings of flowers and animals, and there was an emerald the size of a walnut let into the top of the hilt. It was a nice thing if you like pretty toys—I don't.

"This is the Cellini dagger," Gorman said, and there was honey in his voice now. "I want you to return it to Brett's safe and bring away Miss Rux's compact. I realize it is a little unethical, and you will have to act the role of a burglar, but you won't be stealing anything, Mr. Jackson, and the fee is, I suggest, appropriate to the risks. The fee, Mr. Jackson, of a thousand dollars."

I knew I shouldn't touch this with a twenty-foot pole. The alarm bell kept ringing in my mind telling me this fat flesh-peddler was stringing me for a sucker. I was sure the whole lousy tale—the Cellini dagger, the stripper who walked in her sleep, the compact in the safe—was a tissue of lies a half-wit paralytic could have seen through. I should have told him to jump in a lake—into two, if one wasn't big enough to hold him. I wish I had now. It would have saved me a lot of grief and being hunted for murder. But I wanted those ten iron men with a want that tore into my guts, and I thought I was smart enough to play it my way and keep out of trouble. If I hadn't been broke or in a jam, or if Redfern hadn't been squeezing me, it might have been different. But why go on?

I said I'd do it.

CHAPTER TWO

NOW THAT HE HAD ME ON THE dotted line, Gorman wasn't giving me a chance to change my mind. He wanted me out at his place right away. It didn't matter about going back to my rooms to pick up any overnight stuff. I could borrow anything I wanted. He had a car outside, and it wouldn't take long to get to his place, where there were drinks and food and quiet in which to talk things over. I could see he wasn't going to let me out of his sight now or use a telephone or check his story or tell anyone he and I had made a deal. The promise of a drink decided me. I agreed to go along with him.

But before we started we had a little argument over the money. He wanted to pay by results, but I didn't see it that way. Finally I squeezed two of the Cs out of him and persuaded him to agree to part with two more before I did the actual job. I would receive the balance when I handed over the compact.

Just to show him I didn't trust him further than I could throw him, I put the two bills in an envelope with a note to my bank manager, and on the way down to the street level I dropped the envelope into the mail chute. At least, if he tried to double-cross me, he wouldn't get his paws again on those two bills.

An early-vintage Packard Straight Eight cluttered up the street outside the office. The only thing in its favor was its size. I had expected something black and glittering and streamlined to match the diamond, and this old jalopy came as a surprise.

I stood back while Gorman squeezed himself into the backseat. He didn't get in the car: he put it on. I expected the four tires to burst as he settled himself in, but they held. After making sure there was no room in there with him, I got in beside the driver.

We roared out of town, along Ocean Boulevard, into and over the foothills that surrounded the city in the shape of a horseshoe.

I couldn't see much of the driver. He sat low behind the steering wheel and had a chauffeur's cap pulled down over his nose and he stared straight ahead. All the time we drove through the darkness he neither spoke nor looked at me.

We zigzagged through the foothills for a while, then turned off into a canyon and drove along a dirt road, bordered by thick scrub. I hadn't been out this way before. Every so often we'd pass a house. There were no lights showing.

After a while I gave up trying to memorize the route and let my mind dwell on the two hundred bucks I'd mailed to the bank. At last I would have something to wave at the wolf when next he called at the office.

I wasn't kidding myself what this job was about. I'd been hired to rob a safe. Never mind the elaborate build-up: the poor little stripper, scared of the big, bad millionaire, or the phoney dagger made by Mr. Cellini. I didn't believe one word of that tall tale. Gorman wanted something that Brett had in the safe. Maybe it was a powder compact. I didn't know, but whatever it was, he wanted it badly, and had come to me with this cooked-up yarn so as to have a back door to duck through in case I turned

him down. He hadn't the nerve to tell me he wanted me
to rob Brett's safe. But that's what he was paying me to
do. I had taken the money, but that didn't mean I was
going through with it. He said I was tricky and smooth.
Maybe I am. I'd go along with him so far, but I wasn't
going to jump into anything without seeing where I was
going to land. Anyway, that's what I told myself, and at
that time I believed it.

We were at the far end of the canyon now. It was damp
down there and dark, and a thin white mist hung above
the ground. The car headlights bounced off the mist and
it wasn't easy to see what was ahead. Somewhere in the
mist and darkness I could hear the frogs croaking.
Through the misty windshield the moon looked like a
dead man's face and the stars like paste diamonds.

The car suddenly swung through a narrow gateway, up
a steep driveway, screened on either side by a high, thick
hedge. A moment later we turned a bend and I saw lighted
windows hanging in space. It was too dark even to see
the outline of the house and everything around us was
quiet and still and breathless—it was as lonely out there
as the condemned cell at San Quentin.

A light in a wrought-iron coach lantern sprang up over
the front door as the car pulled up with a crunch of tires
on gravel. The light shone down on two stone lions
crouching one on either side of the porch. The front door
was studded with brass-headed nails and looked strong
enough to withstand a battering ram.

The chauffeur ran around to the rear door and helped
Gorman out. The light from the lantern fell on his face
and I looked him over. There was something about his
hooked nose and thick lips that struck a chord in my
memory. I'd seen him somewhere before, but I couldn't
place him.

"Get the car away," Gorman growled at him. "And let us have some sandwiches, and remember to wash your hands before you touch the bread."

"Yes, sir," the chauffeur said and gave Gorman a look that should have dropped him in his tracks. It wasn't hard to see he hated Gorman. I was glad to know that. When you're playing it the way I had it figured out, it's a sound thing to know who is on whose side.

Gorman opened the front door, edged in his bulk and I followed. We entered a large hall; at the far end was a broad staircase leading to the upper rooms. On the left were double doors to a lounge.

No butler came to greet us. No one seemed interested in us now we had arrived. Gorman took off his hat and struggled out of his coat. He looked just as impressive without the hat, and as dangerous. He had a bald spot on the top of his head, but his hair was clipped so close it didn't matter. His pink scalp glistened through the white bristles so you scarcely noticed where the hair left off.

I tossed my hat on a hall chair.

"Come in, Mr. Jackson," he said. "I want you to feel at home."

I went with him into the lounge. Walking at his side made me feel like a tug bringing in an ocean liner. It was a nice room with a couple of chesterfields in red leather and three or four lounging chairs drawn up before a fireplace big enough to sit in. On the polished boards were Persian rugs that made rich pools of color, and along the wall facing the French windows was a carved sideboard on which was displayed a comprehensive collection of bottles and glasses.

A thin, elegantly dressed man pulled himself out of a lounging chair by the window.

"Dominic, this is Mr. Floyd Jackson," Gorman said; and to me he went on, "Mr. Dominic Parker, my partner."

My attention was riveted on the bottles, but I gave him a nod to be friendly. Mr. Parker didn't even nod. He looked me over and his lips curled superciliously and he didn't look friendly at all.

"Oh, the detective," he said with a sneer, and glanced at his fingernails the way women do when they're giving you the brush-off.

I hitched myself up against one of the chesterfields and looked him over. He was tall and slender, and his honey-colored hair was taken straight back and slicked down. He had a long, narrow face, washed-out blue eyes and a soft chin that would have looked a lot better on a woman. From the wrinkles under his eyes and a little sag of flesh at his throat, I guessed he wouldn't see forty again.

He was a natty dresser, if you care for the effeminate touch. He had on a pearl-gray flannel suit, a pale green silk shirt, a bottle-green tie and reverse calf shoes of the same color. A white carnation decorated his buttonhole and a fat, oval, gold-tipped cigarette hung from his over-red lips.

Gorman had planted himself in front of the fireplace. He stared at me with empty eyes as if he were suddenly bored with me.

"You'd like a drink?" he said, then glanced at Parker. "A drink for Mr. Jackson, don't you think?"

"Let him get it himself," Parker said sharply. "I'm not in the habit of waiting on servants."

"Is that what I am?" I asked.

"You wouldn't be here unless you were being paid, and that makes you a servant," he told me in his super-cilious voice.

"So it does." I crossed over to the sideboard and mixed myself a drink big enough to float a canoe. "Like the little guy who was told to wash his hands."

"It'll be all right with me if you talk when you're spoken to," he said, his face tight with rage.

Gorman said, "Don't get excited, Dominic."

The hoarse, scratchy voice had an effect on Parker. He sat down again and frowned at his fingernails. There was a pause. I lifted my glass, waved it at Gorman and drank. The Scotch was as good as the diamond.

"Is he going to do it?" Parker asked suddenly without looking up.

"Tomorrow night," Gorman said. "Explain it to him. I'm going to bed." He included me in the conversation by pointing a finger the size of a banana at me. "Mr. Parker will tell you all you want to know. Good night, Mr. Jackson."

I said good-night.

At the door, he turned to look at me again.

"Please cooperate with Mr. Parker. He has my complete confidence. He understands what has to be done and what he tells you is an order from me."

"Sure," I said.

We listened to Gorman's heavy tread as he climbed the stairs. The room seemed empty without him.

"Go ahead," I said, dropping into one of the lounging chairs. "You have my complete confidence, too."

"We won't have any funny stuff, Jackson." Parker was sitting up very stiff in his chair. His fists were clenched. "You're being paid for this job and paid well. I don't want any impertinence from you. Understand?"

"So far I've only received two hundred dollars," I said, smiling at him. "If you don't like me the way I am, send me home. The retainer will cover the time I've wasted coming out here. Suit yourself."

A tap on the door saved his dignity. He said to come in, in his cold, spiteful voice, and thrust his clenched fists into his trouser pockets.

The chauffeur came in, carrying a tray. He had changed into a white drill jacket that was a shade too large for him. On the tray was a pile of sandwiches, cut thick.

I recognized him now that he wasn't wearing the cap. I'd seen him working at the harbor. He was a dark, sad-looking little man with a hooked nose and sad, moist eyes. I wondered what he was doing here. I remembered seeing him painting a boat along the waterfront a few days ago. He must be as new to this job as I was. As he came in, he gave a quick look and a puzzled expression jumped into his eyes.

"What's that supposed to be?" Parker snapped, pointing to the tray.

"Mr. Gorman ordered sandwiches, sir."

Parker stood up, took the plate and stared at the sandwiches. He lifted one with a finicky finger and thumb, frowned at it in shocked disgust.

"Who do you think can eat stuff like this?" he demanded angrily. "Can't you get into your gutter mind sandwiches should be cut thin—thin as paper, you stupid oaf. Cut some more!" With a quick flick of his wrist he shot the contents of the plate into the little guy's face. Bread and chicken dripped over him, a piece of chicken lodged in his hair. He stood very still and went white.

Parker stalked to the French windows, wrenched back the curtains and stared out into the night. He kept his back turned until the chauffeur had cleared up the mess.

I said, "We don't want anything to eat, bud. You needn't come back."

The chauffeur went out without looking at me. His back was stiff with rage.

Parker said over his shoulder, "I'll trouble you not to give orders to my servants."

"If you're going to act like an hysterical old woman

I'm going to bed. If you have anything to tell me, let's have it. Only make up your mind."

He came away from the French windows. Rage made him look old and ugly.

"I warned Gorman you'd be difficult," he said, trying to control his voice. "I told him to leave you alone. A cheap crook like you is no use to anyone."

I grinned at him.

"I've been hired to do a job and I'm going to do it. But I'm doing it my way, and I'm not taking a lot of bull from you. That goes for Fatso, too. If you want this job done, say so and get on with it."

He struggled with his temper and then, to my surprise, calmed down.

"All right, Jackson," he said mildly. "There's no sense in quarrelling."

I watched him walk stiff-legged to the sideboard, jerk open a drawer and take out a long roll of blue paper. He tossed it on the table.

"That's the plan of Brett's house. Look at it."

I helped myself to another drink and one of his fat cigarettes I found in a box on the sideboard. Then I unrolled the paper and studied the plan. It was an architect's blueprint. Parker leaned over the table and pointed out the way in, and where the safe was located.

"Two guards patrol the house," he said. "They're ex-policemen and quick on the trigger. There's an elaborate system of burglar alarms, but they are only fixed to the windows and safe. I've arranged for you to enter by the back door. That's it, here." His long finger pointed on the plan. "You follow this passage, go up the stairs, along here to Brett's study. The safe's here, where I've marked it in red."

"Hey, wait a minute," I said sharply. "Gorman didn't

say anything about guards and alarms. How is it the Rux dame didn't touch off the alarm?"

He was expecting that one, for he answered without hesitation. "When Brett returned the dagger to the safe he forgot to reset it."

"Think it's still unset?"

"It's possible, but you mustn't rely on it."

"And the guards? How did she miss them?"

"They were in another wing of the house at the time."

I wasn't too happy about this. Ex-policemen guards can be tough.

"I have a key that'll fit the back door," he said casually. "You needn't worry about that."

"You have? You work fast, don't you?"

He didn't say anything to that.

I wandered over to the fireplace, leaned against the mantel.

"What happens if I'm caught?"

"We wouldn't have chosen you for the job if we thought you'd be caught," he said, and smiled through his teeth.

"That still doesn't answer my question."

He lifted his elegant shoulders. "You must tell the truth."

"You mean about this babe walking in her sleep?"

"Certainly."

"Persuading Redfern to believe a yarn like that should be fun."

"If you are careful it won't come to that."

"I hope it doesn't." I finished my drink, rolled up the blueprint. "I'll study this in bed. Anything else?"

"Do you carry a gun?"

"Sometimes."

"You better not carry it tomorrow night."

We studied each other.

"I won't."

"Then that's all. We'll go out tomorrow morning and look Brett's place over. The lay of the land is important."

"It strikes me it'd be easier to let that stripper do it in her sleep. According to Fatso, if she has anything on her mind she sleepwalks at the drop of a hat. I could give her something for her mind."

"You're being impertinent again."

"So I am." I collected a bottle of Scotch and a glass from the sideboard. "I'll finish my supper in bed."

"We don't encourage people we hire to drink." He was very distant and contemptuous again.

"I don't need any encouragement. Where do I sleep?"

Once more he had to struggle with his temper, and went out of the room with a little flounce that told me how mad he was.

I followed him up the broad stairs, along a passage to a bedroom that smelled as if it had been shut up for a long time. Apart from the stuffy, stale air, there was nothing wrong with the room.

"Good night, Jackson," he said curtly and went away.

I poured myself out a small Scotch, drank it, made another and walked to the window. I threw it open and leaned out. All I could see were treetops and darkness. The brilliant moonlight didn't penetrate through the trees or shrubs. Below me I made out a flat roof, a projection over the bay windows that ran the width of the house. For something better to do I climbed out of the window and lowered myself onto the roof. At the far end of the projection I had a clear view of the big stretch of lawn. A lily pond that looked like a sheet of beaten silver in the moonlight held my attention. It was surrounded by a low wall. Someone was sitting on the wall. It looked like a girl, but I was too far away to be sure. I could make out a tiny spark of a burning cigarette. If it hadn't been for the cigarette, I would have thought the figure was a statue, so still was it sitting. I watched for some time, but nothing happened. I went back the way I had come.

The chauffeur was sitting on my bed waiting for me as I climbed in through the window.

"Just getting some fresh air," I said as I hooked my leg over the sill. I didn't show I was startled. "Kind of stuffy in here, isn't it?"

"Kind of," he said, keeping his voice low. "I've seen you somewhere before, ain't I?"

"Along the waterfront. Jackson's the name."

"The dick?"

I grinned. "That was a month ago. I'm not working that racket anymore."

"Yeah, I heard about that. The cops picked on you, didn't they?"

"The cops picked on me." I found another glass, made two stiff drinks. "Want one?"

His hand shot out.

"Can't stay long. They wouldn't like me being up here."

"Did you come for a drink?"

He shook his head. "Couldn't place you. It sort of worried me. I heard the way you spoke to that heel Parker. I thought you and me might get together."

"Yeah," I said. "We might. What's your name?"

"Max Otis."

"Been working here long?"

"Started today." He made it sound as if it was a day too long. "The dough's all right, but they kick me around. I'm quitting at the end of the week."

"Told them?"

"Not going to. I'll just take it on the lam. Parker's

worse than Gorman. He's always picking on me. You saw the way he behaved...."

"Yeah." I hadn't time to listen to his grievances. I wanted information.

"What do you do around here?"

His smile was bitter. "Everything. Cook, clean the house, run the car, look after that heel Parker's clothes, buy groceries, the drinks. I don't mind the job—it's them."

"How long have they been here?"

"Like I said—a day. I moved them in."

"Furniture and all?"

"No...they've rented the place as it stands."

"For how long?"

"Search me. I wouldn't know. They only give me orders. They don't tell me nothing."

"Just the two of them?"

"And the girl."

So there was a girl.

I finished my drink and made two more.

"Seen her?"

He nodded. "Rates high on looks, but keeps to herself. Calls herself Veda Rux. She likes Parker the way I do."

"That her out in the garden by the pond?"

"Could be. She sits around all day."

"Who gave you the job?"

"Parker. I ran into him downtown. He knew all about me. He said he'd been making enquiries and would I like to earn some solid money." He scowled down at his glass. "I wouldn't have touched it if I'd known the kind of rat he is. If it wasn't for the gun he carries, I'd take a poke at him."

"So he carries a gun?"

"Holster job, under his left arm. He carries it as if he could use it."

"These two guys in business?"

"Don't seem to be, but your guess is as good as mine. No one's called or written. No one telephones. They seem to be waiting for something to happen."

I grinned. Something was going to happen all right.

"Okay, pally, you shoot off to bed. Keep your ears open. We might learn something if we're smart."

"Don't you know anything? What are you here for? What's cooking? I don't like any of this. I want to know where I stand."

"I'll tell you something. This Rux frail walks in her sleep."

He looked startled. "You mean that?"

"That's why I'm here. And another thing, she takes off her clothes at the drop of a hat."

He chewed this over. He seemed to like it. "I thought there was something different about her," he said.

"Play safe and take your hat to bed with you," I said, easing him to the door. "You might be in luck."

CHAPTER THREE

IT WASN'T UNTIL THE following afternoon that I met Veda Rux.

In the morning, Parker and I drove over in the Packard to Brett's house. We went around the back of the foot-hills and up the twisting mountain road to the summit where Ocean Rise has its swaggering terminus.

Parker drove. He took the bends in the mountain road too fast for comfort, and twice the car skidded and the rear wheels came unpleasantly near to the edge of the overhang. I didn't say anything; if he could stand it, I could. He drove disdainfully, his fingertips resting on the steering wheel as if he were afraid of getting them soiled.

Long before you reached it, you could see Brett's house. Although surrounded by twelve-foot walls, the house itself was built on high ground and you could get a good view of it from the mountain road. But when you reached the gates the screen of trees, flowering shrubs and hedges hid it from sight. Halfway up the road, Parker stopped the car so I could get an idea of the layout. We had brought the blueprint with us, and he showed me where the back door was in relation to the house and the plan. It meant scaling the wall, he told me, but as he hadn't to do it, he didn't seem to think that would be anything to worry about. There was a barbed-wire fence on the top of the wall, he added, but that, too, was something that could be taken care of. He was a lot happier than I was about the setup. But that was natural. I was doing the job.

There was a guard standing before the big iron gates. He was nearly fifty, but looked tough, and his hard, alert eyes held us as we pulled up where the road petered out about fifty yards beyond the gates.

Parker said, "I'll talk to him. Leave him to me."

The guard strolled toward us as Parker made a U-turn. He was short and thickset, with shoulders on him like a prizefighter's. He had on a brown shirt, brown corduroy breeches and a peaked cap, and his short thick legs were encased in jackboots.

"I thought this was the road to Santa Medina," Parker said, poking his slick head out of the car window.

The guard rested one polished boot on the running board. He stared hard at Parker, then at me. If I hadn't been told he was an ex-cop, I would have known it by the sneering toughness in his eyes.

"This is a private road," he said with elaborate sarcasm. "It says so a half a mile back. The Santa Medina road branches to the left, and there's a notice four yards square telling you just that little thing. What do you want up here?"

While he was shooting off his mouth, I had time to study the walls. They were as smooth as glass, and on top was a three-stranded barbed-wire fence. The prickles on the wire looked sharp enough to slice meat—my meat at that.

"I thought the road to the left was the private road," Parker was saying. He smiled emptily at the guard. "Sorry if we're trespassing."

I saw something else, too: a dog sitting by the guard's lodge—a wolfhound. It was yawning in the sunlight. You could hang a hat on its fangs.

"Beat it," the guard said. "When you've got the time, learn yourself to read. You're missing a lot."

Around the guard's thick waist was a revolver belt. There was no flap to the holster and the butt of the .45 was shiny with use.

"You don't have to be impertinent," Parker returned gently. He was still very distant and polite. "We all make mistakes."

"Yeah, your mother made a beauty," the guard said and laughed.

Parker flushed pink.

"That's an objectionable remark," he said sharply. "I'll complain to your employer."

"Scram," the guard said, growling. "Take this lump of iron the hell out of here or I'll give you something to complain about."

We drove away the way we had come. I watched the guard in the rearview mirror. He stood in the middle of the road, his hands on his hips, staring after us: a real twelve-minute egg.

"Nice fella," I said and grinned.

"There's another like him. They're both on duty at night."

"See the dog?"

"Dog?" He glanced at me. "No. What dog?"

"Just a dog. Nice teeth. If anything he looked a little tougher than the guard and sort of hungry. And the barbed wire. Good stuff. Sharp. I guess I'll have to ask for a little more dough. I've got to get me insured."

"You're not going to get any more money from us, if that's what you mean," Parker snapped.

"That's what I do mean. Pity you missed the dog. It should be a lot of fun having that cutie roaming around in the dark. Yeah, I guess you'll have to dip into your sock again, brother."

"A thousand or nothing," Parker said, his face hardening. "Please yourself."

"You'll have to revise your ideas. I'm in a buyer's market. You know, Brett might pay me for information. Don't tell me to please myself unless you want me to." I glanced at him, saw his eyes narrow. That hit him where it hurt.

"Don't try that stuff with me, Jackson."

"Talk it over with Fatso. I want another five hundred or I don't go ahead. Fatso didn't tell me about the guards or the dog or the alarms or the wire. He made out it was a soft job—a job you could do in your sleep."

"I'm warning you, Jackson," Parker said between his teeth. "You can't monkey with us. You made a deal and you've accepted part payment. You're going through with it."

"That's right. But the fee's jacked up to fifteen centuries. My union don't let me fool around with dogs."

"You'll take your thousand or you'll be sorry," he said, and his hands gripped the steering wheel until his knuckles turned white. "I'm not going to be blackmailed by you, you cheap crook."

"Don't blame me. Blame Fatso. I'm not a sucker."

He began to drive fast and we got back to the house in half the time it took us to leave it.

"We'll see Gorman," he said.

We saw Gorman.

Fatso sat in a chair and stroked his hard pink face and listened.

"I told him he couldn't make a monkey out of us," Parker said. He was white and his eyes had a feverish look.

Gorman stared at me.

"You'd better not try any tricks, Mr. Jackson."

"No tricks," I said, smiling at him. "Just another five

hundred to take care of the insurance. You want to see the guard and you want to take a gander at the dog. When you've seen them, you've seen plenty."

He brooded for a long minute.

"All right," he said suddenly. "I didn't know about the guards or the dog myself. I'll make it another five hundred, but it's the last you'll get."

Parker let out a little explosion of sound.

"Don't get excited, Dominic," Gorman said, frowning at him. "If you knew about the guards you should have told me."

"He's blackmailing us!" Parker stormed. "You're crazy to pay him. Where's it going to stop?"

"Leave this to me," Gorman said, cool as a cucumber.

Parker stood glaring at me, then he went out.

"I'll have the dough now," I said. "It wouldn't be much use to me if I run into that dog."

We argued back and forth. After a while we agreed to split it and Gorman handed over two hundred and fifty.

I borrowed an envelope and a sheet of notepaper and prepared another surprise for my bank manager. There was a mailbox just outside the house. I went down the drive and mailed the letter while Gorman watched me from the window.

Well, I was coming along. I had collected four hundred and fifty iron men for nothing so far, and they were where neither of these guys could reach them.

All the same I didn't like the easy way Gorman had parted with the money. I knew I wouldn't have screwed it out of Parker. But Gorman was a lot trickier than Parker. When he had parted with the money, his face had been expressionless. But that didn't fool me. I began to think it was going to be a lot harder to collect the balance of the money when I had handed over the compact. I was all right now, but the moment I had handed it over I had a feeling Gorman would go into action. I felt it the way you feel a hunch, and it kept growing. I remembered what Max had said about Parker's gun. Right now they wanted me to do a job Gorman was too fat to do and Parker hadn't the guts to do. But when I'd done it, I'd be of no further use to them. I'd be a danger to them. That's when I should have to watch out. And I told myself I'd watch out all right.

Later, Max came to tell me lunch was ready. I was sitting on the terrace overlooking the lawn, and when I was going to speak to him he frowned a warning.

I glanced over my shoulder and there was my pal Parker standing in the French windows watching us. He came over, a little stiff, but controlled.

"I have everything you need for tonight," he said when Max had gone away. "I'll come with you as far as the wall and I'll wait there in the car."

"Come in with me. You can take care of the dog."

He ignored this, and we went into the dining room. The lunch was nothing to rave about. While we toyed with the food, Parker told me what he had got together for me.

"You'll want a knotted rope for the wall. I have that with a hook at one end. I have a good pair of cutters for the wire. You'll need a flashlight. Anything else?"

"How about the dog?"

"A leaded cane will take care of the dog," Gorman put in. "I'll tell Max to get one."

"And the combination of the safe?"

"I've written that down for you," Parker said. "You'll find a wire running along the side of the safe. Before you touch the safe, cut the wire. That'll put the alarm out of action. Don't touch any of the windows."

"Sounds simple, doesn't it?" I said.

"For a man of your experience it is simple," Gorman said smoothly. "But don't take any chances, Mr. Jackson. I don't want any trouble."

"That makes two of us," I said.

After lunch I told them I'd take a nap in the garden, and that's when I met Veda Rux. I went down to the lily pond hoping I'd run into her and that's where I found her. She was sitting on the low wall surrounding the pond the way she had been sitting the previous night. Her feet in sandals hung a few inches above the water. She wore a pair of canary-colored corduroy slacks and a thin silk shirt of the same color. Her almost black hair hung loose to her shoulders in a kind of Dutch bob, only she had waves in it. She was small and compact and curved, and there was strength in her. It wasn't that she was muscular; it was something you guessed at rather than saw. You had the impression her wrists had steel in them and the curve of her thighs would be as hard as granite if you touched them.

Her face was pale and small and serious. Her lapis-lazuli eyes were alert and watchful. Plenty of girls have pretty faces and curves you can't improve upon. You look them over, get ideas about them, and forget them as soon as they're out of sight. But this girl you wouldn't forget. Don't ask me why. She had something. She was as different as gin is to water. And the difference, as you know, is there's a kick in one of them. Veda Rux carried a kick like a mule.

As soon as I saw her I knew there was going to be trouble. If I'd had any sense I'd have quit there and then. I should have told Gorman I'd changed my mind, given him back his money and got out of this house like a bat out of hell. That would have been the sensible thing to have done. I should have known from the way this girl made me feel that from now on I was going to have only half my mind on my job. And when a guy gets that way he's leaving himself wide open for a sucker punch. I knew it, and I didn't even care.

"Hello," I said. "I've heard about you. You walk in your sleep."

She studied me thoughtfully. No welcome. No smile.

"I've heard about you, too," she said.

That seemed to take care of that. There was a long blank pause while we looked at each other. She didn't move. It was uncanny how still she could sit: not a blink to show she was alive. You couldn't even see she was breathing.

"You know why I'm here?" I asked. "You know what I'm going to do?"

"Yes, I know that, too," she said.

Well, that also took care of that. There didn't seem much else to say. I looked down into the lily pond. I could see her reflection in the water. She looked good that way, too.

I had the idea I was having the same effect on her as she was having on me. I wasn't sure, but I had a hunch I had touched off a spark in her, and it wouldn't need a lot of work to fan it into a flame.

I've been around and I've known a lot of women in my time. They've given me a lot of fun and a lot of grief. Now women are funny animals. You never know where you are with them—they don't often know where they are with themselves. It's no good trying to find out what makes them tick. It just can't be done. They have more moods than an army of cats have lives, and all you can hope for is to spot the mood you're after when it turns up and step in quick. Hesitate, and you're a dead duck, unless you're one of those guys who likes a slow approach that might get you somewhere in a week or a month or even a year. But that's not the way I like it. I like it quick and sudden: like a shot in the back.

I had come around the pool and was close to her now. She sat like a statue, her hands folded in her lap, and I could smell her perfume; nothing you could put a name to, but nice—heady and elusive.

And all of a sudden my heart was slamming against my ribs and my mouth was dry. I stood close behind her and waited. It was as if I'd got hold of a live wire in my hands and it was pulling me to pieces and I couldn't let go. Then she turned her head slowly and raised her face. I caught her in my arms and my mouth covered hers. She was in the mood all right. Her mouth was half-open and hard against mine. I felt her breath at the back of my throat. Five seconds—long enough to find out how good she was, with her firm young other hand gripping my arm; then she pushed me away. She had steel in her wrists all right.

We looked at each other. The lapis-lazuli eyes were as unruffled and as impersonal as the lily pond.

"Do you usually work as fast as that?" she asked and touched her mouth gently with slim fingers.

There was a weight on my chest that made me breathless. When I spoke I had a croak in my voice a frog would have envied.

"It seemed the thing to do," I said. "We might do it again sometime."

She swung her legs over the wall and stood up. The top of her sleek dark head was a little above my shoulder. She stood very still and straight.

"We might," she said and walked away. I watched her go. Her slim body was upright and graceful and she didn't look back. I watched her until she had disappeared into the house, then I sat on the wall and lit a cigarette. My hands were as steady as an aspen leaf.

For the rest of the afternoon I stayed right there by the lily pond. Nothing happened. No one came near me. No one peeped at me from the windows. I had all the time in the world to think out what I was going to do that night, how I was going to evade the guards and the dog, how I was going to climb that wall without being seen, and how I was going to open the safe. But I didn't think about any of that stuff. I thought about Veda Rux. I was still thinking about her when the sun dropped behind the tall pine trees and the shadows lengthened on the lawn. I was still thinking about her when Parker came out of the house and down to the pond.

I looked at him blankly because he had gone right out of my mind. It was as if he had never existed. That was the effect she had on me.

"You'd better come in now," he said abruptly. "We'll run through the final arrangements before we have supper. We want to get off about nine o'clock when the moon's right."

We went back into the house. There was no sign of her in the hall or the lounge where Gorman was waiting. I kept listening for sounds of her, but the house was as still and as quiet as a morgue.

"Dominic will carry the dagger," Gorman said. "When you're up on the wall he'll hand it to you. Be careful with it. I don't want the case scratched."

Parker gave me a key which he said unlocked the back door. We went over the architect's plan once more.

"I have another two hundred bucks coming to me before I go in there," I reminded Gorman. "You can give it to me now if that's okay with you."

"Dominic will give it to you at the same time as he gives you the dagger," Gorman said. "You've had too much of my money without working for it, Mr. Jackson.

I want some action from you before I part with any more."

I grinned. "Right, only I don't go over the wall without it."

I expected to see her at supper, but she wasn't there. Halfway through the meal I found I just had to know where she was. I said casually I'd seen a girl in the garden and was that Miss Rux and wasn't she coming in for a bite of food?

Parker turned a greenish white. His fists clenched until the knuckles seemed to be bursting out of his skin. He started to say something in a voice that was drowned in rage, but Gorman put in quickly, "Don't excite yourself, Dominic."

I didn't like the look of Parker, and I pushed back my chair. He looked mad enough to take a sock at me. I don't like a guy to sock me when I'm sitting down—even a clown like Parker.

"You're hired to do a job, Jackson," Parker said, leaning across the table and glaring at me. "Keep your damned nose out of what doesn't concern you! Miss Rux doesn't want anything to do with a cheap crook like you, and I'll see her wishes are carried out. Don't bring her name into this conversation!"

Because of what had happened out there by the pond, I didn't play it the way I should.

"Don't tell me that number I saw in the fancy pants could fall for a stooge like you," I said and laughed at him. I had my heel against the rung of the chair and I was about to kick it away and land him a poke in his snout when I found myself looking down the barrel of a .38 police special that had jumped into his hand. Max had said he carried a gun as if he could use it. That draw was the quickest thing outside the movies I'd ever seen.

"Dominic!" Gorman said quietly.

I didn't move. There was a blank, sightless look in Parker's washed-out blue eyes that told me he was going to shoot. It was a nasty moment. The gun barrel looked as big as the Brooklyn Battery tunnel and twice as steady. I could see the thin finger taking in the slack on the trigger.

"Dominic!" Gorman shouted and brought his great fist crashing down on the table.

The gun barrel dropped and Parker blinked at me as if he couldn't understand what had happened. His vacant, bewildered look sent a chill up my spine. This guy was slaphappy. I'd seen that dazed, vacant expression duplicated on a row of faces in the psychopathic ward in the county jail. You couldn't mistake it once you'd seen it: the face of a paranoiac killer.

"Don't get excited, Dominic," Gorman said in his thin, scratchy voice. He hadn't turned a hair, and I began to understand why he kept telling Parker to take it easy. It was his way of controlling him when he was getting out of hand.

Parker got slowly to his feet, stared at the gun as if he couldn't understand what it was doing in his hand and walked quietly out of the room.

I took out my handkerchief and touched my forehead with it. I was sweating: not much, but I was sweating.

"You want to watch that guy," I said evenly. "One of these days they'll take him away, strapped to a stretcher."

"You have only yourself to blame, Mr. Jackson," Gorman said, his eyes cold. "He's all right if you handle him right. You happen to be the quarrelsome type. Have some more coffee?"

I grinned. "I'm going to have a drink. He was going to shoot. Don't kid me. You want to take that gun away from him before there's an accident."

Gorman watched me pour the drink. There was an empty expression on his fat face.

"You mustn't take him too seriously, Mr. Jackson. He's become attached to Miss Rux. I shouldn't mention her again in your conversation."

"That guy? And what does she think of him?"

"I don't see what that has to do with you."

I took a drink and came back to the table.

"Maybe you're right," I said.

At nine o'clock Parker brought the car around to the front door. He was distant and calm and seemed to have got over his little spell.

Gorman came down the steps to see us off.

"Good luck, Mr. Jackson. Parker will give you last-minute instructions. I'll have your money for you when you return."

I was looking up at the dark windows hoping to see her and I didn't pay much attention to what he was saying. She wasn't there.

"We should be back in a couple of hours," Parker said to Gorman. I could tell his nerves were jangling by the shake in his voice. "If we're not, you know what to do."

"You'll be back," Gorman returned. His nerves were in better shape. "Mr. Jackson won't make a mistake."

I hoped I wouldn't. As we drove away into the darkness, I leaned out of the window and looked back at the house. I still couldn't see her.

CHAPTER FOUR

WE SAT IN THE CAR close to the twelve-foot wall that skirted the back of Brett's house. It was cold and quiet up there on the mountain, and dark. We couldn't see the wall or the car or each other. It was as if we were suspended in black space.

"All right," Parker said softly. "You know what to do. Take your time. Give me a whistle when you're coming back. I'll flash a light so you'll find the rope again."

I breathed gently into the darkness. Even now I hadn't decided what to do. I didn't want to go in there. I knew once I was over the wall, I would have put myself out on a limb, and if I slipped up, the least I could hope for was a stretch in jail. Redfern would fall over himself to put me away. He was only waiting for me to step out of line.

Parker turned on the shaded dashboard lamp. I could see his hands and the shadowy outline of his head and shoulders.

"Here's the combination of the safe," he said. "It's easy to remember. I've put it on a card. One full turn to the right, half a turn back, another full turn to the right, and a half turn to the right again. Stop between each turn to give the tumblers a chance to drop into place. Don't rush it. The only way to open the safe is to wait between each turn."

He gave me the card.

"How about my dough?" I asked.

"That's all you think about," he said with a snarl in his voice. He was wrong there, but it wasn't the time or the place to tell him about Veda Rux. "Here, take it, and keep your mind on what you're to do."

He handed over two one-hundred-dollar bills. I folded them small and put them in my cigarette case. I should have clipped him on the jaw then, shoved him out of the car and driven away, but I wanted to see Veda again. I could still feel her mouth against mine.

"When you've opened the safe, you'll find the compact on the second shelf. You can't miss it. It's a small gold case, about half an inch thick. You know the kind—hundreds of women have them. Put the dagger in its place."

"It would have saved a lot of trouble if that babe had slept with a chain on her ankle," I said. "You might pass the idea on."

He opened the car door and slid out into the darkness. I followed. Out in the open I could just make out the top of the wall. We stood listening for a moment or so. There wasn't a sound. I wondered if the dog was loose on the grounds—just thinking about that dog gave me the shakes.

"Ready?" Parker said impatiently. "We want to get this over before the moon is up."

"Yeah," I said and swung the leaded cane. I wished now I carried a gun.

He uncoiled the length of rope, and I took the hook in my hand. At the third throw the hook caught on the wire and held.

"Well, so long," I said. "Keep your ears open. I may be coming out a damn sight faster than I go in."

"Don't make any mistakes, Jackson," he said. I couldn't see his face but by the way his voice sounded he was talking through locked teeth. "You won't get any more money out of us if you don't bring out that compact."

"As if I didn't know," I said and took hold of the rope. "Got the dagger?"

"I'll hand it up to you. Be careful with it. Don't knock it against anything. There mustn't be a mark on it."

I climbed up the rope until I reached the wire. My feet gripped one of the knots in the rope and I went to work on the wire with the cutters. The wire was strung tight and I had to watch out it didn't snap back and slash me. I got it cut after a while.

"Okay," I said into the darkness and drew myself up until I was sitting astride the wall. I looked toward the house, but it was like looking into a pit a mile deep.

"Here's the case," Parker whispered. "Handle it carefully."

I leaned down, fumbled about until my fingers closed around it.

"I have it," I said and took it from him. While I was shoving it into my coat pocket, I went on. "It's as black as a hat down there. It'll take me some time to locate the way in."

"No, it won't," Parker said impatiently. "There's a path a few yards from the wall. It'll take you to the back door. Keep to your right. You can't go wrong."

"You've really made a study of this thing, haven't you?" I said, pulling up the rope, and sliding down the other side of the wall into the garden.

I stood in the darkness, my hand against the wall, my feet on the grass verge, and listened. All I could hear was my own breathing and the thump of my heart against my ribs. I had left it late to make up my mind what I was going to do. I had to make a decision now. I could either stay right where I was for a while and then climb back

over the wall and tell Parker I couldn't open the safe or
it was too well guarded or something, or I could go ahead
and do the job and take a chance of running into the dog
and the guards.

Once I had the compact, and if the guards caught me,
nothing could save me from Redfern. But I was curious.
I was sure the whole setup was phoney. A guy as smart
as Gorman wouldn't be gambling away fifteen hundred
bucks to help a woman out of a mess. He wasn't the type.
The compact or whatever it was he wanted out of Brett's
safe was worth a pile of jack. There could be no other ex-
planation. If it was worth money to him, it might be
worth money to me. I was sick of San Luis Beach, sick
of being pushed around, sick of having no money. If I
used my head I might make a killing with this job. I
might collect enough dough to take it easy for years. It
was worth the gamble. I decided to go ahead.

All this took about five seconds to go through my
mind; a second later I was on the path and heading toward
the house. I had on rubber-soled shoes and I made less
noise than a ghost, and I was listening all the time. I
didn't hurry and I crouched as I moved, the flashlight in
one hand and the leaded cane ready for business in the
other. After a while I came out of the trees. Away to my
left I could make out the shape of the house: a vast black
bulk of stone against the sky. No lights showed.

I kept moving, following the path that circled the lawn,
and I kept thinking about the wolfhound. It was nervy
work walking into that thick darkness—a police dog
doesn't bark. It moves along almost on its belly, very fast
and quiet, and the first and last time you know it's there
is when its fangs are tearing your throat out. My shirt
stuck to my back, and my nerves were poking out of my
skin by the time I reached the end of the path. I was close

to the house now. The path led to the terrace steps. I knew from the plan that to reach the back entrance you had to walk along the terrace, up some more steps, along another terrace, pass a row of French windows, around the corner and there you were. Once on the terrace you had as much cover to duck behind as a bubble dancer has when her bubble bursts.

I stood near the last tree of the path and probed the terrace and the steps until my eyes hurt. At first I couldn't see a thing, then I began to make out the broad white steps and the balustrade of the terrace. I kept on looking and listening and straining into the darkness because I knew once I moved out into the open there was no turning back. I had to be sure no one was there. I had to be doubly sure the dog wasn't up there waiting for me.

Now that I was close to the house, I could see chinks of light from one of the downstairs curtained windows. I could hear the whisper of dance music. The sound of that music made me feel lonely.

I still couldn't make up my mind to leave the shelter of the tree. I had a hunch it wasn't as safe up there as it looked. I kept staring and waiting, and then I saw the guard. By now my eyes had become used to the dark—and besides, the moon was coming up behind the house. He had been standing close to what looked like a big stone bird on a pedestal at the top of the steps. He had been merged into the design of the bird and I hadn't seen him, although he had been there all the time. Now that he had moved away from the bird I could see the outline of his cap against the white background of the terrace. I sucked in a lungful of air. He stood looking into the garden for a while, and then walked leisurely along the terrace, away from the back entrance.

I had to take a chance. He might turn and come back,

but I didn't think he would. I sprinted for the steps. I ran
on tiptoe and I gained the terrace without him having the
slightest idea he wasn't up there alone anymore. I could
still see him as I crouched by the balustrade. He had
reached the far end of the terrace and was standing with
his back turned to me, looking into the garden like a
ship's captain on his bridge. I didn't wait; keeping low,
I ran up more steps and reached the terrace above him.

I could hear the radio distinctly now. Ernie Caceres
was tearing a hole in "Persian Rug" on an alto sax. But
I had other things to do than to listen to Ernie, and I went
past the French windows, round the corner of the house
the way I had seen it on the blueprint.

I was a few yards from the back entrance when I heard
footsteps. My heart flopped around inside my hat and I
stood against the wall. I heard more footsteps—coming
toward me.

"You down there, Harry?" a voice called out of the
darkness. I thought I recognized it. It belonged to the
guard we had run into outside the gates. He couldn't
have been ten yards from me.

"Yeah," a voice called back.

I could see the guard now. He was leaning over the
balustrade, looking down at the other guard on the lower
terrace. The other guard had turned on a flashlight.

"All quiet?"

"Quiet enough. Dark as pitch down here."

"Keep your ears open, Harry. I don't want trouble
tonight."

"What's biting you, Ned?" The other guard's voice
sounded impatient. "Got the shakes or something?"

"You keep your damned eyes open like I say. Those
two guys are on my mind."

"Aw, forget them. They lost their way, didn't they?

Every time a guy loses his way and gets up here you have to act nervy. Take it easy, can't you?"

"I didn't like the look of them," Ned said. "While the blockhead was sounding off, the other guy was using his eyes. He looked tough to me."

"Okay, okay. I'm on my way around the grounds now. If I run into your tough guy I'll fertilize the soil with him."

"Take the dog," Ned said. "Where is he, anyway?"

"Chained up, but I'll take him. See you here in half an hour."

"Right."

I listened to all this as I stood like a statue in the dark. Ned stayed where he was, his back to me, his hands on his hips, looking out across the vast stretch of lawn.

Slowly I began to edge along the wall, away from him. I kept going, making no sound, until I lost sight of him in the darkness. After a few more steps I came to a door. I fumbled about until I found the iron ring that lifted the latch, turned it and pushed, but the door was locked. I transferred the leaded cane from one hand to the other, felt in my pocket and drew out the key Parker had given me. I daren't show a light. I began to feel up and down the door for the keyhole, and all the time I kept my ears cocked in case Ned took it into his head to come back. I found the keyhole, slid in the key, turned it gently. The lock eased back with a faint click. To me it sounded like a gun going off. I waited, listened, heard nothing, turned the ring again and pushed. The door opened. I edged my way into more darkness. Then I removed the key, shut the door, locked it from the inside and pocketed the key.

Now that I was inside the house, I was suddenly as cool and as calm as a tray of ice cubes. I was out of reach of that dog and that took a weight off my mind.

I knew exactly where to go. I had facing me, although I couldn't see them, five steps and a long passage. At the end of the passage there were more steps, and then a sharp right would bring me to Brett's study and the safe.

I listened for a moment or so. Ernie Caceres was showing his versatility by playing the clarinet solo in the "Anvil Chorus." I reckoned any noise I might make would be cancelled out by his high notes. I turned on the flash, got my bearings, went up the stairs and along the passage as fast as I could lick. There was a light at the head of the second flight of stairs. I shot up them, turned a sharp right into a little lobby that was glassed in on the garden side. A door faced me. It led to Brett's study. On my right was a broad flight of stairs to the upper rooms.

There was a sudden giggle at the head of the stairs. I didn't jump more than a foot.

A girl said, "Don't you dare! Oh!"

Fun and games among the staff, I thought, and wiped the sweat out of my eyes. The girl yelped again. Feet pounded overhead. There was another yelp and then a door slammed.

I waited some more but it got quiet then: no screams, no yelps. I thought it was time Brett got back. His staff was having too good a time. I didn't wait any longer, beetled over to the study door, turned the handle and peered in. No one yelled for help—no one was there. I went in and closed the door. The beam of the flashlight took me to the safe. It was right where the plan had said it was; so was the wire running down its side. If I hadn't been looking for the wire I wouldn't have seen it. It was what they call artfully concealed.

I cut the wire, expecting a peal of bells to start up all over the house, but nothing happened. It looked as if Parker had either cased the joint with expert thoroughness or else the alarm was still unset. I didn't know and didn't care.

I took the card from my pocket, checked the combination and then started on the dial. I held the flashlight on the dial and turned carefully: one full turn to the right, a two-second wait, one half turn back, another wait, a full turn to the right, another wait and a half turn to the right again. Just the way Parker had said. Then I took hold of the knob and pulled gently. I didn't expect anything to happen, but it did. The safe opened.

I whistled through my teeth, shone the beam of the flashlight into the steel-lined cabinet. On the second shelf in the corner was a small gold box, about three inches square—very neat and modern and expensive looking. I picked it up, balanced it in my hand. It was weighty for its size. There was no button or catch to open it. I fiddled with it for a second or so then dropped it into my pocket. There was no time to waste. I could examine it when I was out of the house.

I took the dagger case from my pocket. Up to now I had been too busy avoiding the guards and thinking about the dog to give the case any attention, but now I had it in my hand my brain began to function.

The dagger was the only thing about Gorman's story that didn't click. I was as sure as Parker was loony that the girl hadn't taken the dagger from Brett's safe, and that the compact wasn't her property. I had seen the dagger. It looked genuine enough. I didn't know anything about antiques, but I did know gold when I saw it, and the dagger was gold—that made it expensive. Then why was Gorman getting me to put a valuable antique in Brett's safe—an antique that I was certain didn't belong to Brett? Why? A thing like that could be easily traced. Why hire me to steal the compact and leave something in its place of equal value and which would give the police a clue that might take them to Gorman? There was something wrong here, something out of tune.

I looked at the case in the light of the flash. Maybe they had fooled me and the dagger wasn't in it. I tried to open the case, but it wouldn't budge. It was too heavy for an empty case. I continued to examine it, and suddenly it occurred to me that it was thicker and a shade longer than the case Gorman had shown me. I wasn't sure, but it looked that way to me. Then I heard something that brought me out in a rush of cold sweat. There was a faint but distant ticking coming from the case. I nearly dropped it.

No wonder those two smart punks had told me to handle it carefully. I knew what it was now. It was a bomb! They had made up the bomb to look like the dagger case, figuring I would be in such a hurry to get rid of it I wouldn't spot the exchange. I put it in the safe as fast as you'd have got rid of a tarantula dropped in your lap.

I had no idea, of course, when the bomb was timed to explode, but when it did, I knew it would blow everything in the safe to atoms. That's the way they had it figured. Brett wouldn't know whether or not the compact had been stolen. For all he could tell, an attempt had been made to blow open the safe, but too much T.N.T. had been used and the contents of the safe had been liquidated. It was a bright idea—an idea worthy of Gorman. But when I thought of climbing that wall, coming up here, wasting time dodging the guards with a bomb ticking in my pocket, I came out in another rush of cold sweat. I shut the safe and spun the dial. My one thought was to get as far away from the safe as I could before the bomb went off. Maybe I was a little panicky. You would have felt the same. Bombs are tricky things, and a homemade bomb is the trickiest of them all. I didn't doubt that Parker—if Parker was responsible for the thing—had timed it to go off sometime after we were well clear of the house; but I wouldn't trust anyone to be accurate when it comes to bomb mechanism. So far as I was concerned that bomb was likely to go off right now.

I shot to the door, jerked it open and walked out just as Ned, the guard, walked in.

I have a reputation for fast action when it comes to a fight. I don't have to think what to do when I step into that kind of trouble. My reflexes take care of the work long before my brain goes into action. I had Ned by his thick throat, throttling his yell, before I had gotten over the shock of running into him.

His reflexes were a mile behind mine. He just stood there for a split second, unable to move, letting me throttle him. I'll say this for him: he made a remarkable recovery. As soon as he realized what was happening, he caught hold of my wrists and I knew by his grip I wouldn't be able to hold him. He was as strong as a bear.

Only one thing mattered to me. I had to stop this guy from yelling. He tore one of my hands off his throat and swung a fist that felt like a lump of pig iron into the side of my neck. It hurt and got me mad. I socked him twice about the body. His ribs weren't made of concrete but they felt like it. He grunted, drew in a breath and I socked him again before he could yell. He sagged a bit at the knees, ducked under another smack I let fly at him and grabbed me around the body. We went to the floor, in slow motion, and settled on the carpet with scarcely a bump. We fought like a couple of animals then. He was as tough and as dirty as an all-in wrestler, and as savage. But I kept socking them into his body and I knew he wasn't built to take much of that stuff. I grabbed hold of his head and slammed it on the floor. He twisted away, gave me a kick in the chest that flattened me and let out a yell like a foghorn.

I jumped him and we sent a table crashing to the floor. I was rattled now. If the other guard came in with the dog, it wouldn't be so good. I hit Ned in the face with two punches that nearly bust my fists. He flopped to his side, groaning. I didn't blame him. Those smacks even hurt me.

Then the light went on and the other guard came in and that seemed to be that.

I kicked Ned away, half rose on my knee, paused. The .45 pointing at me looked a lot larger than a 240 milli-meter howitzer and twice as deadly.

"Hold it!" Harry said, his voice squeaky with fright.

I held it while Ned got unsteadily to his feet.

"What the hell is going on?" Harry demanded. He was a fat-faced, dumb-looking hick, but built like a bullock.

All I could think of was the bomb.

"Watch him, Harry," Ned croaked. "Just let me get my breath. I told you, didn't I? It's the same guy."

Harry gaped at me. His finger tightened on the trigger.

"We'd better call the cops," he said. "You all right, Ned?"

Ned cursed him and cursed me. Then he kicked me in my ribs before I could block his boot. I went sprawling across the room and I guess that saved me.

The bomb went off.

I was vaguely aware of a lot of noise, a flash of blind-ing light and a rush of air that flung me up against the wall. Then plaster crashed down on me, windows fell out, the room swayed and shook.

I found I was clutching the flashlight I'd dropped

when I had grabbed Ned. I knew I had to get out of there fast, but I had to see what had happened to the guards. I needn't have worried. They had been in a direct line of the safe door as it was blown off its hinges. I recognized Ned by his boots, but I didn't recognize Harry at all.

I stumbled through the broken French windows out onto the terrace. I was punch-drunk, slaphappy and scared witless, but my brain still functioned.

I was going to double-cross Gorman before he double-crossed me. The exploding bomb had made it easy for me.

I staggered over to the stone bird that guarded the top of the terrace steps. I don't know how I managed to climb up to the place where its wings joined its body, but I did. I put the compact in the little hollow between the wings, scrambled down, and began to run toward where I hoped I'd find Parker.

My legs felt as if the bones had been taken out of them and my ears sang. It looked a long way across that lawn to the wall and I wasn't sure if I could make it.

The moon had climbed above the house now and the garden was full of silvery light. You could see every blade of grass, every flower, every stone in the gravel paths. There was nothing you couldn't see. But I saw only one thing: the wolfhound coming straight at me like an express train.

I let out a yell you could have heard in San Francisco, turned to run, changed my mind, spun around to face the brute. He came over the lawn, low to the ground, his eyes like red-hot embers, his teeth as white as orange pith in the moonlight. I still dream about that dog, and I still wake up, sweating, thinking he's coming at me, feeling his teeth in my throat. He stopped dead within ten yards of me, dropped flat, turned to stone. I stood there, sweat dripping off me, my knees buckling, too scared even to breathe. I knew one flicker out of me and he'd come.

We stared at each other for maybe ten seconds. It seemed like a hundred years to me. I could see his tail stiffening and his back legs tightening for his spring, then there was a sharp crack of an automatic. I heard the slug whine past my head. The dog rolled over on its side, snarling and biting, its teeth snapping horribly at empty air.

I didn't wait to assess the damage. I ran toward the beam of the flashlight that flashed from the top of the wall. I got there, pulled myself up and fell with a thud on the far side.

Parker grabbed me around the waist, half dragged, half carried me to the car. I rolled in, slammed the door as he let in the clutch.

"Keep going!" I yelled at him. "They're right behind. They've got a car and they'll be after us."

I wanted to get him rattled so he wouldn't ask questions until we had gone too far to go back. I got him rattled.

He drove down the hills like he was crazy. That guy certainly could drive. Why we didn't go over the mountain road beats me. We tore down the road, took hairpin bends at eighty, our wheels inches from the overhang.

At the end of the mountain road he suddenly slammed on his brakes, skidded across the road, straightened up and turned on me as if he were out of his mind.

"Did you get it?" he screamed at me, grabbing my coat lapels and shaking me. "Where is it, damn you! Did you get it?"

I put my hand in the middle of his chest and gave him a shove that nearly sent him out of the car.

"You and your damned bomb!" I yelled back at him. "You crazy dumb cluck! You nearly killed me!"

"Did you get it?" he bawled, beating on the steering wheel with his clenched fists.

"The bomb blew it to hell," I told him. "That's what your bomb did. It blew the whole safe and everything in it to hell," and I hit him flush on the button as he came at me.

CHAPTER FIVE

I CAUGHT A GLIMPSE of myself in the mirror over the mantel as I came into the lounge. I was smothered in white plaster dust, my hair hung over my eyes, the sleeve of my coat was ripped, one knee showed through my trouser leg. If that wasn't enough, blood ran down my face from a cut above my eye and the side of my neck where Ned had socked me was turning a nice shade of purple. With the elegant Parker draped over my shoulder, it wasn't hard to see we had run into trouble, and plenty of it.

Gorman sat motionless in an armchair, facing the door. His great arms rested on the arms of the chair, his thick fingers gripped the chair arms as if he wanted to squeeze the wood to pulp. His fat face was as stony as a cobbled sidewalk.

In another chair by the fireplace sat Veda Rux, stiff and upright, her lips pressed tightly together, her eyes carefully blank, but wide open. She was dressed in white: a strapless gown that held itself up by willpower or suction or something—the kind of gown you'd keep watching in case you missed anything.

I swung Parker off my shoulder and dumped him on the chesterfield. Neither Gorman nor Veda said anything. The tension in the room was terrific.

"He threw an ing-bing and I had to slug him," I explained to nobody in particular and started to dust myself down.

"Did you get it?" Gorman asked. He didn't look at Parker.

"No."

I went over to the sideboard, poured myself a drink and sat down in a chair facing them. I knew I shouldn't have come back to this house. I should have dumped Parker, picked up the compact when things had cooled off and had it all my own way. But playing it safe would have lost me Veda, and I didn't reckon to lose her if I could help it.

Gorman didn't move. The chair arms creaked as his grip tightened. I shot a quick look at Veda. She was relaxed now. A muscle in her cheek twitched. It kept pulling one side of her mouth out of shape.

I emptied the glass at a swallow. I wanted that drink. As I set down the glass, Parker stirred, groaned and tried to sit up. Nobody looked at him. He might have been at the bottom of the sea for all anyone cared, and that included me.

"I didn't get it," I said to Gorman, "and I'll tell you why. Right from the start you've been too smart and too tricky. You and your stooge hadn't the guts to get that compact for yourselves. So you put your smart minds together and you thought up an idea to get it so you'd be in the clear, and the sucker you picked on to do the job would be way out on a limb if he failed. It wasn't a bad idea—a little elaborate, but still, not a bad idea. It might have worked, but it didn't because you knew all the answers and you kept them to yourself. You picked on me because I was in a jam. You found out the cops were waiting for a chance to throw a hook into me. You found out I was broke, and there wasn't much I wouldn't do for solid money.

"Where you slipped up was you didn't take the trouble to find out just how far I'd go for money. You knew I'd been mixed up in a couple of shady deals, but even at that you were scared to put your cards on the table and tell me you wanted me to steal something from Brett. You thought if it came to a proposition like that I'd buckle at the knees and squeal to the cops. But I wouldn't have done that, Gorman. Cracking a safe wouldn't have scared me away from a thousand bucks, but you weren't smart enough to know it."

Veda made a sudden little movement. It could have been a warning gesture or it might have been a nervous reflex. I didn't know.

I went right on. "You don't think I was sucked in by the sleepwalking act and the Cellini dagger, do you? I wasn't. I knew the compact belonged to Brett, and for some reason or other you wanted it. I wouldn't have given a damn one way or the other. I wanted your dough—that was all I cared about. But you weren't smart enough to know it. If you'd told me the dagger case was a bomb I would have known what to do, but you didn't. And when I found out it was a bomb I got rattled. Everything happened at once. I heard the ticking of the bomb and the guard coming all at the same time. I'd just opened the safe. All I could think of was to get rid of that bomb. I shoved it in the safe, locked the safe and went for the guard as he came in. I saw the compact in the safe, but I didn't touch it. It was still there when I closed the door of the safe. I could have handled the guard, only the second guard showed up.

"It looked as if I was in a mess, and then your homemade bomb went off. The safe door was blown off its hinges and it went through those two guards the way a hot knife goes through butter. It wrecked the room, too. It was a good bomb, Gorman. Whoever made it can be happy about that. I stayed long enough to see nothing but dust was left in the safe. The compact simply doesn't exist anymore. Then I came away." I got up, walked to the sideboard, poured another drink.

Parker was sitting up now, his hand to his jaw. He stared at me fixedly, his face white and drawn, his eyes vicious.

"He's lying," he said to Gorman. "I know he's lying."

Gorman released a little puff of breath.

"I hope he is," he said in his scratchy voice.

"Go and look for yourself," I said. "Take a look at those two guards. That's murder, Gorman."

"Never mind the guards," Gorman said. "It's the compact I'm interested in. Why did you leave it in the safe when you heard the guard coming?"

"I'd be a sucker to let him find it on me, wouldn't I?" I said evenly. "Look at it this way. If I was caught and they found nothing on me it'd make a difference to the sentence I'd get. I thought of that. I could have taken the compact after I'd settled the guard."

"On the other hand," Gorman said smoothly, "you might have put the compact in your pocket and chanced being caught."

Did he think I'd come back here with the compact in my pocket? Did he think I was that much of a sucker? The way I was playing it put me in a sweet position. He might think until he was blue in the face that I had the compact but he couldn't prove it.

"Go ahead and search me," I said. "Look me over if it'll set your mind at rest."

Gorman nodded to Parker.

"Search him," he said.

Parker went over me as if he'd like to tear me to pieces. I could feel his hot breath on the back of my neck as his hands ran over my clothes. It was an uncomfortable feeling. I expected him to bite me.

"Nothing," he said, his voice harsh with fury. "Is it likely the rat would have it on him?"

"Now look," I said, stepping away from him, "you guys are sore. All right, I understand that. But don't take it out on me. I did what I was paid to do. It's not my funeral you had to act smart and mix a bomb up in this."

Parker turned on Gorman. He was shaking with rage. "I told you not to go to him. I warned you, didn't I? I said over and over again we didn't want a man with his record. You knew he was tricky. Now look where he's landed us. We don't know whether he's lying or not. We don't even know if the case was blown to bits as he says or whether he's hidden it somewhere."

"Don't get excited, Dominic," Gorman said and looked across at me. "He's right, Mr. Jackson. We don't know if you're lying. But we can find out." He lifted his hand out of his pocket. The blue-nosed automatic looked like a toy in his thick fingers. "And don't think I wouldn't shoot, my friend. No one knows you're here. We could bury you in the garden and it might be years before you were found. You might never be found. So don't try any tricks."

"I told you what happened," I said. "If you don't believe it, that's your lookout. Waving a gun at me won't get you anywhere."

"Sit down, Mr. Jackson," Gorman said gently, "and let's talk this over." He suddenly seemed to be aware that Veda was still in the room. "Leave us, my dear," he said to her. "We want to talk to Mr. Jackson. You would only be in the way."

She went out quickly. The room seemed empty without her. I listened to the sound of her feet on the stairs, and heard something else: the swish of a club, and I ducked. A light exploded inside my head. I guess I ducked too late.

Before Parker belted me, I had noticed the hands of the clock on the mantel showed ten minutes past eleven. When I looked again it showed half past eleven and Parker was throwing water in my face. I shook my head, stared at the clock fuzzily. My head hurt and I felt a little sick. What really bothered me was finding that I was tied to the chair.

Gorman was standing by the fireplace watching me. Parker stood over me, a jug of water in his hand, a vicious, snarling expression on his face.

"Now, Mr. Jackson," Gorman said breathlessly, "let's talk about the compact. This time you'll tell me the truth or I'll have to persuade you."

"There's no fresh news on the compact, brother," I said steadily. "No stop press—no nothing."

"The weakness of your story is obvious," Gorman told me. "No one as smart as you would have left the compact in the safe once you had opened the safe. You would have grabbed it and chanced fighting your way out or you would have hidden it somewhere in the room where you could get at it quickly after you had liquidated the guard. You would never have left it in the safe, Mr. Jackson."

He was right, of course, but he couldn't prove anything and I grinned at him.

"I left it in the safe," I said. "The bomb had me rattled."

"Let me see if I can persuade you to change your story," he said and came toward me.

I watched him come. Now you see what I mean when I said having a woman on your mind leaves you wide open to a sucker punch. As I looked into his tight fat face, I told myself what a mug I'd been to come back here. I might have known he would have turned tough. Then I thought of Veda in that white dress and thought maybe I wasn't such a mug.

He was standing over me now, his eyes like wet stones.

"Are you going to tell me what you did with the compact, or will I have to choke it out of you, Mr. Jackson?"

"I looked carefully. That compact was a heap of dust," I told him. I tried to pull away from his hands, but the rope held me.

Thick fingers circled my chin and neck.

"You'd better change your mind, Mr. Jackson," he said in my ear. "Where's the compact?"

I looked across at Parker, who was standing by the fireplace. He was watching, a spiteful smile on his face. I braced myself.

"Nothing to add, brother," I said and waited for the squeeze. I'd said that if ever that thug got his hands on my throat he'd make blood come out of my ears. He nearly did. Just when I thought the top of my head was coming off, he relaxed. I dragged in a lungful of air, tried to blink away the bright lights that swam before my eyes.

"Where's the compact, Mr. Jackson?" His voice sounded a long way away and that bothered me.

I didn't say anything and he squeezed again. It was worse than being strangled. I felt the bone in my jaw creak under the pressure. I seemed to fade after that. It got dark and breathless like I was drowning.

More water hit me in the face. I came to the surface gasping. Gorman was still there. He was breathing strenuously.

"You're being foolish, Mr. Jackson," he said. "Very, very foolish. Tell me where the compact is and I'll give you the balance of the money and you can go. I'm trying to be fair with you. Where is the compact?"

I cursed him, trying to wrench away from his hand and the squeeze started all over again. After minutes of choking, flashes of pain and a horrible sensation of being slowly crushed, I passed out again.

The hands of the clock on the mantel showed twelve-ten when I opened my eyes. The room was very still and quiet. The only light came from a reading lamp at the far end of the room. Without moving my head, I looked about the room. Parker was sitting under the lamp, reading a book, a fat cigarette hanging from his lips. There was no sign of Gorman. On the table at Parker's elbow was a heavy club with a wrist thong attached.

I didn't make a move to tell him I was with him in spirit as well as in flesh. I had a feeling if he knew I'd come to the surface he'd start working on me. My neck felt as if the Empire State Building had fallen on it, and my nose dripped blood. I felt as lively and as fit as a ten-day-old corpse.

I heard the door open and I played dead, shutting my eyes and sitting as still as a dummy in a shop window. I smelled her perfume as she paused to look at me. I heard her go over to Parker.

"You shouldn't be here," he said sharply. "What do you want? You should be in bed."

"Has he said anything?" she demanded.

"Not yet, but he will."

He sounded too confident—much, much too confident.

"Is he conscious?" she asked.

"I don't know and I don't care. Go to bed."

She came back to stand close to me. She had changed out of her white dress and was wearing the canary-colored slacks again. I looked up at her. She was pale and her eyes were overbright. For a brief second our eyes met, then she turned quickly away.

"He's still unconscious," she said to Parker. "He looks very bad."

I felt a tingle run up my spine.

"Not half as bad as he'll look when Gorman gets back. Go away. You shouldn't be here."

"Where is Cornelius?"

"He's gone to Brett's place to see if he can find out anything."

"But what can he find out? The police will be there, won't they?"

"How do I know?" His voice snapped at her. "Go to bed. I don't want you here with him."

"You're not angry with me, Dominic?"

I moved my head slowly so I could watch them. She was standing over him, her slim fingers playing with the club, her eyes on his face.

"No, I'm not angry," he said. "But go to bed. You can't do anything."

"Do you think he's hidden it?"

Parker clenched his fists.

"I don't know. That's the trouble. That's where he's been so smart. It could have been destroyed. All this trouble—all these plans, and now we don't know." He thumped the arm of his chair. "Cornelius was crazy to trust this cheap, tricky crook."

"Yes." She was swinging the club idly in her hand now. "But Cornelius won't be able to get near the house, will he? I don't understand why he has gone."

"He can't do anything. I told him that, but he wouldn't listen. He can't rest until he knows. If he doesn't find out anything he'll kill Jackson. I don't care what he does. I'm past caring."

She pointed down at his feet.

"Is that something of yours?"

It was well done, casual and quiet—an ordinary every-day question. It fooled Parker; it nearly fooled me. He leaned forward to look. The back of his head was a perfect target. He spread out on his face on the floor. He didn't even groan.

She stepped back, dropped the club; one hand went to her face.

"I liked your follow-through," I said.

She turned swiftly to look at me.

"What happens now?" I asked.

She continued to stare at me. "There's nothing else I could do, was there?" she said. Her words tumbled over themselves. "I couldn't let them torture you."

"That's right," I said. "How about cutting me loose?"

She moved quickly to the sideboard, found a knife and came over to me.

"I have a car outside. If only I knew where to go," she said as she sawed at the ropes.

"You mean you want to come with me?" I knew she couldn't stay here after clobbering Parker, but I wanted to hear her say she would go with me.

"What else can I do?" she asked impatiently. "If Cornelius ever finds me after this—I don't know what he'll do to me."

I threw off the last rope, got unsteadily to my feet.

"That's fine," I said, feeling my throat with tender fingers. "The moment I saw you I knew you and me were going to tie up. We'll make a fine partnership." I tottered over to the sideboard, poured myself a large drink. It hurt as it went down but it did me a power of good when it was down. "We'll talk when we get out of here. I can't go like this. Where does Parker keep his clothes?"

"The door facing the top of the stairs. Will he be all right?"

"Sure. He'll sleep for hours. Wait for me. I won't be long."

I went over to Parker, turned him over, relieved him of his gun and stuck it in my hip pocket.

"I'll be right with you," I said and left her.

It took me ten minutes to wash and change into one of Parker's less fancy suits. It was a little tight across the shoulders, but it would do in a pinch. I found a white silk scarf that I wound round my throat to hide the bruises. My head ached and my neck felt as if it'd been fed through a wringer, but taking me by and large, I felt pretty good.

I ran down the stairs, back into the lounge. She was waiting for me. There was an alert, watchful expression in her eyes and she was still pale.

I looked from her to Parker. He wouldn't come to for hours.

"All set?" I asked, smiling at her.

"Where are we going?"

"Santa Medina. That'll do us for tonight. We can make plans when we know more about each other. Taking anything with you?"

"My bag's in the car."

"Sounds like premeditation."

"As soon as Cornelius left I knew what I was going to do."

My heart was beginning to hammer against my ribs again.

"Now I wonder why you picked on me?" I asked.

She didn't say anything and didn't look at me.

"Maybe we'd better go," I said after I'd given her time to answer if she was going to answer.

"Kiss me," she said.

Well, that certainly took care of that. She had an unnerving effect on me. I was shaking when she pushed me away.

"Now we'll go," she said and went with me to the door.

We both stopped abruptly as we opened the front door. Gorman was standing at the foot of the steps, looking up at us. He was as startled as we were. I beat him to the draw.

"Watch it!" I said. My voice sounded like someone ripping a sunblind in half.

Gorman dropped his hands. His little black eyes went from me to Veda. His face was empty.

Max was in the car. He stared out of the window at me, his eyes wide with fright.

"You," I said. "Get out of that. There's a gun in his right-hand pocket. Get it."

Max got out of the car, went up behind Gorman, dipped into his pocket and fished out the gun.

"Take it from him," I said to Veda.

She went down the steps. Max held the gun out to her, butt first. She took it.

"You foolish child," Gorman said to her. "You'll be sorry for this."

"Cut it out!" I said. "She's coming with me."

"Well, you're lucky this time, Mr. Jackson," he said quietly, "but I shall find you again, and I shall find you, too, Veda." He was very calm and controlled—it made him all the more dangerous. "I shall find you again. You can be sure of that."

"Go in and keep Parker company. He's kind of lonely in there. And I'll have the ring. I'm a little pressed for cash."

He looked down at the diamond and then at me.

"If you want it, you must take it," he said and closed his hand into a gigantic fist.

"You forget I have the gun," I pointed out. "A guy with a gun always gets his own way."

"Not this time, Mr. Jackson."

"Hand it over, pally."

He didn't move.

I felt Veda's eyes on me. If I let this fat thug get away

with it, I'd lose caste. Besides, I needed the ring. But I wasn't going near him. I knew if he got his hand on me I wouldn't stand a chance.

"I'm sorry about this, Fatso," I said and meant it. "But I want the ring. You'll get a smashed foot if you don't hand it over. I'll give you three seconds."

He stared at me, then his mouth twitched. It was the only sign of rage he had shown up to now. He saw I wasn't fooling.

"Then take it, Mr. Jackson," he said, pulling the ring off his finger. He threw it at my feet. "It'll make it harder for you when next we meet."

I picked up the ring and put it in my pocket. It's a funny thing, but now I had it I knew all along I'd made up my mind to take it off him—the moment I'd seen it when he first came to my office.

We left him standing on the steps looking after us. Veda drove. Her car was an open coupe, fast and slick. I knelt on the seat, the gun in my hand, watching Fatso until I lost him in the darkness.

I had an uneasy feeling I'd meet him again.

CHAPTER SIX

No tourists ever go to Santa Medina and the million-aires shun it like a plague spot. After you've seen San Luis Beach, I guess Santa Medina looks like a plague spot.

The only thing that thrives in this small compact town of wooden buildings, sun-bleached awnings and beer saloons is Mick Casy's gambling joint, where sooner or later every crook, twister, con man and gambler from the four corners of the States looks in to say hello and shoot craps. Casy's joint is famous along the whole of the Pacific Coast. They say if it wasn't for Mick Casy, Santa Medina would have folded up long ago, and some think the sooner Casy clears out of town and lets it fold up the better.

The gambling joint dominates the town. You can see its big electric sign long before you even know there's a town down there in the darkness. It is the only brick-tile building in the town, and it stands in a vacant lot with a broad concrete driveway up to the entrance.

I've known Casy for a long time. I ran into him years ago before he was in the money. He used to play pool for a living in those days. There wasn't a smarter guy with a cue in the country, but his reputation went ahead of him and he had trouble getting a sucker to play with him. He was always broke at that time, and when I ran into him he had got himself mixed up in a shooting affair in a place on the San Francisco waterfront. It had been a political killing, and the cops were looking for a fall guy. They picked on Casy, and the frame would have stuck if I hadn't come forward as the surprise witness at the trial. I proved Casy didn't do the shooting because I swore he was with me at the time. He wasn't, but it didn't seem right to me that because a guy was broke and had no influence, the cops could pick on him to save the neck of some greasy politician who was too weak in the head to hold his liquor.

My testimony swayed the jury, and they threw out the case. Casy and I had to leave town fast. The cops would have given us a going-over if they'd've caught us, but we were too quick for them.

Casy took himself very seriously. He swore I'd saved his life. He said he'd never forget it, and he didn't. Whenever I looked him up everything was on the house, and he'd get mad if I wanted even to settle my gambling debts. It embarrassed me and I gave up seeing him. I hadn't seen him now for maybe six months.

Until I found out more about the compact and why Gorman wanted it so badly, I decided to hole up with Casy. I'd be safe there and so would Veda. If Gorman tried any tricks, he'd find he wasn't only bucking me but Casy and the whole town as well.

I explained to Veda about Casy as she drove down the mountain road to Santa Medina.

"All right," she said out of the darkness. I could just see the outline of her head and the red spark of the cigarette she had in her mouth. "But I don't want to talk now. I want to think. Do you mind if I think? We can talk later, can't we?"

I didn't get anything else out of her until she pulled up outside Casy's joint.

"Is this it?" she asked.

I helped her out of the car and pointed to the electric sign. It was twenty-four feet square, and even from where we stood we could feel the heat from the neon lights.

"Speaks for itself, doesn't it?" I said. "Come on in and meet Casy."

The guard at the door gave me a quick, hard look, then touched his cap. He was paid to know who could go in there without a frisk and who couldn't. I guess he earned his money.

"The boss around?" I asked him.

"In the office."

"Thanks."

I took Veda's arm and we went through the lobby, across a sea of drugget carpet, past one of the five bars and down a passage that led to Casy's quarters. Close by a very hot band was playing. There was a smell of tobacco smoke and whisky in the air.

It wasn't a luxury joint, but it served its purpose. You could find anything you wanted within its walls from a willing blonde to a poker chip. Casy catered for all vices. The only reason the cops hadn't slammed the place shut was the police chief himself had a kink and Casy looked after him.

A guy with a profile like Byron, only better, in a nifty white flannel suit and with a cornflower in his buttonhole, drifted out of a room and minced toward us. He looked at Veda with eyes like Disney's Bambi, fluttered long lashes at her and minced on.

The expression on her face made me laugh. I took her into the bar that was reserved for Casy's friends. The room was full of men and tobacco smoke. Joe, Casy's bodyguard, a short, thickset guy with a flat, ugly puss and eyes like chips of ice, heaved himself away from the bar and came scowling toward me. But he grinned when he recognized me and gave me a light punch on the chest. Then he saw Veda and he pursed his thick lips.

"Hello, chummy," he said to me. "Where did you spring from? Ain't seen you in months."

"Casy around?"

He jerked his head to the door at the far end of the room.

"Go ahead. He ain't doing nothing."

All the men had stopped talking and were staring at Veda. I didn't blame them. I guess if she took a walk through a burial ground the graves would give up their dead. But I hunched my shoulders and looked tough just to let them know it wouldn't be healthy to get the wrong ideas. She walked past those guys as if they were poles in a sheep fence.

"That door there," I said to her, and she turned the handle and walked right in.

Casy was sitting at his desk, a bottle of Scotch at his elbow, a cigar in his small white teeth. He was in shirtsleeves and his tie hung loose and his collar was open. His thick black hair looked as if he'd just run his fingers through it.

"Floyd!" He jumped to his feet. "Well, what do you know! How are you, soldier?"

I shook hands and we tried to crack each other's bones. Casy has quite a clutch.

"I'd like you to meet Miss Rux," I said, grinning at him. "Veda, this is Mick Casy, the guy I told you about."

"Glad to know you," Casy said, a little uneasy. "Sit down. Have a drink?"

Veda sat down. She seemed to throw Casy out of his stride. He began to do up his collar and retie his tie.

"You'll excuse me. I wasn't expecting visitors."

"Be yourself, Mick," I said, pulling up another chair. "Veda's a regular fellow. You wait until you know her like I do."

Casy smiled uneasily. I could see Veda had knocked him.

"Is that right? Well, you certainly can find 'em, Floyd. Damn it, have a drink?"

While he set up glasses, Veda studied him. Casy was short, with a chest like a barrel, nearing fifty and looked what he was: the owner of a successful gambling joint.

"Where've you been all this time, Floyd?" he asked, shooting me a puzzled glance. "I haven't seen you in months. What's cooking?"

"Trouble in one form and another," I said, and picked up the glass he had pushed towards me, shot the whisky down my throat. "A couple of guys are being difficult, Mick. I want to hole up for a while."

"Cops?" Casy again glanced at Veda as if he couldn't place her.

I shook my head. "Not yet it isn't cops, but it could be later."

"Two guys, huh? Like me to take care of them? For the love of Pete, Floyd, use your head. What do you want to hole up for? Joe will take care of anyone bothering you, you know that."

"Yeah, but this is a kind of a family affair. I'll take care of them when the time comes, but the time hasn't come yet. Veda and I just want to stay out of sight for a few days. Can you fix it for us?"

Casy ran his fingers through his hair, frowned. "Sure I can. Come over to the hotel with me if you like. Plenty of protection, drinks and nice beds. You'd like it. That suit you?"

I shook my head. "I was sort of figuring on being alone."

He took another look at Veda. This time he smiled.

"Yeah, I should have thought of that. There's the pent-house on the top floor. A couple of boys are in there now, but they can come out. How's about it?"

I knew the penthouse. I was hoping he'd let me have it.

"Fine," I said.

He seemed glad to show what he could do for me. He shouted for Joe.

"Big shot," I said to Veda. "Watch his smoke."

Veda didn't say anything. She had gone back to her statue act. Her eyes were watchful and she sat very still.

Joe came in.

"Get those two punks out of the penthouse, Joe," Casy ordered, "and have someone clean up the place. Make it snappy. Floyd's moving in."

Joe looked surprised, but he didn't ask questions.

"Sure, boss," he said and went away.

"Anything else I can do?" Casy asked. "If there is, just name it."

I produced Gorman's diamond, tossed it on the blotter.

"I'd like to raise a little folding money on that, Mick."

He picked up the diamond, held it under the light, frowned at it. "Nice stone."

"Yeah, but it's hot."

He looked up sharply, his frown deepening.

"Not a copper job, Mick. I took it off the guy who's making trouble for me. He won't go to the cops."

Casy's frown went away. "Okay. What do you want?"

"It's worth four, five grand. Three will do."

"Cash?"

"Yeah."

He went to an open safe, dug out a wad of notes, tossed a thick packet on the desk in front of me.

"There's a grand there. That'll hold you, won't it? You can have the rest whenever you want it."

I stuffed the notes away in my hip pockets.

"You're a pal, Mick."

"Sure, I'm a pal." He looked at Veda. "He saved my life once. He's a good guy. I'm telling you. Don't let anyone tell you different."

"I won't," Veda said.

Casy poured more drinks.

"About these two guys," he said. "Sure you wouldn't want me to take care of them?"

I shook my head.

"Not yet. Still, you never know. One of them is tough."

"I like them tough," Casy said simply, and meant it.

Joe put his head round the door.

"All clear up there. I've taken your bags up, miss." He leered at Veda.

She thanked him. In spite of her calm, I could see she was a little bewildered by all the attention.

"Come on then," Casy said, struggling out of his chair. "We'll go up."

I put my hand on his shoulders and shoved him down again.

"I'll see you tomorrow, Mick. We'll have a little talk then. Right now I have business with the brunette."

Joe coughed behind his hand. Casy looked startled.

"I guess I'm slipping," he said apologetically. "Why sure, you go right on ahead."

"That's the idea," I said and took Veda's arm. "Let's go," I said to her.

At the door I looked back.

Casy was staring, his mouth a little open. Joe was kissing his thick fingers to the ceiling.

"And thanks, Mick," I said, opened the door and followed Veda across the bar.

The guys all stopped talking again. They x-rayed Veda as she walked to the far door. One fella gave a low long whistle. I scowled at him. He cut the whistle short.

I showed her to the elevator in the lobby and we rode up together to the roof level.

A bellhop with a big friendly smile opened the door of the penthouse for us. He said it was all ready, and after showing me where the whisky was, he went away, rolling his eyes.

The penthouse was a gaudy little love nest that at one time Casy had thought of using for himself. Although he had plenty of ideas about women, he had never found one that could interest him for more than a couple of hours. He was always too busy thinking up new ways of making money to take a woman seriously, and when he bought up the local hotel, he took over the largest suite and lived there, surrounded by hard-drinking, hard-swearing gamblers who shared his itch for money. The penthouse, as far as Casy was concerned, was a white elephant, but it came in handy for his friends—it was seldom empty.

It consisted of a big lounge, a bedroom, bathroom, kitchen and a roof garden. It had been decorated and furnished by a swank firm in Los Angeles, and it *looked* as if it had been decorated and furnished by a swank firm in Los Angeles.

Veda looked around the lounge, her hands in her pockets, her head on one side.

"Like it?" I asked.

She turned slowly on her heels to face me.

"What have you done with the compact?" she asked.

"Sit down." I went over to the cocktail cabinet. "Before we talk about the compact, we'll talk about you. Where do you figure in this?"

She sat down, crossed her legs and frowned at her slim hands.

"I want to know about the compact," she said. "What have you done with it?"

"One thing at a time." I mixed a couple of highballs, came over to her. "Who are you? Let's begin at the beginning. How did you get mixed up in this?"

She took the drink, brooded for a moment, then said, "I couldn't help myself. I wanted money."

I sat opposite her, lowered half the highball, set the glass on the floor by my feet, reached for a carton of cigarettes on a nearby table, threw her one, lit up and tossed the matches over to her.

"How did you run into Gorman?"

"He's my agent."

I studied her.

"He told me you were a stripper. That right?"

"Yes."

"Look, don't make me drag it out of you like I was pulling out your teeth. Start in from the beginning. I want to know as much about you as you know yourself."

She sipped her highball and studied me. She had a way of looking at you from under her lashes. You couldn't see her eyes when she looked at you like this—but you could feel them.

"Why should I tell you anything about myself?"

"Why shouldn't you?"

She shifted her gaze from me to the opposite wall. There was a thoughtful, faraway expression in her eyes; she began to talk.

Her old man was a farmer, she told me. He had a small farm near Waukomis, Oklahoma. There was her ma, four brothers and five sisters. Ever since she could remember, things had been tough. The farm was a ruin; her old man had done what he could to hold the place together, but it licked him. It licked her ma, too, and she was hard and bitter with the misery of it all. The kids were half starved and wild. When Veda was sixteen they found her old man by a waterhole. He'd worked himself to a standstill and had fallen facedown in four inches of water and had drowned. He hadn't had the strength left in him to turn his face for air.

The family split up after that. Veda got a job in a roadside restaurant, washing dishes and serving meals to hungry truckers who came in at all hours of the day and night.

She was crazy about the movies and her one thought was to get to Hollywood. She was sure she'd get a job as an extra and then when someone important saw her she'd be made a star. She talked to a trucker about her chances. He told her she couldn't miss. A girl with her looks, he said, and with her figure, was a snap for the movies, and offered to take her to the strip.

At first she couldn't believe him, but he assured her he wasn't kidding. Of course, he told her, looking at her with his hard, intent eyes, there was a little ceremony attached to the offer. She couldn't expect him to give her the money, but she wouldn't mind earning it, now would she? There was a sweaty animal look on his face that turned her cold.

How's about it, kid? he wanted to know. How's about it?

She felt in her bones if she could get to Hollywood she'd be a star. She wouldn't have to wash dishes or smell stale cooking or wash her own clothes or go to the outhouse in the cold and the dark; she wouldn't have to do any of those things again if she could get to Hollywood. She wouldn't have to make do on five dollars a week if she got to Hollywood. She said she'd meet him in the barn that night.

Of course he gypped her out of the dough, but she got to Hollywood a year later. It took her three weeks to do the trip. She hitchhiked all the way, and paid her fare like any other of the hundreds of road floozies travelling that route, and she landed in Hollywood with a veneer you couldn't crack with a steam hammer.

She got a job as a waitress in a smart café opposite one of the big film studios. After a while of playing around with various studio technicians, she met one of the lesser-known directors. He traded a film test for a weekend in his caravan, and was honest enough to tell her, although she looked fine in the flesh, she just didn't photograph. He let her see the test, and she was smart enough to see he was right.

The director had practically promised her a job on the screen and he felt bad when he saw the way the test turned out. He told her he wanted to do something for her and gave her an introduction to Gorman.

Gorman, he told her, ran a team of strippers who were in big demand at stags, reunions and wherever a party of men had got together to celebrate. The job was worth fifty to a hundred bucks a night and all she'd have to do was to sit in a bathtub full of champagne or in a glass bowl or dance on a table or stuff like that. She'd be unlucky if she didn't get one or two engagements a week.

Gorman signed her up and she worked with him for a year or so. She soon got used to the work and she was popular and in demand. She earned money, spent money and never had any money. Then Gorman came to her with a proposition.

All the time she'd been talking she had stared at the wall. It was as if she had been talking to herself. When she came to Gorman's proposition she got up for a cigarette, and when she had lit it she said, "He told me he'd fixed up for me to do my act at Lindsay Brett's in San Luis Beach. I didn't think anything of it. I was used to going to people's houses and around the country. Then he said I could make myself a lot of money if I found out the combination of the safe in this house, and if there were any alarms and what the routine of the guards were and stuff like that. I thought he was fooling at first. There'd never been anything like that before. But he wasn't fooling. He said it'd be worth a thousand dollars to me if I got the information he wanted. I said I'd think it over."

She wandered around the room, her hands in her pockets, the cigarette held tightly in her lips, showing herself off. She had a shape to set a man crazy.

"I told him I'd do it," she said, paused to look at me and then continued her prowling. "It was easy. Brett opened the safe to show his friends a diamond he'd bought. He had the combination on a card he took from his wallet. It was easy to get hold of the wallet and copy the combination without him knowing it. He got pretty drunk as the evening went on. They all did—it was some evening. I asked him about the alarms and he showed me how they worked. He was proud of them and got a lot of fun out of making the bells ring and bringing the guards arunning. I even took a wax impression of the back door key. I was pretty efficient, and they were all as drunk as an Irishman on St. Patrick's Day."

"So you didn't walk in your sleep?"

She laughed. It was a hard little sound without humor. "That's one of the few things I don't do."

"And then what happened?"

"I told Gorman I knew the combination of the safe, and how the alarms worked and that I'd taken a wax impression of the key. He was pleased until I asked him what it was all about." She pursed her lips, frowning as she recollected the scene. "He wasn't so pleased when I told him he'd have to cut me in on his racket or he wouldn't get the information."

I was listening attentively now. "Did he?"

"Yes." She flicked ash onto the carpet. "It didn't come as easy as that, of course, but he came across in the end."

"And what did he tell you?"

She rested her elbows on the mantel and pushed her chest out at me.

"He told me why he wanted the compact, and what he was going to do when he'd got it. He told me how much the compact was worth and how he was going to get the money. He agreed to trade a one-third share of whatever he got for my information."

"Why did he want the compact?" I asked casually— a little too casually.

"What did you do with it?" she asked, also casually.

This was where I'd come in. "Yeah, that's what you said before. You needn't worry about the compact. That's been taken care of. Finish your story. Why did he want it?"

"Why do you think I ratted on Gorman?" she returned and surveyed me with her alert, cool eyes.

"You didn't want him to torture me," I said. "Remember?"

She laughed; the sound jeered at me. "Guess again."

"You thought Gorman would gyp you out of your share. You knew Parker was screwy, and you didn't put it past him after they had the compact to twist your pretty neck and stick you headfirst in the lily pond."

Her lapis-lazuli eyes brooded. "Go on."

"You also thought one third wasn't as good as half, and when I turned up, you thought I was the kind of guy you could do things with. And when I came back with the yarn that the compact had gone up in smoke, you were sure I was the guy for you."

She pushed her chest out at me. "I have information to sell. It'll cost you half of whatever you get out of Brett if you want to buy it."

I got up, yawned. "Come on, kid, we're going to bed. We've talked enough for tonight. I'll show you where we'll lay our weary heads."

Alarm and doubt flickered into her eyes.

"Don't you want my information?" she asked sharply.

"I'll think about it," I said, took her arm and led her across to the bedroom. "Maybe I can do without your help."

"No, you can't," she said, pulling away. "It's no good thinking you can. The compact means nothing to anyone unless they know what I know."

"So you say," I said, sitting on the bed. "But I have an inquiring mind. I was a dick once. It's my business to find out things, and you'd be surprised at the things I have found out."

She faced me; two angry red spots of color showed on her cheeks. She was no longer calm and alert—she was rattled.

"I want half—" she began, but I pulled her down on the bed.

"Don't go shrill on me, sweetheart," I said. "I'm not interested in business anymore tonight. I want a little fun."

"You're not getting it from me like this!" she said through her clenched teeth and tried to break my hold, but she wasn't the only one with steel in her wrists. "Let me go!" she went on furiously. "I'll scream!"

"Go ahead," I said, gripping her arms. "What's a scream or two in this joint? Someone's always screaming here, it's part of the setup. Scream as much as you like if you want to."

"Let me go—damn you!"

She wrenched an arm free and I collected a punch in the jaw that jerked my head back. She kicked my shin and thumped my sore neck with her clenched fist, but she didn't scream and her wriggling only seemed to bring her body closer to mine.

I'd been punched around plenty during the past twenty-four hours. I was supposed to be a tough guy, but up to now everyone had been using me as a door scraper. It was about time something went my way.

"This is how it is," I said, leaning over her. "We've been suckers long enough. Now it's our turn, Blue Eyes, to get what we want. This is what I want and I hope you'll like it."

"You beast!" she panted, struggling up and closer still.

I grabbed her shoulders. She tried to bite, but she didn't try very hard. After a while her arms slid around my neck and she held on like she was scared of losing me. Her lips parted against mine. Her eyes were shining like two blue stars.

Like I said, women are funny animals.

CHAPTER SEVEN

THE CLANG OF THE TELEPHONE clapper brought me upright in bed. Another jackrabbit popped out of the pillows beside me.

"No fire," I said. "Only the telephone. Did it scare you?"

Veda pulled away from my clutch.

"Not as much as it seems to have scared you," she retorted, and as the telephone was at her side of the bed, she reached for it.

I put an arm across her chest, flattening her into the pillows. "I'll take it. You rest yourself."

I had to lean on her to reach the receiver, so I leaned on her.

"You have the manners of a hog," she gasped, "and that's insulting the hog."

I smiled down into fierce blue eyes, and lifted the receiver off its prong.

"I'm at my best with cripples and very, very old ladies," I assured her. Into the phone I yawned a hello.

Casy's voice barked in my ear. "Come on down, Floyd. The lid's aching to fly off this can, but I'm holding it on till you get here."

"What can?" I said. "And don't shout, Mick, my nerves are jangling." They were, too. I felt I could duck under a duck and not ruffle its feathers.

Casy let out a bellow.

"To hell with your nerves. Come on down and shake the ants outa your pants. Give you five minutes," and he hung up.

I replaced the receiver gently, ran my fingers through my hair and looked down at the small pale face buried in the pillows. Most dames would have looked a little wilted, but Veda didn't. She still looked great enough to eat.

"Hello?" I said. "Remember me?"

"If I don't my collapsed lungs will," she returned tartly. "Get off, you big oaf. You're crushing the life out of me."

"Swell death," I said, heaved myself out of bed, stretched, yawned and made a jump for the bottle. "Like a little of the dog that bit you?"

"No, thank you." She raised herself up on her elbow. "Who was that?"

"Casy. I have to go down. I'll have some coffee sent up for you."

"What's he want?" Her tone was sharp.

"He didn't say. Maybe he's lonely." I found my wrist-watch amongst the junk I'd dumped on the dressing table. It was twenty minutes past eleven. "Hey! We've slept away most of the morning!"

"Isn't that what mornings are for?" she asked and curled down in the bed again.

I took another slug at the bottle before taking a shower. Ten minutes later I entered Casy's office. I was all in one piece, but my nerves still twittered and my neck felt like it'd been boffed with a meat ax.

Casy was standing by the window, a cigar in his teeth, his hands clasped behind his back. There was a sullen expression in his eyes and the corners of his mouth were down.

A short, bland-looking man sat on the edge of the most uncomfortable chair in the room and smiled at the black hat resting on his knees. Everything about him was neat: his hair, his clothes, his shave and his shoes. His smile was the neatest of them all.

Casy grunted as I came in.

"You've taken your time. This is O'Readen, Chief of Police."

I got ready to duck, but the bland-faced man jumped up hurriedly and held out his hand.

"Glad to know you, Mr. Jackson," he said—even his handshake was neat. "Mighty glad to know you."

Usually when chiefs of police meet me they start tearing up the floorboards to hunt out a skunk, so this reception surprised me.

"I'm glad to have you know me," I said and disentangled my hand. I put it in my pocket for safekeeping.

Casy stamped over to his desk and sat down.

"Park yourself, Floyd," he said and pulled at his short, thick nose. He stared at O'Readen with sullen anger. "Tell him," he barked.

O'Readen smiled at nobody in particular. "A little trouble broke out on Ocean Rise last night," he said. He seemed to be confiding the news to his hat, but I didn't miss a word. "The San Luis Beach Homicide Bureau called me this morning and asked for my co-operation. An attempt was made to open the safe belonging to Lindsay Brett and two guards were killed."

"What's this?" I asked Casy. "A subscription for their wreaths or something?"

"O'Readen is a good friend of mine." Casy glared at O'Readen as if he could eat him. "He takes care of my headaches. It's part of his job."

O'Readen continued to smile, but the edges of the smile were a little frayed.

"I do what I can," he explained to his hat; then, in

case he hadn't made himself plain, he added, "What little I can do, I do."

I selected an armchair, folded myself down in it and set fire to a cigarette. This was the kind of police chief I liked.

"And what he does for me," Casy continued grimly, "he'll do for you. Right, O'Readen?"

The smile wobbled, but came through. "That's why I'm here, Mr. Jackson," O'Readen said. "You see, Redfern—you know Lieutenant Redfern?"

I said I knew Redfern.

"Yes." O'Readen shook his head. "Well, Redfern has been on to me. He's connecting you with the robbery at Brett's place."

I didn't jump more than a foot. I knew Redfern was smart, but not all that smart. I wondered if Gorman had turned me in.

"Why pick on me?" I said after the silence had become embarrassing.

"The guards at Brett's place keep a log," O'Readen explained apologetically. "It seems you and another man drove up to Brett's house yesterday morning. You were both reported in the log as suspicious characters. There's a comprehensive description of you. Redfern says he recognized you by the tie you wore. He says you're the only character he knows who wears horses' heads on your ties."

"There must be others," I pointed out.

"Yes, but the rest of the description would convince a jury, he tells me. These guards were police trained. They didn't miss much."

I looked over at Casy.

"Were you up there yesterday morning?" he asked.

"Sure."

O'Readen's smile went a little limp.

"Brett's got a lot of influence," he said uneasily. "He arrived back this morning and is yelling for blood."

"To hell with Brett!" Casy snapped. "Now listen. Jackson was here last night. He arrived around seven-thirty and he played poker until two o'clock in the morning. He played with me and Joe and you, O'Readen."

The smile slipped a foot. O'Readen couldn't even jack it into place. "I don't think he played with me," he said gently, like he was tiptoeing across a floor. "I'm not much of a poker player."

"That's right. You're a lousy player. He took fifty dollars off you."

I flicked ash all over the carpet. It was a pretty nice feeling to know I played poker with a chief of police: a nice, safe feeling.

"This is a murder charge," O'Readen said painfully. "Redfern could stick a knife into me. You know I'd help if I could, but I wouldn't want him to know I play poker here."

Casy chewed his cigar—anger and contempt brooded in his eyes. "You and me and Joe and Jackson played poker here last night from seven-thirty until two," he said savagely. "What the hell do you think I pay you for? I don't give a damn if Redfern sticks a knife into you. He can stick a harpoon into you for all I care. That's our story and you're stuck with it. Now get the hell out of here and earn some of that dough I'm putting in your bank."

O'Readen got up, smiled at his hat again. His face was the color of a fish's belly and he looked as if he were getting over a long and painful illness.

"Well, if that's how you feel," he said. "I'll see what I can do."

"You'll do better than that. You'll do what I tell you,"

Casy snarled. His voice sounded like a buzz saw tearing into a wood knot.

We watched O'Readen all the way across the room to the door. He didn't look back and walked a little flat-footed. When the door closed, Casy spat viciously into the brass spittoon by the desk.

"I pay that punk a hundred bucks a week to keep me in the clear, and every time I want him to take care of anything he squawks."

"Nice work, Mick," I said admiringly. "I didn't know you owned the town. You've pulled me out of a hole bigger than the one you were in. That makes us quits."

"Like hell it does," he said, but his face brightened. "Listen, soldier, when you pulled me out of my hole you didn't know me from a dog's flea. That's what makes what you did something, and I ain't forgetting it."

I stubbed out my cigarette, lit another.

"And please yourself what you tell me," Casy went on, "but if you want to tell me, now's the time."

I didn't hesitate. I could trust Casy and he might be useful.

"I was up there last night," I said. "It's a cockeyed yarn—you'd better hear it."

I took him through the story from Gorman's proposition to the time Veda and I had come to Santa Medina last night. He sat smoking; his frown deepened as the story unfolded. Even to me it sounded as phoney as O'Readen's smile.

"That's it," I concluded. "Make what you like of it, but I smell money somewhere in all this and I mean to be at the head of the queue."

"Not in my line," he said. "It's crazy. But you watch out. Brett's big-time. You be careful how you monkey with him. I'll take care of Gorman and Parker if you like."

"No. You're doing all I want you to do right now. I can't do a thing until I get this compact or whatever it is. The frail upstairs says she knows what it's all about." I shook my head thoughtfully. "I don't know what to make of her, Mick. She's an enigma."

"That's your lookout. You were always a sucker for a woman. Anything I can do?"

I grinned at him. "I'm going over to San Luis Beach. I want to get some clothes for one thing. I want to see Redfern, too. Will O'Readen play?"

"Sure he'll play. You heard what I told him. Redfern won't bust your alibi."

"That's fine. I'll go over there and iron things out with him and maybe have a look around. Can I borrow a car?"

Casy nodded.

"Then there's the frail upstairs. She'd better stay put until I come back. I don't want her to run out on me. Can you get a guy to keep an eye on her?"

"Joe can do it. He ain't doing anything." Casy raised his voice and bawled for Joe.

"I want her to stay right where she is. I'll lock her in, but a lock mightn't keep her there if she takes it into her head to take a powder. If Joe can keep an eye on her..."

Joe came in.

"Miss Rux is to stay where she is until Jackson's say-so," Casy told him. "You're to see she stays."

Joe gave a soft grunt. Dismay showed in his eyes, but he was well trained.

"Check," he said.

"And watch her, pally," I told him. "She's as tricky as a sackful of rattlesnakes. Every time she snaps her garters some guy comes arunning."

"If she snaps anything at me I'll snap right back," Joe said with a cold little grin.

"I'll have a word with her and then I'll get off," I said to Casy. "Will that car be ready?"

"Sure—right outside in five minutes."

Veda, in sky-blue pajamas and red mules, was looking over the wooden roofs of Santa Medina from the roof garden when I came in. She swung around on her heels and her chest pointed at me.

"Coffee coming up," I said. "I'll have to go out. You stay here until I return."

"I might." She looked over her shoulder to the distant summit of Ocean Rise. "I'll think about it."

"You'll stay, unless you want to jump off the roof."

She turned quickly. "And what does that mean?"

The friendly-looking bellhop came in with a tray of hot rolls and coffee. He ducked his head at us, said it was a fine morning, and shuffled away.

I poured the coffee, added cream and sugar and handed her a cup.

"I don't want you floating around footloose," I explained. "Take it easy. I'm locking the door when I go out in case you start sleepwalking again."

"You'll do nothing of the kind!" Her blue eyes flashed. "You're having it too much your own way."

"Sure, and there's nothing you can do about it. If you go out and run into Parker, what do you think he'll do to you? Use your head. You stay here until I see what's cooking."

She brooded, then she said abruptly, "Where's the compact?"

"We'll talk about that some other time," I said and finished my coffee. "Right now I've other things on my mind."

She studied me thoughtfully.

"If it hadn't been for me you'd be filling a hole in the ground," she said. "Can't you show a little gratitude?"

"Some other time." I picked up my hat. "We'll get together before long. Just take it easy. If you want anything, use the telephone. Joe's looking after you. Don't try any tricks with him. He's got a heart of stone."

She beat me to the door, grabbed the key and tried to twist it out of my clutch.

"Take it easy," I said and scooped her up, running her to the bed. On the way she pounded the top of my hat with clenched fists.

"Let me go!" she stormed. "How I hate you right now, you heel!"

I tossed her on the bed, knelt on her while I squeezed her fingers and took the key.

"Can't you quit fighting?" I asked, scowling at her. "Now lay off and act like a lady."

I made a rush for the door. A clock and a vase helped me on my way. I got outside and turned the key as she began to pound on the panels. The names she called me would have made a taxi driver blush.

Joe came along the passage, paused to listen.

"Snapping her garters, huh?" he said. "The jobs I get. If she calls me names like that I'll tape her mouth shut."

"Not a bad idea," I said and handed him the key. "Give her anything she wants except a gun and poison. Okay?"

He put the key in his vest pocket and sighed. "I guess so. See you before long I hope."

I went down to Casy's office. The long, fragile-looking guy with the profile like Byron and the cornflower in his buttonhole was draped up against the wall, his hands in his pockets. He was watching Casy reading his mail.

"This is Lu Farrel, Floyd," Casy said. "He'll take care of any trouble you might run into. Take him along with you. He can drive the car."

"Thanks all the same," I said hastily, "but I can handle my own trouble. All I want is the car."

"Better take him along," Casy advised. "He's a good guy with a rod."

Judging by that flower, he'd be better with a garden hoe, I thought, but didn't say so. I didn't want to hurt Casy's feelings or make Lu cry.

"That's okay, but I'd rather go along on my own. No hard feelings," I went on to Lu.

"Not at all, dear," he said and sniffed at his cornflower.

Casy grinned. "Don't let Lu kid you. His appearance is against him."

"Something is," I agreed darkly and went out.

A big black-and-chromium Cadillac was parked outside. The doorman guarding it smirked when he saw my expression.

"The boss says for you to use her," he said and held the door open for me.

In that beauty it took me a little over half an hour to reach my rooms. I had a small apartment in a three-story house in the less prosperous quarter of San Luis Beach. It was comfortable enough: a little shabby, but clean, and Mrs. Baxter who looked after me was no more dishonest than the other landladies in the street.

A closed car was parked on the opposite side of the street to the house. I parked the Cad outside the front door, looked the closed car over and grinned to myself. The guy sitting at the wheel, reading a sporting sheet, had "cop" written all over him.

I got out slow, allowed him to take a good look at me, then went on up the stairs to my rooms.

I unlocked the door and went in. They had taken some trouble not to leave signs of a search, but it wasn't hard to see they'd been over the joint with a fine comb and a small earthquake to help them.

I made sure my last bottle of whisky hadn't been tampered with, then I started to pack my bags. I was through in half an hour. As I was closing the last bag, heavy footsteps creaked up the stairs and knuckles with plenty of authority rapped on the door.

I called, "Come in," and went on strapping my bag.

Lieutenant of the Police Redfern and a plainclothes dick named Summers stalked in, closed the door and regarded me the way tigers regard their dinner.

Redfern was a nice-looking guy as far as cops go. He was middle-aged, middle-height, square-shouldered and clean-shaven. He had eyes like the points of gimlets. Two thick wings of chalk-white hair showed below his gray slouch hat. His brown suit had a pinstripe of red and plenty of good tailoring in it, and his shoes looked like they were varnished. He was a good steady cop, wise to all the rackets, a little tired of being honest, but keeping that way in spite of a lot of pressure from the political group that ran the town—and a hard, mean, dangerous character to run up against if he disliked you. He hated me worse than an abscess in the ear.

"Hello, there," I said cheerfully. "You've just caught me. I'm leaving this burg. How do you like that?"

There were no frills on Redfern. He came to the point with his usual bluntness. "Did you go to Lindsay Brett's house yesterday morning?" He had a quiet voice. He never shouted, but he managed to get a chill in his voice that could unsettle a guilty conscience faster than anything I know.

"Sure," I said, and dumped the bag with the other two. "So what?"

Summers cleared his throat menacingly. He was big and fleshy and tough. On the middle finger of his right hand he wore a flat cameo ring. It came in handy when he punched a suspect in the teeth. A ring like that could do plenty of damage and he could always plead the excitement of the moment made him forget to take it off.

"Why did you go up there?" Redfern asked curtly.

"I was on my way to see my friend Casy—you know Casy?"

"I know him. Casy doesn't live anywhere near Ocean Rise."

"That's right. I was waiting for a bus and a guy came along and gave me a lift. I told him how to get to Santa Medina but he was too smart to listen. He said he knew his way around and promptly took the wrong turning. I was in no hurry so I let him sort himself out of the mess. We landed up outside Brett's place and a guard got sarcastic. Then I told this guy where he'd gone wrong and he went right. That's all there's to it."

"Listen, you cheap—" Summers began, but Redfern waved impatiently at him.

"I'll handle this," he said and stared at me woodenly. "Who was this fellow who gave you a ride?"

"No idea. He looked like a drummer to me, but I may be wrong. I didn't ask his name. He dropped me off at Santa Medina and I lost sight of him."

Redfern wandered around the room. "Where were you last night?" he demanded and jerked round to look at me.

"With Casy."

"You'll have to do better than that, Jackson. I think you were up at Brett's place last night."

"Well, there's no harm in you thinking so, so long as you don't believe it," I said, slipped the bottle of Scotch in my pocket and glanced around to make sure I hadn't forgotten anything. "I was playing poker with Casy. You ask him. There was a pal of yours there, too. Chief of Police O'Readen. I took fifty dollars off him."

Redfern stood very still while he looked at me, then he glanced down at his nicely manicured nails.

"O'Readen?" he repeated.

"That's the fella. Good cop, too, by the look of him. Nice cheerful guy—always smiling."

Summers flexed his muscles. I could see he was having to make an awful effort not to sock me with his ring.

"And O'Readen was playing poker with you last night? How long did the game last?"

"From seven-thirty till two," I said cheerfully.

Again there was a long pause, then Redfern shrugged. He looked suddenly tired and a little sad.

"Okay, Jackson, that lets you out." He stuck his hands into his trouser pockets. Only his eyes showed how mean he was feeling. "Where are you going now?"

"Got myself a frail and I'm using Casy's penthouse for an unofficial honeymoon. Look in some time, pally. Casy would like to have you over."

"Let's go," Redfern said to Summers and moved to the door.

"Can't I give this heel a tap, Chief?" Summers pleaded.

"I said let's go," Redfern snapped and went out.

Summers paused at the door. He looked like a tiger that had its dinner snatched away.

"One of these days I'll have you where I want you, you smart punk—then, watch out."

"Don't put off till tomorrow what you can do today,"

I said, grinning at him. "Start something now, and see where it gets you."

"Come on!" Redfern called from the bottom of the stairs.

Summers gave me a bleak look and went out, his face slack with rage. The door slammed violently behind him.

I gave them a few minutes to get out of the way, went down to the basement and paid up my rent, told Mrs. B. I was pulling out and scuttled from the house before she could kiss me or maybe slug me with a bottle.

I piled my bags in the back of the Cad, climbed in and drove over to my office. The number of girls who smiled at me as I drove along was an education. I could have had a carload if I hadn't been busy. I told myself I'd borrow this car when I had some time on my hands and drive along Ocean Boulevard and see what I caught. I wouldn't need a net.

A crowd of kids came from the vacant lot and swarmed around the car as I pulled up outside the office. I picked the biggest and toughest-looking of them and held up three nickels.

"Listen, killer," I said, "keep these kids off this car and you're on my payroll."

The kid said he would, and I left him glaring ferociously at the other kids, his clenched fists threatening them. He looked so tough I didn't know if I'd have the nerve to ask him for the car back.

The telephone bell was ringing as I unlocked the office door. I kicked the door shut, reached for the receiver as the bell stopped.

I didn't worry. No one had called me up in weeks. It was probably a wrong number.

I cleared out my desk drawers, stuck my .38 police special in my hip pocket, dropped the Scotch bottle from the desk cupboard into the trash basket, closed all the drawers a little regretfully. It wasn't much of a room, but I liked having an office of my own. Casy's penthouse was all right, but it didn't belong to me and that makes a big difference.

As I turned to the door, the telephone bell started up again. I was going to leave it, then changed my mind.

A girl's voice asked, "Is that Mr. Floyd Jackson?"

I had to think for a moment before I told her it was. No one had called me "mister" on the telephone for months.

"Will you hold on, please?"

She had a nice voice: quiet, musical and a lilt in it.

"Mr. Lindsay Brett is calling," she added.

I clutched the telephone. "Mr.—who?"

"Mr. Lindsay Brett." There was a click on the line, then she said, "You're through, Mr. Brett. Mr. Jackson is on the line."

A crisp, tense voice demanded, "Jackson?"

That was more like it. That's the way it'd been for the past months. *"Jackson?"* Some copper looking for trouble. Redfern snarling at me. Now Brett.

"Yeah," I said.

"I want to talk to you, Jackson. Come over to my place on Ocean Rise right away. I'll expect you in an hour."

I stared at the big ad on the wall. It showed a girl with a lot of cleavage in a swimsuit that looked like it was put on with a spray gun. She had a cute smile and I winked at her. She didn't wink back.

"I shouldn't, Mr. Brett," I said.

"What? What was that?" The bark in his voice would have scared his secretary or the guys who worked for him. But I wasn't his secretary nor did I work for him, so it didn't scare me.

"You shouldn't expect me," I said, as polite as a receptionist booking a room, "because I won't be there."

There was a pause. Icicles seemed to drip from the mouthpiece, but maybe I was just imagining it.

"I want to talk to you." There was a shade less bounce in his voice now. Not much, but enough for me to notice.

"If it's that important, maybe you'd better come down here," I said. "I'm leaving San Luis Beach in about an hour. I'm leaving for good."

"Don't leave until I get down," he said—much, much softer now, almost human.

"I'll be gone in an hour," I said and hung up.

CHAPTER EIGHT

I WALKED DOWN the six flights of stairs to the street level, paid off Little Sir Echo who was guarding the Cad, took it around to a nearby garage and crawled up the six flights again. I was fighting for my breath after the climb when I heard a rush of feet along the passage.

To get from Ocean Rise to this dump in twenty-five minutes was fast going. I expected Brett to come into the office with congestion of the lungs and a heart murmur; but he didn't. He looked the kind of guy who spends a lot of time being athletic, and six flights of stairs was just a warm-up to him. He could have run to the Matterhorn and still have had enough breath to whistle "Dixie."

He didn't knock or stand on ceremony. He burst in on me like a runaway cyclone.

He was about six foot two and all of it hard muscle. At a guess he could be thirty or so, good-looking if you like the well-fed, rich face that a millionaire usually carries around with him. I could see why women went for him. He was the dominant type, with a personality that ran away with a lot of voltage, and was slightly overpowering at close quarters. His eyes were sharp, keen and alert. You had the impression you'd have to get up very early to trap him into anything and then you'd probably fail. By the set of his shoulders, the line of his mouth and his way of talking, you knew without being told that he was in the money.

"Are you Floyd Jackson?" he barked and planked down his hat and stick on the desk.

"Yeah," I said. "Mr. Brett, of course."

He didn't bother to answer that one, and glanced around the office, giving each stick of furniture an exclusive sneer.

"You blew the door off my safe last night and killed two of my guards," he went on, glaring at me.

"Did I?" I groped for a cigarette and set fire to it. "Now why did I do that?"

He caught hold of the visitor's chair, jerked it up to the desk and sat on it.

"And don't think that alibi of yours is any good. I know all about O'Readen. He's a crook. You weren't playing poker with him last night. You were up at my place."

He sounded so convincing I was inclined to believe him.

"Redfern didn't seem to think so," I pointed out. I felt he might want to argue.

He took out a cigar, cut the end, lit it and blew a stream of rich-smelling smoke at me.

"I don't give a damn what Redfern thinks. I don't have to be impressed by a chief of police even if Redfern is. I want the dagger back and I'm going to get it back. That's why I'm here."

I became suddenly very attentive.

"What dagger is that, Mr. Brett?" I asked.

"Now look, Jackson, you're not going to act dumb with me. You know what I'm talking about. You stole the Cellini dagger from my safe last night and you're going to give it back. This is a business transaction. The police don't come into it."

A tingle ran up my spine and I was aware of a feeling

of suppressed excitement and I knew I'd have to step carefully. This could be either a ticket to the gas chamber or the means of collecting a lot of dough. It depended how I played it.

"And why don't the police come into it?" I asked cautiously.

"Because they can't do anything about it, but I can. I don't give a damn for those guards. I don't give a damn whether you go to jail or not. All I'm interested in is getting the dagger back, and I'm going to get it back. Make no mistake about it! Here's my proposition. Bring the dagger to me before ten o'clock tonight and I'll pay you twenty-five thousand dollars. If you're not at my house by ten o'clock, I'll start something that'll surprise you."

"Such as what, Mr. Brett?" I asked.

"I'll break O'Readen," he said bleakly. "It'll take a little time and it'll cost money, but I'll do it. When I've broken him we'll see how your alibi stands up in court. I'll have you sent to the gas chamber if I have to buy the judge and jury." He leaned forward and tapped on the ink-stained blotter. "You'll find it doesn't do to monkey with me, Jackson. I have a lot of influence around here. Please yourself what you do. I want the dagger."

"And what dagger are you talking about?" I asked mildly.

He studied me for a long moment. I thought he was going to fly into a rage but he didn't, although it was a near thing.

"The Cellini dagger," he said in a voice you could crack a nut on. "If they didn't tell you its history, you'd better hear it now. Cellini was commissioned to make a pair of gold daggers for Cardinal Jacobacci. One of them eventually found its way to the Uffizzi, the other disappeared, believed stolen. It turned up a few months ago and I bought it. It is a collector's piece and valuable, and I took the precaution to inform the authorities that I had bought it and its description has been widely circulated. It's impossible for anyone to sell it. You might just as well try to sell the *Mona Lisa*. You were commissioned to steal it by an unscrupulous collector. I can even make a guess who it is, but I won't. I haven't the evidence, although I'm pretty sure who has it. Only a dishonest collector would risk stealing it.

"Collectors are funny people, Jackson. If anything is rare enough, they just have to have it, even if they have to keep it under lock and key. I'm sure of one thing. You stole the dagger and you were paid to do so by a collector. You stole it because you were in a jam. You were up at my place yesterday morning and your bank account, which has been at zero for the past months, has now a substantial balance. That's how I know you stole it."

"How do you know about my bank balance?" I asked mildly.

He gave me a hard little smile.

"I own the bank, Jackson, and I had your account examined."

"Looks as if I'll have to change my bank, doesn't it?"

He got to his feet. "That's my offer. No questions asked, no trouble and twenty-five thousand dollars for the dagger. I don't care how you get it, but get it. If you're not at my place by ten tonight, look out. You'll find you've been meddling with dynamite."

"And suppose I get a break and find the dagger and bring it out to your place; what guarantee have I that Redfern won't be there to hang a frame on me?"

"My word," he said curtly.

We looked at each other.

"Okay," I said and shrugged. "If that's the best you can do, I'll take the risk."

He took out his wallet, dropped a card on the desk. "That's my telephone number. When you have the dagger, give me a ring. I'll arrange for the guard to let you up to the house."

I tucked the card into my vest pocket. "Maybe I'll be seeing you," I said. "But don't bet on it."

"I'll be seeing you all right," he said grimly and stamped to the door.

"And what else was stolen from the safe, Mr. Brett?" I asked casually. "Any other offers?"

I watched him narrowly. I didn't know if he would jump or turn pale or sag at the knees or even have a stroke. According to Gorman and Parker and Veda, he should have done one or even two of these things. He didn't do any of them. He looked over his shoulder and frowned.

"What are you talking about?" he demanded.

I wasn't going to mention the compact just in case I had been given a bum steer, but I gave him another hint. "Wasn't there something else in the safe besides the dagger that was of value to you, Mr. Brett?"

He looked bewildered. It wasn't an act. He just happened to be bewildered. "Are you trying to be funny?"

I was trying not to be bewildered myself. "I guess I am," I said. "Think nothing of it. I haven't been sleeping too well recently."

He gave me a hard stare and went out. I waited until I heard him running down the stairs, then I fished out the bottle of Scotch, poured three inches of it into the office glass and drank most of it without drawing breath. The kids screamed and yelled as they fought each other amongst the rubbish in the vacant lot. A car started up in the street below and drove away with an open exhaust. A mouse popped out of its hole and sneered at me. The girl on the wall continued to smile. She seemed to enjoy the joke.

"Yeah, it's funny," I said to her. "It's very, very funny and you can laugh all you like. You're not in this mess—I am."

I lifted my feet and placed them tenderly on the blotter and tried to sort it out. So there was a dagger after all, and the compact meant nothing to Brett.

"How do you like that?" I said to the girl on the wall. "That's what comes of being smart. No one to blame but Jackson, the boy detective, Sherlock the second, the punk with a paralyzed brain. So I'm right back where I came in, and maybe Fatso's yarn was true. Maybe that female enigma did walk in her sleep and steal the dagger and leave her compact in the safe. Maybe that's why Fatso wanted the compact so badly, because Brett would know when he found it in the safe that it was Veda who had swiped the dagger. Maybe I'd better start from the beginning again. Maybe I'd better take this thick skull of mine and swap it for a bottle of Scotch. Maybe no one would want to swap it for a bottle of Scotch. I wouldn't." I set fire to a cigarette, rubbed my face with a hot hand and transferred my stare from Miss Cleavage to the telephone. I had a feeling Brett wasn't bluffing when he said he'd start after me if I didn't produce the dagger by ten o'clock. If he cracked O'Readen I'd be in a nasty jam. And he was big and rich enough to crack that smiling copper. I pulled the telephone towards me, dialed and waited.

A voice with an accent like a tin can rolling downstairs hit my ear. "Hollywood Banner."

"Give me Al Ryan."

After a lot of delay, Al asked crossly, "Who is it?"

"This is Floyd Jackson," I told him. "How are you, Al?"

"Terrible," Al said with conviction. "Don't bother me now. Call me next week. I'll be on vacation then."

"I want a little information, Al," I said firmly.

"Not interested. I'm busy. Be a pal and throw yourself under a train. No one would miss you."

"Very, very funny. How's your wife, Al?"

"Still horrible. Why drag my wife into this?" Al sounded suspicious.

"And how's that little redhead with dimples in her knees I saw you with at the Brown Derby last week?"

There was a long, hurt silence. "That's blackmail, Jackson. You wouldn't stand for blackmail, would you?"

"I want some information, Al," I said gently.

"Well, why didn't you say so? You know I'm always ready to help a guy if I can. What do you want to know?"

Miss Cleavage and I exchanged smiles.

"What do you know about a fat flesh-peddler who calls himself Cornelius Gorman?"

"Not much. He has an office in the Wiltshire Building on Wiltshire Boulevard, been in business five or six years, smart agent, handles a bunch of strippers and makes a good thing out of it. Got into trouble last year with the Mothers' League for Good Morals and beat a Mann Act prostitution rap a couple of months ago, but a guy in his racket is always running into some kind of trouble."

I frowned at the mouthpiece of the telephone. Nothing new—nothing I didn't know already.

"Does he run any other rackets, Al?"

"Not that I know of. I don't think so. He makes a lot of solid dough out of his girls. He might, of course."

"Ever heard of a girl who calls herself Veda Rux?"

"Sure have." He sounded enthusiastic. "She's one of

Gorman's strippers. I've seen her toss off her clothes. It's a nice experience."

I was getting nowhere fast.

"Do you happen to know if Gorman has a pal who collects antiques?" I asked hopefully.

"Antique women?" Al asked, puzzled.

"No, you dumb cluck. Antiques—pictures, jewellery, stuff like that."

"How should I know? He's pretty thick with Dominic Boyd, who has a lot of jack and a big place on Beverly Hills. Maybe he collects antiques."

I pricked up my ears.

"Is he a tall guy with slicked-down fair hair and a face like a lady horse?"

"Could be. Natty dresser and a little jumpy."

"That's the fella." I was excited now. "Who is he, Al?"

"I don't know where he came from. He just arrived out of the blue four or five years ago. Some guy I know told me he was one of the booze barons from the North. Made a million or so out of running moonshine in the prohibition days. He's a dangerous character from what I hear. The same guy said he was a fugitive from an asylum for the insane, but I don't believe all I hear."

I thought all this over.

"Well, thanks, Al, that's about all, I guess. Sorry to have bothered you."

"And forget about that redhead. That was just a business dinner we were having."

"And I suppose you were cuddling her because she was cold?" I said and hung up.

So Gorman was a theatrical agent and Veda was a stripper after all, but my old pal Dominic wasn't Gorman's partner—he was a slaphappy ex-booze king by the name of Boyd.

I turned the whole thing over in my mind for twenty minutes or so. It got me a nice set of theories, but nothing I could take to the bank and cash into hard currency. One thing I was sure about: I would have to produce the dagger by ten o'clock tonight. I wasn't going to call Brett's bluff.

That stuff about the gas chamber worried me. I'd have to persuade Gorman to part with the dagger. I sat for ten minutes or so working out how I was to do it. There were ways and means; the most obvious one would be to go out to Boyd's place and steal the thing, but I decided against that. I'd have to play this one safe. I thought some more, then pushed back my chair, closed the window, took a last look round and walked down the six flights of stairs to the street level.

It took me an hour and a half driving fast to reach Gorman's office on Wiltshire Boulevard. The layout of the place made me think I might do a lot worse than become a flesh-peddler myself. The office was located on the eighth floor of the Wiltshire Building. You go through revolving doors into a vast lobby of chromium and green and white rubber block flooring. A row of elevators is on your right; facing you is an arcade of shops where you can buy a flower for your buttonhole or a diamond tiara, according to your bank balance and inclination. To your left is an enquiry desk, a row of telephone booths and a theater ticket agency. A sign at the head of a broad flight of stairs leading to the basement tells you you can have a haircut, shave, turkish bath and a meal if you can be bothered to walk that far.

I rode to the eighth floor in an express elevator and walked along some more green and white rubber blocks before I reached double plate-glass doors with *Cornelius* on one door and *Gorman* on the other. I looked through the glass at a cute little blonde at a switchboard and behind a railing, well out of reach of clutching hands. The rest of the room was given up to four rows of armchairs. A number of nifty-looking young women were sitting in the chairs and doing nothing in particular.

I pushed open the swing doors and sauntered over to the switchboard. The young women watched me come. I didn't hurry. Waiting to be taken on as a stripper can't be a lot of fun, and if they could get a thrill out of seeing a hundred and eighty pounds of bone and muscle and hot red blood snaking into their gray young lives, that was all right with me.

"Mr. Gorman," I said to the blonde trick and leered into her big brown eyes.

She gave me a look full of repressed yearning and asked if I had an appointment.

"No," I told her, "but he'll see me. Tell him the name's Floyd Jackson and I'm in a rush."

I glanced over my shoulder to see how the young women were taking the news. They stared back at me with intent, expectant expressions.

The blonde trick said regretfully, "Mr. Gorman never sees anyone without an appointment, Mr. Jackson. I'm sorry."

"Ask him," I coaxed. "Call him and tell him I'm here. You're in for a big surprise, honey. Fatso and I shared the same cell together. You ask him."

She giggled nervously. "You wouldn't be kidding? Mr. Gorman doesn't like to be interrupted."

"Tell him. I have a fatal fascination for him. Go ahead, honey, whisper the good news to him."

She put through the call while the rest of the young women listened on tiptoe.

"There's a Mr. Floyd Jackson asking for you," she said timidly into the receiver. "He says you'll see him." She listened for a moment, her eyes growing big, then she hung up. "Will you wait, Mr. Jackson? He won't keep you long."

I thanked her and edged my way toward the young women, but before I could select a chair, the door near the railed-off portion of the office opened and a slim, dark girl with a cold, hard face came out.

"Mr. Jackson?" she asked sharply.

I moved toward her.

"Go in, please. Mr. Gorman will see you now."

I looked past her to the blonde trick, whose mouth was hanging open, and I winked, then I strolled into a big airy room full of light and cigar smoke and photographs of nice-looking cuties with very little on.

Gorman sat behind a vast desk covered with papers that may or may not have been contracts, cigar ash and still more photographs. His ball-round face was as empty as a pauper's purse, and his little black eyes that peered at me over ridges of pink fat were suspicious and alert.

"An unexpected visit, Mr. Jackson," he said smoothly. "I must confess I didn't expect to see you so soon."

"Came as a surprise to me, too," I said and drew up a leather-padded chair and sat down.

"Perhaps you have come to return my ring?" he asked and chuckled the way an orangutan might chuckle before he snaps off your arm.

"I sold that," I said regretfully. "I was short of money. A guy promised me fifteen hundred bucks and never paid up."

"I see." He stared thoughtfully, went on. "And yet, Mr. Jackson, you have obviously come here for a reason."

"Why, sure," I said, lit a cigarette and placed the match end carefully in the onyx ashtray. "Yeah, I didn't blow in to pass the time. How's Dominic?"

Gorman lifted one immense hand and studied his well-manicured nails. He was very calm and cool. "He's well enough, Mr. Jackson. A dangerous man, of course. I'm afraid he's a little annoyed with you. I should keep clear of him if I were you."

"It's a wonder they let him out of that asylum," I said. "His name's Boyd, isn't it? And he's a collector of antiques."

Gorman frowned at his nails. "You have been making enquiries then, Mr. Jackson?"

"I was a private eye once. Difficult to keep one's nose out of other people's business once you get the urge." I flicked ash on the desk to keep the other ash company. "Veda sends her love. Nice girl—a little hotheaded, but nice."

"Foolish," Gorman said, and there was a rasp in his voice.

"Well, you know how these kids act. She didn't mean anything by it. Any self-respecting girl would want to slug a thug like Dominic."

"Suppose you get to the point?" Gorman said. "If you haven't come to return the ring, why are you here?"

I smiled at him. "I've come for the dagger."

There was a moment's silence. The little black eyes flickered.

"I don't think I know what you mean," he said at last.

"I've seen Brett." I stubbed out my cigarette, lit another. "Ever met Lindsay Brett?"

Gorman said he hadn't met Brett.

"Pity—he has a compelling presence. He's big-time, and doesn't ever let you forget it, and he has also a persuasive manner—a might persuasive manner. He wants the dagger back, and he's convinced me he'll get it back. So I thought I'd drop by and pick it up."

Gorman studied me.

"And what makes you think I have it?" he asked smoothly.

"You don't," I said. "Boyd has it, but you're a pal of his, and you're in a jam, so I thought it'd be easier for me to persuade you to persuade him to part with it."

"Am I in a jam?" The black eyes glittered like bits of painted glass.

"You certainly are," I said and hitched my chair forward. "Brett's put his cards on the table. If I play with him I'm in the clear. He guarantees me a clean bill. All he wants is the dagger. If he doesn't get it, then I'm for the high jump and that includes the gas chamber. So what do I do? I make the same proposition to you. Hand over the dagger or I'll turn you in. All I have to do is to tell Brett the whole story. He already suspects Boyd is at the back of this. I have Veda tucked away, and she'll be the principal witness. To save her skin she'll throw you two guys to the wolves so fast you'll be sniffing cyanide before you know the trial's over. The cards are stacked against you. I have the story, I have Veda, I have the compact and Brett's guarantee to keep me in the clear. If you can't persuade Boyd to hand over the dagger, you and he are sunk."

He took out his gold cigarette case and helped himself to a cigarette. As he lit it his eyes searched my face. He kept pretty cool, but I could see he wasn't very happy.

"Would Brett pay any reward if the dagger was returned?" he asked, and his voice sounded very thin and very scratchy. I grinned at him.

"You bet," I said cheerfully. "Twenty-five grand."

"I see." For a moment his face lit up. "We might divide the reward between us, Mr. Jackson. Mr. Boyd wouldn't care about the money. It would be between you and me."

"I'm afraid not," I said, easing myself back in my chair. "You don't get anything out of this, Fatso. You once said I was tricky and smooth, and that makes me tricky and smooth. Your job is to get the dagger from Boyd. I don't have to pay you anything because I hold five aces."

His face turned the color of cold mutton fat. "I think it would be wiser for you to share the spoils," he said and leaned forward. "Think again, Mr. Jackson."

I kicked back my chair and stood up.

"I'll be back here at four o'clock, Fatso. Have the dagger here by then or take the consequences. You've played me for a sucker long enough. It's time you got wise. I'm not taking any excuses. The dagger's either here at four, or you and your pal can explain your little plot to Redfern. And don't try any tricks. I've put the whole story down in writing and Veda is holding on to it. If I'm not back with her by six tonight, she turns the yarn over to Brett."

We stared at each other for a long moment, then I walked out, leaving him sitting behind the desk as quiet and as cold and as deadly as a cobra coiled up in a bush.

The young women watched me as I came out of the office. They flinched with horror when I slammed the door behind me. The cute blonde trick was still openmouthed. The hard-faced number who had told me to go into Gorman's office looked at me with calculating eyes.

I sauntered across the room, pulled open the glass door and walked into the passage. I let the doors swing to. They were still staring as I moved toward the elevator. I rode down to the street level, opened the door of the Cad and looked up. Eight floors above me, three windows pushed up. The young women, the blonde trick and the hard-faced number stared down at me intently. The blonde trick's mouth fell open another inch.

It crossed my mind as I got into the car that all those frails would remember me. It was a cosy thought. Even a punk with a paralyzed brain hates to be forgotten.

CHAPTER NINE

I HAD THREE HOURS TO KILL before I saw Gorman again, but that's not a hardship when you're in Hollywood. I spent one of them climbing outside the best meal I'd had in years. Nothing was too good or too expensive for Mrs. Jackson's favorite son that sunny afternoon.

With still a couple of hours to use up, I left the restaurant and drove over to the Paramount Film Studios and parked outside the main gates. In case you don't know, this is as good a way as another to pass the time if you have time to pass. There is always a steady flow of nice-looking frails passing in and out, and they like being whistled at, and there's always the possibility that Dorothy Lamour might appear in her sarong, but you mustn't count on it. I saw a lot of cuties who looked like fun, but I was choosy that afternoon. It had to be Lamour or nobody—it turned out to be nobody.

While I waited and leered out of the car window, I made plans for the future. Before very long, I should have in my pocket a roll worth twenty-five grand; and that's a lot of dough. After a little thought I decided I'd take Veda to Miami. I've always wanted to go to Miami and act the way millionaires act. I felt it would be good for my general state of health and my inferiority complex. I'd been a poor, trashy dick too long.

Taking a broad view of the whole setup, I failed to see where I could go wrong. Boyd would have to hand over the dagger—he couldn't help himself, unless he wanted a stretch in jail. Brett would hand over the twenty-five grand. He had given his word, and when a guy of his standing gives his word, he keeps it. I thought it would be nice to lie about on golden sands with Veda in a swimsuit. She had the kind of figure a swimsuit likes. I told myself as soon as Brett paid up, I'd nip into a travel agency and book a couple of seats in the first aircraft out to Miami the following day.

Time was getting on now. Maybe someone had tipped Lamour I was waiting outside. I regretfully started the engine and drove away. The clock on the dashboard of the Cadillac said it was two minutes to four o'clock when I pulled up outside the Wiltshire Building again. There wasn't going to be any nonsense this time. I was coming out with the dagger or else. I shot my cuffs, tipped my hat to a more becoming angle and strode across the sidewalk, through the revolving doors to the elevator.

No young women sat in the four rows of armchairs when I paused outside Gorman's double glass doors. The cute blonde trick sat huddled up by her switchboard and her mouth was closed. She sprang off her seat when I pushed open the doors and clutched at the rail that penned her in.

"The same name and the same guy," I said, wondering what was eating her. She appeared to be suffering from shock, and her face was the color of a freshly laundered sheet. I didn't know whether she'd been caught dipping into the petty cash or whether it was due to seeing me again.

"Go in." The words popped out of her as if someone had suddenly kicked her sharply with a nail-studded boot. She waved to Gorman's door, then grabbed up her hat and coat that was lying on a chair, jerked open the little gate and bolted to the swing doors.

I turned to watch her hurried flight. She didn't wait for the elevator, but scooted down the stairs as if she'd heard someone was giving nylons away free on the floor below.

The outer office seemed very quiet and empty without her. I looked at the closed door that led to Gorman's office. I looked at the four rows of vacant armchairs, and I had a feeling that things were not what they seemed. My hand slid around to my hip pocket to clutch my gun when a voice with a tin larynx said, "Hold it, mug!"

I looked cautiously over my shoulder. A lean, tall bird in a gray check suit stood behind the last row of armchairs. That would account for the blonde trick's agitation. He had been snooping there out of sight, waiting for me to arrive. The face under the black slouch hat was better shaved than the face of a rat, but not so attractive to look at.

"Speaking to me?" I asked and was careful not to make a sudden move. The hood looked nervous, and by the whiteness of his knuckle I knew he'd taken in all the trigger slack there was to be taken in.

"Get in there," he said and pointed to Gorman's office. "And watch it."

It crossed my mind that I might not be going to Miami after all, and was glad I hadn't been impulsive and bought the tickets. I hate throwing good money away. Reluctantly I pushed open Gorman's door, went in, followed by the hood.

Parker—or Boyd as I'd better call him now—sat in Gorman's chair. He looked very cold and distant and contemptuous. Standing by the window was another tough who nursed a blue-nose automatic. He was short and fat and shabby, and looked like any second-rate gunsel in any third-rate movie. Cornelius Gorman was conspicuous by his absence.

"Hello, pally," I said to Boyd. "How's your poor head?"

"This is the one time you've been too smart and too tricky, Jackson," he said. There was a lot of vinegar in his voice. "I'm not going to waste time talking to you. You're not getting the dagger, and you're not leaving this room alive. You're going to answer a question, and then you're going to have a little accident. You can answer the question right away or I'll force it out of you. You can please yourself, but whichever way you decide you're going headfirst out of that window as soon as you've answered it."

Being tossed out of an eighth-floor window wasn't my idea of fun, but it didn't seem worthwhile to tell him so.

"That won't get you anywhere," I said as calmly as I could. "I told Fatso I've left a statement. It'll be in Redfern's hands if anything happens to me, and then a lot of things will happen to you."

He sneered distantly. "I don't think so. After we've dealt with you, we'll destroy the statement if it exists, but I very much doubt it does."

"Now why didn't I think of that?" I said, wondering if I could get my gun out before the lean bird filled me with lead. I doubted it. "Of course you'll have to find it first, and by then it may be too late."

"That brings me to my question. Where is Veda Rux?"

The lean bird must have been a thought reader. He poked his gun into my spine and lifted my gun out of my hip pocket.

"You won't need this anymore, lug," he said in my ear.

"Where is Veda Rux?" Boyd repeated. He was very frigid and controlled, but I didn't like the blank look in his eyes.

"Where you won't get your paws on her," I told him.

"I'm used to making men talk. Have you ever been hit on the head with a rubber hose? It hurts and doesn't leave marks. I'll use your skull for a drum if you don't answer that question."

The fat tough pushed himself away from the window and yanked out a tube of solid rubber. He balanced it thoughtfully in his hand and looked mean enough to use it.

It occurred to me that this wasn't the place to let off a lot of guns. The Wiltshire Building was packed with respectable people who would want to know what was cooking if a heater popped off, and besides, these shabby hoods annoyed me. I hoped the lean bird had also considered the folly of making a noise, and I spun around and took a sock at his jaw.

A lot of things happened at once. The lean bird crashed to the floor, the fat tough came at me like a charging buffalo, Boyd kicked back his chair and stood up, and the door opened and Lu Farrel wandered in, gun in hand.

"Hell," he said to me, "are these boys bothering you?"

I ducked under the club and hit the fat tough very hard in the middle of his vest. He went reeling away, tripped over a chair and sat heavily. The lean bird cursed and struggled to his feet. A long, shiny sticker jumped into his hand. There was a soft *pop!* And the sticker fell to the floor. The lean bird stared at his shattered hand, then let out a howl that rattled the windows.

Lu waved his gun at Boyd and the fat tough. There was an efficient-looking silencer screwed to the barrel.

"Don't be hasty," he implored them and fluttered his Bambi eyes at them. "Look what I've done to your little pal."

I took a quick step up to Boyd and hit him.

He fell over backward, and I snatched up a desk lamp and smashed it down on top of him. I threw the onyx ashtray and a couple of big photographs of nude cuties at him, and looked around for something else to hit him with. I was feeling pretty mean by this time. I didn't doubt he would have pitched me out of that window if he'd had the chance, and that gave me a rush of blood to the head.

Lu snickered. "Don't lose your temper," he said, and waved his gun at the fat tough, who had got to his feet and was now standing awkwardly against the wall like a wall-flower at a party.

I clutched hold of Boyd's collar and hauled him to his feet. He spat at me and tried to claw my face, but I brushed his hands aside and socked him again. Then I shook him back and forth and slammed him down in the desk chair. He sat gasping, most of the fight knocked out of him, but to make sure, I hauled off and belted him in the jaw so he and the chair went over backward. That finished him. He lay as still as death. I went over and looked at him, then dusted myself down, eased my muscles and shot my cuffs. I felt a lot better.

"Hello," I said to Lu. "Where did you spring from?"

"Mick told me to follow you around," he said and simpered. "I saw Dorothy Lamour. She came out two minutes after you left, and that lovely man Crosby was with her."

"Was she wearing her sarong?" I asked, stiffening to attention.

"Not her sarong," Lu said, shocked. "She had on a nifty scroll-shouldered suit of sharkskin. You should have seen it." He cast a pensive look at the lean bird, who continued to bleed onto the carpet. "Were you thinking of leaving?" he asked me. "Or shall we rough up these boys some more?"

"I'm leaving," I said and went over to Boyd. I hauled him to his feet. He cringed away from me.

"Where's the dagger?" I demanded, waving my fist at him.

His bruised face was slack with rage and fright.

"At my place," he mumbled and tried to pull away.

"Then that's where we're going." I shoved him toward the door and jerked my head at Lu. "I'll feel safe with you around. Come on, gorgeous, keep me company."

We left the fat tough staring bleakly at the thin bird.

Neither of them showed any further interest in us.

I caught hold of Boyd's arm and walked him to the elevator. Lu kept close.

"Any more tricks from you," I said to Boyd as we waited for the elevator, "and I'll turn you over to Redfern."

He leaned up against the wall and dabbed at his face with his handkerchief. He was too tired and too hurt to be dangerous.

We rode down to the street level. The elevator attendant kept staring at Boyd's face, but he was too well-trained to pass remarks, or maybe he didn't like the scowl I gave him.

We crossed the sidewalk and I shoved Boyd into the back of the car, getting in beside him.

"You drive," I said to Lu.

Boyd gave me the address in a shaky voice. I didn't even have to ask him.

We drove along Wiltshire and Santa Monica Boulevards to Beverly Hills. Boyd's place was on Mulholland Drive. We shot up a long driveway, skirting a lawn big enough for a polo field, to an impressive-looking house that could have been Buckingham Palace if it had a couple more rooms.

"Come on," I said to Lu as he pulled up outside the

massive front door. "I'm not taking any chances with this punk. If he acts funny, crack him over the noggin with the gun."

But Boyd was past acting funny. He could scarcely walk, and we had to help him up the steps to the front door and into a lobby the size of an aircraft hangar.

"The dagger," I said sharply, "and make it snappy."

A white-headed old gentleman who looked like a bishop and acted like a butler materialized. He gaped at Boyd, started forward, stopped when he ran into my scowl.

"Tell him to go launch a ship," I said to Boyd.

"It's all right, John," Boyd said, waving at him. "Go away."

The old gentleman hesitated, then stalked off down the passage, his back stiff with disapproval.

"Come on, Dominic," I said, poking Boyd in the ribs. "Let's have the dagger. This atmosphere's too rich for me."

He took us into a nearby room, opened a safe and produced the dagger case. He handed it to me without a word, but his taut, white face spoke volumes. I opened the case, stared down at the dagger and snapped the case shut before Lu could see it. It was a pretty toy, and I didn't want Lu to get ideas about it.

"Right," I said. "I'm handing this over to Brett. Keep out of my way and you'll hear nothing more about it, but if you start anything I'll let Brett know you stole it, and you can guess what he'll do to you."

"Get out!" Boyd snarled and sank into a chair, his face in his hands. That's the way we left him. He was a pretty tough guy so long as you didn't hit him, but a punch or two broke him up. The beating I had given him made him look like a jigsaw puzzle someone had spilled on the floor.

We got back to Casy's joint a few minutes before seven o'clock, and before going up to Veda I gave Lu a little speech in which I called him a number of flattering names and thanked him for taking care of me. Then before he could fall on my neck, I slid into the elevator and hurriedly shut the door.

I found Joe playing a patience game outside the front door of the penthouse. When he saw me, he scooped up the cards, stood up and stretched himself.

"And am I glad to see you again," he said with a grin. "Brother, this nursemaid stuff sure gives me a pain."

"Any trouble?" I asked and nodded to the front door.

"Nothing I couldn't deal with," he said smugly and handed me the key. "She raised Cain at first, but when I offered to sock her, she quieted down."

"I guess you're right. I'm going out again at eight-thirty. I want you to take over when I've gone."

"For the love of Pete!" he exclaimed. "What's the sense? She can't get out. Why should I waste my time sitting out here?"

"That's something you can discuss with Mick. I want you out here tonight, but I can't make you if you won't."

He shrugged in disgust. "Okay, okay. I'll be here at eight-thirty. Anything you say," and he went into the elevator and slammed the door.

I found Veda lying on the settee. There was a highball on the table near her and a pile of picture magazines lay on the floor. It looked as if Joe had given her service as well as threats.

She was still wearing the pale blue pajamas, and in the bright light that flooded down on her from the reading lamp, they were interestingly transparent.

"Oh, so you're back," she said, laid down her magazines and stared up at me.

"That's right, I'm back," I said. "Have you been all right?"

"A little tired of my own company. Do we go out tonight or have I still to be Monte Cristo in his dungeon?"

"Not tonight. Tomorrow night perhaps. Tonight I have things to do."

"What have you been doing today?"

I made myself a highball.

"I've been getting around. I missed seeing Dorothy Lamour by two minutes. It didn't matter. She wasn't wearing her sarong."

"You may think you're bright and funny, but I don't." There was a hard note in her voice. "I think you're a small-time dick who's peeped through so many keyholes his brains have been blown away by the draught."

"That's exactly what I thought until this afternoon," I said, coming to sit by her side on the settee. "Then I changed my opinion."

"Did you? I wonder why."

I lapped down half the highball and set the glass on the table.

"Did you sleepwalk when you were a kid or is this something new?"

The lapis-lazuli eyes hardened; the full red lips tightened.

"Still trying to be funny?"

"Maybe. Depends what you call funny." I finished the highball, then lit a cigarette. "Take a look at this." I fished out the red leather case, opened it and laid the dagger in her lap.

There was a long awkward silence. She didn't touch the dagger; she didn't move—she didn't seem to breathe.

"Now suppose you tell me the story as it happened," I said. "I've seen Brett. If I give him back the dagger, no one gets into trouble. I'm going out there at ten o'clock tonight. He's paying me a nice little sum for returning this bauble, and if you play pretty, I'll take you along with me on a vacation. Only I'm curious to know what happened at Brett's place before Gorman came to see me. So suppose you get it off your chest, and this time tell me the truth."

She pushed the dagger away with a little grimace. "How did you get it?"

"From Boyd. You knew Parker was Boyd, didn't you?"

She said she did.

"He handed it over when I assured him Brett wasn't looking for trouble. All Brett wants is the dagger. He doesn't care a hoot what happens to you or Gorman or Boyd. He doesn't even know any of you figure in this."

"He will if he finds my compact," she said uneasily.

"He won't find it. I took it from the safe and hid it in the wings of a stone griffin at the head of the terrace. I'll pick it up when I leave him tonight and you can have it back if you want it."

She clutched hold of my arm.

"You really mean that?"

"Why, sure. You've made too much fuss about the compact. Don't worry about it. Now listen. I like you. You have your funny ways, but I like you in spite of them. I was thinking you and me might take a trip to Miami and spend some money. Would you like that?"

She stared at me for a long moment, then suddenly laughed. And this time she laughed as if she meant it.

"Why, I'd love it. If only I was sure you weren't kidding."

"I'm no kidder, and I'll prove it."

I went over to the telephone and put through a call to the Pan-American Airways. When I got my connection, I booked two seats on the eleven o'clock plane to Greater Miami. I gave the name as Mr. and Mrs. Floyd Jackson.

Her eyes were very bright and excited when I sat down at her side again.

"There it is," I said and took her hand. "If that doesn't clinch it, I give up. Now come on, let's have it."

"Give me a cigarette and I'll tell you."

While she was lighting the cigarette, I could see she was thinking, then with a sudden shrug of her shoulders she began to talk. It had happened, she said, just the way Gorman had told me. She had gone to Brett's place to do her act and Brett had shown her the dagger. If ever she was worried or upset she walked in her sleep; she had done so ever since she'd been a child. Brett had forced his attentions on her and she had fought him off. She was worried he wouldn't give her her fee and she went to sleep worried. She had taken the dagger in her sleep and left the compact in its place. So far her story and Gorman's matched. She left the next morning, knowing Brett was going to San Francisco. When she got home she found the Cellini dagger at the bottom of her bag and her compact missing. She guessed what had happened and was scared out of her wits. Gorman was the only person she could think of to get her out of the mess and she went around to see him. She told him the story and showed him the dagger. He laughed at her. There was nothing to worry about, he said. He'd call Brett and explain what had happened. Brett would be so glad to get the dagger back he wouldn't think anything of how she had taken it. It was while Gorman was trying to get Brett on the telephone that Dominic Boyd walked in. The dagger was on the table and he recognized it. He heard the story.

If Veda and Gorman wanted to make a little money, he told them, now was the time. He wanted the dagger. Brett had beaten him by a short head in his search for it. Neither

of them must do anything hasty until he had thought of
how he could keep the dagger without getting anyone into
trouble.

Veda didn't like this, but Gorman handled her. After
a while Boyd had worked out his idea. Someone would
have to get the compact. That was the first thing. As Brett
hadn't opened the safe he didn't know the dagger was
missing or that the compact was there. Someone would
have to put a bomb in the safe so when it went off Brett
and the police would assume that was when the robbery
had taken place and to give Veda a watertight alibi, she
should be at a nightclub when the bomb went off. It was
left to Gorman to find a sucker to get the compact and
plant the bomb. He picked on me.

"You see," she concluded, "if the compact was found,
Brett would know I'd taken the dagger and Boyd knew
I'd give him away in a showdown. Now he had the
dagger, he wasn't going to part with it and that's why he
wanted the compact so badly. It was the only thing that
connected me with the dagger, and he knew he couldn't
rely on me if the police questioned me. Then when you
acted smart and pretended the compact had been destroyed, I got scared. Boyd knew you had the compact.
If he couldn't get it from you, the simplest thing would
be to get rid of me, and I didn't like the way he began to
look at me. He's crazy, and I felt he might do anything.
That's why I helped you escape."

"But why didn't you tell me all this before? Why did
you invent the phoney story about the compact being
valuable to Brett?"

"Because I'd promised Boyd not to give him away. I
was scared of him. But now you've found out who he is,
it doesn't matter, does it?"

I turned the story over in my mind, and I couldn't find

any fault with it. This time, I was pretty sure, she had told me the truth.

"So there's no money in the compact?" I asked, giving her a mercenary look.

"Of course not. It belongs to me. Naturally I want it back."

"And so you shall. Maybe I'd better call Brett. I'm going out there tonight and I don't want to run into any more of his tough guards or tougher dogs." I fished out the card he had given me, frowned at it. Then I turned it over and found printed on the other side his name and telephone number. I reversed the card again, frowned some more. Written on the back of the card in a small, neat fist were the unexpected words: *For Alma from Verne. "A man's best friend is his wife."*

"Now that's a damn funny thing for a man like Brett to write on a card," I said and tossed the card into Veda's lap. As she picked it up, I went over to the telephone, called Brett's number and got my connection almost immediately.

The same nice musical voice with the lilt in it announced, "This is Mr. Brett's residence."

"This is Floyd Jackson. Will you tell Mr. Brett to expect me at ten o'clock tonight? Tell him I have what he wants."

"Why, yes, Mr. Jackson," she said, then added, "I'm so pleased."

"That makes two of us," I told her, wondered if she was as pretty as she sounded and reluctantly hung up.

Veda was mixing two highballs. With the light behind her, there was no doubt about the transparency of her pajamas. Before giving them my undivided attention, I picked up Brett's card again and frowned some more at it.

"Would you say a man's best friend is his wife?" I asked.

"I wouldn't know." She brought me the highball and

looked at me. There was a faraway look in her eyes. "I've never been a wife."

I flicked the card with my nails.

"Alma…and Verne…I wonder who they are." I slipped the card into my pocket.

"If you're so curious, why don't you ask him?" she said indifferently.

"Did you know those pajamas are transparent?"

"They're supposed to be."

That seemed to take care of that. We drank our cocktails. I locked the dagger in a drawer. There was still a lot of time to kill before ten o'clock.

I kept looking at her pajamas.

"They're a lot better than a sarong," I said suddenly.

"They're supposed to be," she repeated and wandered toward the bedroom.

I watched her go. She looked back over her shoulder, raised her eyebrows and then went into the room. I followed her after a while.

That's another good way of passing the time, in case you don't know.

CHAPTER TEN

THE HEADLIGHTS OF THE Cadillac sent two long fingers of white glare up the mountain road that led to Ocean Rise.

Lu Farrel lounged at the wheel and I sat by his side. I didn't want him on this trip, but Casy had insisted. He said he didn't trust Brett. How did I know Brett wouldn't have a reception committee waiting when I arrived? If that kind of trouble was up there, I'd be glad of Lu.

I argued that Brett had given me his word, but that made Casy laugh. The word of a millionaire didn't rate high with him, and he said so with a lot of fancy language. I finally gave way. As it turned out, I was mighty glad to have Lu with me.

It didn't take long before the headlights picked out the twelve-foot wall surrounding Brett's house.

"You stick around outside, Lu," I said, "and be ready for a snappy getaway. Keep in the car. If the guards see you they might molest you."

Lu stopped the car outside the gates. A powerful light flashed on over the guard's lodge and a couple of uniformed guards appeared from nowhere. One of them stood before the iron gates; the other strolled over to the car. I got out as I didn't want them to get a look at Lu.

"Mr. Brett's expecting me," I said. "I'm Floyd Jackson."

The beam of the flashlight hit me in the face.

"I guess you're Jackson all right," the guard said after a lengthy scrutiny. "Come on in and I'll phone the house. Do you want to bring the heap in?"

"It can stay there. I'll walk up."

"Suit yourself, but it's quite a walk."

"I want the exercise. I'm getting fat."

He shrugged and moved to the gates.

"It's okay," he said to the other guard. "It's the party who's expected."

The other guard scowled at me and opened the gate. We passed through and went into the lodge. It was very clean and bare and reminded me of a guardroom in a military camp. There was even a rack by the door that held four businesslike-looking carbines and ammunition belts.

The other guard went over to a wall telephone and muttered into the mouthpiece. He waited a moment, pushed back his hat to the back of his head and eyed me with a blank, disinterested expression. A voice cracking in his ear brought him to attention.

"Jackson's down here, sir," he said. "Yes, sir. I'll have him sent up. I'll see to it, sir. Yes, sir. I'll fix it, sir." He hung up, stroked his nose and gave me a sour grin. "That's a boy who likes to be called sir. A big shot, see? How would you like to be a big shot, comrade? How would you like a fella like me to call you sir?"

"I could stand it if you could."

"Yeah, maybe you could, but one big shot's enough for me, so don't go getting ideas, comrade. One big shot is plenty. Got a gun on you?"

I said I hadn't.

"Gotta see, comrade. The big shot was emphatic about it. You don't mind if I pat you over? No offence, mind. I gotta do what the big shot says."

"Go ahead."

He patted me all over, found the dagger case, lifted it out of my pocket.

"What would this be, comrade?"

"That belongs to the big shot. If you open it I'll have to tell him and he mightn't like it."

"Well, it couldn't hold a gun, could it?" He handed the case back. "There're a lot of things the big shot doesn't like. I wouldn't want to cross him."

I put the case in my pocket.

"Come on, comrade, he's waiting. That's something else he doesn't like."

We began to walk up the long, dark driveway.

"That's a nice car you've got out there, comrade," the guard said suddenly. "I could use a car like that. Must have cost a heap of jack."

"I wouldn't know. I borrowed it."

He spat into the darkness.

"I didn't think somehow a private eye could run to a car like that."

"I'm no dick now. I retired weeks ago."

"That right? Two of our guards got knocked off a couple of nights back. I thought maybe the big shot was hiring help."

"Nothing like that."

"Just sort of private business, huh?"

"Kind of private, yeah."

We walked on in silence after that, but I knew he was bursting with curiosity.

"Too private to talk about, huh?" he said as we neared the house.

"You ask him. He'll tell you if he wants you to know."

He again spat in the darkness.

"That's funny. I've only got to ask him. He'd tell me with the toe of his boot."

"He might at that."

"See that lighted window?" He paused to point. "That's where he is. He said for you to go in the garden entrance. You can find your own way now, can't you, comrade? No need for me to walk up all those steps, is there? I've got kind of tender feet."

I looked toward the terrace. Against the lighted French windows that stood open, I could see the outline of the stone griffin at the head of the steps leading from the terrace.

"Sure," I said. "See you on my way out."

He stood at the bottom of the steps and watched me all the way up. When I reached the stone griffin, I paused to look back. He was still standing there, his hand on his hips, watching. I kept on up the second flight of steps, and when I got to the top I looked back again. He was walking away down the driveway. There was bright moonlight and it was easy to see him. I ducked into the shadow of the house and waited a moment until he had disappeared around the bend of the drive. Then I ran down the steps to the griffin.

I was taking a chance, but if I waited until I was through with Brett, the guard might be up there to see me to the gates. I had to pick my opportunity.

I reached the griffin, took a quick look around. No one holloed at me; no one peeped out of the windows. I climbed up the base and reached into the little hollow between the wings. My questing fingers found nothing. I groped some more, cursed softly, levered myself up to stand on the top of the pedestal. I took out my small flashlight and turned the beam into the hollow. There was a little dirt, a little rainwater, but no compact.

Time stood still while I clung to the stone wings of the griffin and gaped into the empty hollow. Then out of the night came the sharp crash of gunfire—a single shot, too close for comfort, but not directed at me.

I dropped from the pedestal and darted up the steps toward the French windows. The echo of the shot was still whispering in the garden as I reached the open glass doors; a thin wreath of smoke drifted lazily out on the beam of light.

I stood in the doorway and looked into the brightly lit room. It was a nice room—the kind you would expect to be owned by a millionaire. Everything in the room was expensive and neat and good.

Lindsay Brett sat in an armchair facing me. There was a blank look of surprise on his well-fed face, and a small, blue hole in the center of his forehead. His sightless eyes stared at me; his lips were drawn off his teeth in a startled snarl. He didn't look as if he would ever run up the Matterhorn again, nor did he look as if he had any breath left to whistle "Dixie." I didn't have to touch him to know he was dead.

The death weapon, as the newspapers would call it, lay on the desk in front of him. It was a six-shot .25 automatic, and smoke still curled from its short blue barrel.

Whoever had killed Brett had made a swell job of it. The slug had wiped out this millionaire's life as surely as it had wiped out my chances of collecting twenty-five thousand dollars. And that's what I thought about as I stared into the dead, empty eyes. So I wasn't going to be on easy street after all. Mr. and Mrs. Floyd Jackson wouldn't collect their reservations to Miami tomorrow morning. No dough for Jackson, the boy detective. That's the way it is. You make plans, build castles, sit on top of the world, then someone comes along and lets off a heater and bursts the bubble for you.

Then another thought popped into my mind. The cops wouldn't look far for the killer. They'd pick on me. I felt a chill run up my spine and into the roots of my hair. Sure they'd pick on me. They couldn't help themselves. I had come up here alone. I hadn't been up here long before the shooting started. Of course they'd pick on me. Redfern would fall over himself with a setup as sweet as this.

These thoughts took very little time to run through my mind. The smoke was still drifting out of the gun barrel as I began to back slowly away. Then the door of the room opened and a girl burst in. We looked at each other over the top of Brett's dead head. She was tall and slim and fair and nice. She saw the gun, then Brett. Blood was beginning to ooze out of the hole in his head. She stiffened and her hands flew to her face and she screamed. The sound jarred through me and set my nerves jangling.

Feet pounded along the passage outside. I didn't wait. They wouldn't believe me no matter how convincing I was. No one was going to believe me this time. I went down the terrace steps as if I had wings on my feet. The girl screamed, then a man shouted. I didn't look back, and as I ran a penetrating noise of a bell started up.

I ran down the dark driveway toward the gates and the car. The guards would know something was up by the bell, but I had to take a chance on that. I couldn't climb the wall. I couldn't stay in the grounds. If they let the dogs out they'd run me down in no time. I had to get past the guards or I was sunk.

I could see the gates now as I tore down the driveway. They stood open and I could hear the engine of the Cadillac roaring. Then I saw something else and I put on a spurt. The two guards were standing against the wall of the lodge, their hands stiffly above their heads.

"Come on, dear," Lu called from the car. "These boys won't bother you."

I darted past the guards and into the car. Lu was leaning out of the window. He was pointing a sawed-off shotgun at them.

"You drive," he said calmly. "I'll watch these guys."

I engaged gear, shot the Cad into the darkness.

Lu withdrew his head, slid the shotgun onto the backseat.

"Push her along," he said uneasily. "They'll start shooting in a moment."

The words were scarcely out of his mouth when gunfire broke out behind us. A slug smashed the clock on the dashboard, another cut a groove along the off wing— pretty nice shooting.

"Mick's going to be tickled pink having this car shot up," Lu said and giggled. "What did you do to annoy them?"

"I didn't do anything," I said, treading on the gas. "Someone got in ahead of me and shot Brett. They think it's me."

Lu forgot to act soft.

"Is he dead?" he demanded, a rasping note in his voice.

"Very," I said.

The shooting had stopped now, but I didn't slacken speed.

"That guy's influence won't die with him," Lu said and rubbed his jaw with an uneasy hand. "This is going to start something we'll all be sorry about."

He didn't say another word until we reached Casy's joint, then as I got out, he slid under the steering wheel.

"You see Mick," he said. "Tell him I'm going to get this car under cover. Those guards had a good look at it. They'll know it again."

Casy was playing poker when I walked in. One look at my face brought him to his feet.

"All right, boys," he said to the players. "I'll be back in a while. I have a little business right now."

He went straight to his office and I followed.

"Trouble?" he asked and locked the door.

"You bet there's trouble," I said through clenched teeth. I had time now to realize what a jam I was in, and it shook me. "Brett's dead. Someone got there just ahead of me, and as I walked in, whoever it was shot Brett with a .25. And I'm it."

He swore softly and obscenely under his breath.

"See the killer?"

"No, I'm it, I tell you. I was seen gaping at Brett. I've got to get out of here. There's nothing you can do about this, Mick. There's nothing anyone can do."

The telephone began to jangle. Mick scooped up the receiver, barked, "Yes?" He listened, his face a blank, sullen mask. "Okay, okay," he said angrily. "He's not here anyway. Come over and have a look if you want to. I've got nothing to hide." He hung up and his eyes glittered as he looked at me.

"I can guess who that was," I said.

"Yeah. They're after you. There's nothing O'Readen can do. Anyway, that's what he says. They've sewn up the roads. They reckoned you'd come here. O'Readen is on his way over with a bunch of prowl boys."

"I'll need some dough, Mick. You have two grand of mine. Can I have it?"

"Sure." He went to his safe, tossed a packet of notes on the desk. "You can have more if you want it."

"This'll hold me." I ran my fingers through my hair. I hated to admit it, but I was rattled. "They'd better not find Veda here."

Mick grunted, went to the telephone.

"Give me Joe," he bawled. He waited a moment or so, then went on. "Bring Miss Rux down here, Joe, and make it snappy."

"What the hell are we going to do with her?" I said.

"Take it easy, Floyd. This isn't the first time a guy got knocked off," Mick said and put his hand on my arm. "I've got this kind of situation organized. You have to when you play it as close to the chest as I do. There's a hideout under the floor. You and Veda stay down there until the heat cools off. They'll never find you there."

I drew in a deep breath and grinned at him.

"I was getting ready to jump out of my skin, Mick. This has caught me off balance. It's a tough feeling to know you're really in bad with the police. I've fooled around in my time, but murder takes the color out of things."

"Yeah," Mick said. "But don't forget. I was framed for murder once and I beat the rap."

"This is different. I was seen. They have enough witnesses to convince the dumbest jury. If they catch me I'm sunk."

"They won't catch you," Mick said grimly.

There came a rap on the door.

"Who is it?"

"Joe."

Mick unlocked the door. Joe came in with Veda. She was wearing a pair of black slacks and a red shirt. She looked startled.

"Okay, Joe," Mick said and waved him to the door. When he had gone, Mick went to a cupboard that stood in a corner of the room, opened the door, pulled out a lot of junk and knelt.

"What's happened?" Veda asked, staring at me.

"Plenty. I'll tell you later." I went over to Mick.

"There you are. Get down there, you two, and keep quiet." He had pulled up a couple of boards and I could see a flight of wooden stairs leading into darkness.

"Come on," I said to Veda.

"I don't think I want to," she said. "What's happened?"

I caught hold of her wrist as a red light flickered over the door.

"That's the cops," Mick said. "Make it snappy."

"Police?" Veda said, and she caught her breath.

"Come on," I said and yanked her to the cupboard.

"There's a light switch at the foot of the stairs," Mick said as we went down into the darkness.

I found the switch as he dropped the boards into place. The light showed us we were in a low, narrow passage with a dirt floor. At the far end of the passage was a door.

"This way," I said to Veda and took her arm.

I pushed open the door, turned on another light and looked around a small room equipped without much comfort: a bed, two chairs, a table, a radio, a cupboard full of tinned food and several bottles of Scotch. It was a typical hideout for hot characters.

I shut the door, crossed the room, peeped into the bathroom that consisted of a shower and a low-down suite.

"Our new home," I said and sat on a chair.

"What's happened? Did you get the compact?"

"I've told you before—you're making too much fuss about the compact. It ceased to be dangerous when I took it out of Brett's safe. Forget the compact. I didn't get it. Someone was there before me. I don't know who it was and I don't think I care. It doesn't matter. What does matter is Brett's dead. He was shot."

She sat down abruptly.

"Is that why we're hiding from the police?"

"That's right. Now, don't get ideas. I didn't kill him. They think I did, but he was dead when I arrived."

"Why do they think you killed him if you didn't?"

I told her exactly what happened.

"I'd like a drink," she said. "Do you think I could have a drink?"

"I guess so. I could use one myself." I went to the cupboard, tore off the tissue paper around one of the bottles, found two glasses, fixed a couple of shots a duck could have floated on.

"This lets us out," I said as I handed her a glass. "As soon as the police have gone, you can fade away. From now on I have to be on my own."

"So we don't go to Miami." Her voice sounded bitter.

"That's the way it is." I swallowed half the whisky. "When a guy like Brett runs into a bullet there's a lot of trouble. The newspapers will put on pressure. All his friends will raise a squawk. This is the one job the cops can't lie down on. I'll have to keep on the move." I finished the drink, added, "And I haven't much dough. I'm telling you this not because I expect you to stick to me, I don't, but because I'm going back on a promise and I don't like doing that."

"You have all the money you want," she said in a small voice.

"No, I haven't. Brett promised me twenty-five grand for the dagger. He didn't get around to paying out. With twenty-five grand I could have given you a good time. I could have had a good time myself. Now I'll need every nickel I own to keep ahead of the cops."

She leaned forward and pulled the dagger case out of my pocket. For a long moment I stared at it. I had been so busy escaping and getting rattled I had forgotten about it.

"Boyd would give you twenty-five grand for that," she said. "Have you thought of Boyd?"

I said I hadn't, and sat staring at her.

"We could still go to Miami if we could get there."

"You want to keep away from me. I'm hot."

"Do I?"

We looked at each other. My heart began to thump and the old dryness came back in my mouth again.

"You want to keep away from me," I repeated.

She reached out and touched me and I grabbed her. There was no fighting this time. We clung to each other as if it meant something—it did to me.

"If we can get away," she murmured, her fingers touching my face, "I want to be with you for always. I want to start a new life. I'm so tired of being what I am. I want to find happiness. I could with you."

Mick came in to spoil it. He stood in the doorway and scowled at us.

"For the love of Pete, can't you do something else besides grabbing a woman?" he demanded.

"It's one way of passing the time." I unraveled myself from Veda's clutch and stood up. "The Law gone?"

"Yeah. I've fixed it for you to get to the coast. There's a boat waiting to take you to San Francisco. O'Readen's men won't see you when you go through the cordon. I had a little trouble with that punk, but he'll play."

"Tomorrow night, Mick."

"Tonight, I said."

"It's got to be tomorrow night, and she's coming with me."

He ran his fingers through his hair.

"If it's not tonight, it won't be at all," he said in an exasperated voice. "I'm doing a hell of a lot for you. The heat's on and it's like a red-hot stove. It's got to be tonight."

"I'm picking up twenty-five grand. It's my getaway stake. I can't get it until tomorrow."

He gaped at me.

"Twenty-five grand?"

"Yeah."

"Well, that's different. I'll see what I can do." He stared at me, his eyes suddenly alert. "Does this mean more trouble?"

"Maybe, maybe not. I wouldn't know."

"I'll see what I can do."

"I want to use the telephone." I smiled at Veda. "Wait here. I'll be right back. Try to make that bed comfortable. We've got to get us some sleep tonight."

I pushed past Mick to the door.

I had trouble getting Boyd to come to the phone, but after a long delay his voice crackled against my ear.

"I have something you want, Dominic," I said. "You know what it is. Brett doesn't need it now. If you want it, bring twenty-five grand in cash to Casy's joint in Santa Medina before noon tomorrow. As for Casy—don't try any smart tricks or you'll never see the dagger again. It's yours for twenty-five grand. Is it a deal?"

"You killed him!" he shouted. "You're not going to get away with this, Jackson. You've been too smart."

"Is it a deal?" I repeated.

He hesitated, then said it was in a voice you could cut bread on.

I hung up and went back to Veda.

CHAPTER ELEVEN

IF WE HAD DONE AS CASY had planned and had made a break for it on the night of the murder, we might have reached Miami. But by delaying another twenty-four hours to collect what I thought was a getaway stake killed that idea as surely as a .25 slug had killed Brett. O'Readen would have let us through the cordon if we had gone at once, but the delay crippled him. In those wasted hours the manhunt was organized. By then the State Troopers, the FBI and the Los Angeles police had taken the matter out of O'Readen's hands. The politicians were yelling for action. The squawk the newspapers put up the morning following the murder echoed up and down the coast like a thunder clap. They had been waiting for an opportunity to crucify O'Readen, and they grabbed the chance like a starving man grabs a free meal. They demanded instant action or else.

The president of the oil companies owned by Brett added his voice to the uproar by offering ten grand for any information that'd led to the arrest of the killer. All that day the local radio station interrupted its programs to give the latest information on the murder and to broadcast a description of me. The K.G.P.L. police hookup was pouring out instructions to their prowl cars every hour of the day to go to this or that address where it had been reported I had been seen. In those twenty-four hours I'd thrown away, the whole country was whipped into an hysterical frenzy, and the manhunt of the century, as the radio called it, was on.

Dominic Boyd had been over to collect the dagger. I didn't see him. Casy handled the deal for me. He said Boyd handed over the money with scarcely a word. As he was leaving he said he hoped the police would get me, and the vicious fury in his voice had startled Casy. Well, I had collected the getaway stake, but the way things were shaping it didn't seem as if it would help much.

All day Veda and I stayed in the hideout and listened to the radio. The constant reference to me as a vicious killer gave me a sick feeling, but I didn't let her know how rattled I was. When a special broadcast warned mothers to keep their children off the streets, and lock and bolt all doors and windows that night, I couldn't even look at her.

As the hours crept past and the hysteria increased, I began to realize that we wouldn't reach Miami. The distance was too far and the risk too great. If we were to believe what the radio said, every road out from Santa Medina and San Luis Beach was barricaded, and amateur detectives all over the country were on the lookout for me in the hope of earning that reward.

While we were trying to eat a meal Veda had prepared, Casy came in. There was a bleak look in his eyes and his mouth was set in a hard thin line.

"How's it going, Mick?" I asked, not liking his expression. I knew how it was going, but I hoped I was getting hysterical, too, and it wasn't so bad as I thought.

"You're not getting to Miami," he said and sat down. "We've got to face it, Floyd. This is the biggest thing that's happened in a lifetime. Whoever shot Brett might just as well have shot the president. The heat's fierce."

"Yeah," I said and pushed away my plate. The food

had been sticking in my throat anyway. "Some punk was saying on the radio just now I should be shot at sight like a mad dog."

"They've jacked up the reward to thirty grand and that's too much dough," Mick said gravely. "Now look, Floyd, you'll have to get moving. Too many guys know you're here. There's the guard on the door, there's Joe and Lu and there're the guys I was playing poker with when you came in. They all know you're still in the building because they haven't seen you leave. I trust Joe and Lu, but no one else, and thirty grand is too big a temptation. You're not safe here."

I poured myself a shot of whisky, frowned at it, then pushed it impatiently aside.

"I'll get out," I said.

"Redfern has been over. That guy is no fool and he's going to throw a hook into you or bust. If one of my boys squeals, Redfern will be back with a wrecking crew, and he'll take this joint to pieces until he finds you. I hate having to say this, Floyd, but you'll have to move."

I looked at Veda. She was very calm and alert and her eyes were bright with excitement.

"Your only chance is to get across the border," Mick was saying. "Make for Tijuana. That's your quickest way out of trouble. I don't know how you'll get there, but if you can get there, you're safe."

"I'll tell him how to get there," Veda said briskly. "We'll go in my car. They're not looking for me, and Floyd can disguise himself. We'll get through all right."

"No!" I said and stood up. "You're keeping out of this. You're not coming with me. I've changed my mind about you. These boys mean business. There's going to be shooting when they run into me. If we're caught together you'll suffer for it. Keep out of it."

"She's right, Floyd," Casy said. "You might stand a chance of getting through with her. They're looking for you on your own. If she was with you, you two might throw them off."

"I can't help that!" I said and moved restlessly about the room. "She must keep out of this. This is lynch law. I can smell it. You know what they'd do to her if they caught us together."

Casy shrugged. He looked tired and his face was sullen with anger. "Well, what are you going to do?"

"We're going together," Veda said quietly. "Let me talk to him. I'll convince him."

"You won't," I said, raising my voice. "I'm not dragging you into this. Now look, Mick—"

"Think about it," he interrupted. "I'll be back in a while. I'll think about it, too."

He went away before I could stop him.

"I'm coming with you," Veda said. "It's no use arguing. I've made up my mind. The two of us can get through. I'm sure of it."

"Now look, you've heard what they're saying about me. They're calling me a mad dog, a vicious killer, a child murderer—every damn name they can lay their tongues on. If they catch me they're not going to take me to headquarters. They'll string me to a tree or kick me to death. Think what they'll do to you if you're with me."

She caught hold of my coat lapels and pulled my head down and kissed me. "You're rattled, Floyd. Don't lose your nerve. We'll do it together. Think a minute—what will happen to me if you leave me? I can't go back to Cornelius. I haven't any money, and besides, I want to come with you. I'm not scared. This is what we'll do. You must dye your hair and wear a pair of shell spectacles. They'll never suspect you with me. I'm positive, Floyd."

I stared at her. I wanted her along with me if I could be sure I wasn't getting her into a jam. I knew she was talking sense. They would be looking for me on my own. If I did alter my appearance and travel with her, the betting was we'd get through.

"I'm weakening," I said. "I believe you're right."

"I know I am. Let's see what I can do with you." She ran to her bag and brought out an elaborate makeup box. "I have some black hair dye that dries fast. Come into the bathroom, and I'll fix you up."

Twenty minutes later I stood before the mirror and stared at a tall, dark fella who stared back at me a little short-sightedly through a pair of thick horn cheaters. He might have been a distant relative of mine, but he certainly wasn't me.

"Not bad," I said, and for the first time that day I felt a little more confident. "Not bad at all."

"They won't know you," Veda said. "I scarcely recognize you myself." She fished out a road map from her bag and began to study it. She had got down to this escape business with a grim seriousness that impressed me. It was as if she had been running away from the police all her life.

"We'll go out on Highway 395," she announced. "That'll take us through Riverside to San Diego and into Tijuana. We should do it in under five hours."

"You have it all figured out, haven't you?" I said and took her in my arms. "If we get out of this jam, Veda, I'll make you happy."

"You're making me happy now."

A little later Casy rapped on the door and came in. He took one look at me and let out a startled oath. A gun jumped into his hand before I could let out a yap.

"Hey, Mick, take it easy. Is it as good as all that?"

His face was a study as he lowered the gun.

"I'll say it's good. I didn't know you from Adam."

We told him what we planned to do.

"That little car ain't much," he said when we were through. "I can get you something bigger. I have a Buick that's been built for this job—armor plate and bullet-proof windows. If you get in a jam, you can make a run for it and nothing can stop you. It has self-sealing tires and an engine that's geared for fast work. You can knock a hundred and twenty out of her."

"Do you want to trade your car?" I asked Veda.

"For a job like that—yes. We can use my licence plates and tag, can't we?"

"I'll fix 'em myself," Mick said, getting up. "As soon as it gets a little darker, you'd better move." He gave a sly grin. "I've locked up all those boys who know you're here. They're getting difficult to handle, but they'll stay under lock and key until you've gone."

"You're a swell guy, Mick. I don't know what I'd've done without you. I'll square accounts if I ever get out of this jam."

He laughed. "You'll get out of it all right. They won't spot you. Don't worry. It's a cinch now. I'll be back in a while."

The moon was getting up above Ocean Rise when we left the hideout and walked along an alley that led from the back of the gambling joint to a dirt road. It was a hot night, and the stars were like points of steel through blue velvet.

I carried Veda's bags and Mick brought mine. The Road-master Buick looked as big as a house as we came upon it. It wasn't a new job, but we didn't want anything too showy.

"You've got food and drink in the back," Mick told me as he stowed the bags in the boot. "This job was built in Chicago, where they know how to build a car. There's a couple of panels you might like to know about. One's under the driving seat and contains a .45. I've cleaned and oiled her and she's loaded. There's another panel under the dashboard. There's a Sten gun in there with ammunition, and two hand grenades that might come in useful."

"For Pete's sake," I exclaimed, "what do you think this is? The beginning of another war?"

"It might be—for you," he said grimly. "Don't let them catch you, Floyd."

"Okay, Mick, and thanks again."

We shook hands.

"Keep your eye on him," Mick said to Veda. "He's a good guy. Don't let anyone tell you different."

"I've found that out for myself," Veda said, "and you're a good guy, too."

I engaged gear. Before we all burst into tears, I moved the Buick slowly on its way.

Mick jumped on the running board.

"There's a barricade across the bottom of Main Street as you go out and another at Pasadena. Watch out—and good luck."

He dropped off as I trod on the gas and sent the big car leaping forward along the dirt road.

"Well, we've started," I said. "I'll be a lot happier when I've crossed the border."

"If we're questioned, you're my brother John," Veda said. "You better let me do the talking. I'll sex them into letting us through."

"You've got a nerve, kid. Aren't you scared?"

"A little. Not much. I'm trying to get a kick out of this. I can't really believe it's happening to us."

"Yeah," I said, "every now and then it sneaks up on me, then I get the shakes."

I swung the car off the dirt road onto Main Street, and drove along at a steady thirty miles an hour. I could feel an atmosphere of suppressed excitement as we passed through the town. There were groups of men outside every beer saloon. They all looked at us intently. Several of the men carried rifles, and not a few swung pick-handles.

"Looks like the beginning of a lynch mob," I said. "I'm glad we're getting out."

"Lights ahead," Veda said with a slight catch in her voice. "They're stopping the traffic."

I slowed down. Two cars ahead of me had come to a standstill. I drew up behind them. A big truck had been maneuvered across the road to prevent traffic passing. A group of men with lanterns and flashlights and armed with guns stood around the truck while two policemen and a state trooper talked to the drivers of the cars in front of me. They waved the cars on, and came strolling toward me.

I found I was sweating slightly, but there was nothing I could do about that. I was lighting a cigarette as one of the policemen threw a beam on me.

"Where are you going?" he demanded roughly.

"Pasadena," I said.

The beam slipped over me and onto Veda.

"They must be looking for the Brett killer," she said brightly. "That's right, isn't it, officer?" She gave him a smile that rocked him back on his heels.

"That's right, miss," he said, almost human now, "and who are you?"

"Rux is the name. Veda and John. He's my brother."

The beam came onto me again.

"Brother, huh? Lucky guy."

"I'd as soon be her husband," I said, but my grin was a little stiff.

"Don't listen to him, officer," Veda giggled. "He always says the most terrible things."

"That's not so terrible," the policeman said and laughed. He seemed to be enjoying himself. "He's got something there."

The state trooper came up. He looked as hard and as unfriendly as a concrete sidewalk.

"Checked their licence tag?" he demanded.

"Naw, but that guy ain't him. Use your eyes, and don't try to make work."

"Check it," the trooper snapped. "This ain't a picnic. It's a manhunt."

Muttering under his breath, the policeman read the license tag on the wheel, grunted.

"Okay, move along," he said to me, winked at Veda. "I wouldn't want to be your brother, either," he told her.

I drove around the truck, aware of a couple of dozen eyes on me. Some of those guys certainly looked hungry to earn themselves thirty grand. Once clear of the truck, I gave the Buick its head.

"That was easy enough, wasn't it?" Veda said, but there was a little quiver in her voice.

I wiped my face with my handkerchief.

"It was all right while it lasted," I said. "But I don't want any more of it."

We licked along the road at a steady sixty miles an hour. I didn't feel much like talking. I kept thinking of the other barricade at Pasadena.

We went through Glendale without being stopped. There was a big crowd of men at one street corner. A guy in a Stetson hat was standing on the backseat of a car, talking to them. He kept waving his arms and seemed excited. A number of men had pick handles, and I didn't have to wonder who he was talking about.

One of the men in the crowd turned and stared at us. He shouted suddenly, but he was too far away for us to hear what he was yelling. I drove on. It needed a little effort not to increase our speed.

Veda, looking back through the rear window, said the crowd was looking after us.

We got onto the Pasadena road, and after driving for eight or nine miles I saw a red light flickering in the distance.

"There's a light ahead," Veda said sharply.

"Yeah," I said, and tried to make up my mind whether to stop or not. There were no other cars coming, and this was a lonely stretch—too lonely.

"Act natural," she said sharply as if sensing my hesitation. "There's nothing to worry about."

"Who said I was worrying?" I snapped back.

I guess our nerves were sticking out a foot.

The headlights of the Buick picked out a bunch of men standing in the middle of the road. I couldn't see a policeman or a trooper among them, and I felt a chill run up my spine. They looked a tough mob.

"Watch out," I said to Veda and reached down and slid back the panel at my feet.

"Don't start anything," she whispered fiercely. "Please, Floyd…"

I let go of the butt of the .45 and straightened up.

"I don't like the look of them," I said out of the corner of my mouth.

As the Buick stopped, a fat guy, carrying the red lantern, came up. He was big, and his dungarees were ragged and dirty. Four of the others leveled their rifles at the windshield and blinked with intent eyes into the headlights. They also wore ragged dungarees. They looked like a bunch from a mining camp.

"Road up or something?" I said, leaning out of the window. "Or is this a holdup?"

"Come out of it," the fat guy said, "and make it snappy."

"Do what he says," Veda whispered. "We don't want to make them mad."

"Not damn likely," I returned. "Once out there they could do what they liked with us. We're safer in here." I leaned farther out of the window. "What's the idea?" I demanded.

Someone flashed a beam on us.

"'Taint him, Jud," a voice said. "This punk's dark."

The fat guy sneered. He came closer and I could smell beer on his breath.

"Come on out when I tell you," he snarled and pushed the rifle into my face.

I heard Veda's door open and glanced round. She had slid out and was standing in the road. I cursed softly, flipped open the panel under the dashboard and my hand closed around a cold hard object. Very cautiously I lifted it and slipped it into my side pocket. Then I opened the car door and got out.

The fat guy pushed me into the glare of the headlights.

"Take care of him," he said to a little guy with a face like a weasel.

They were all looking at Veda, who smiled at them. They were very still and intent. The little guy pointed a shotgun at me.

"We're looking for the Brett killer," the fat guy said to me. "How do we know you ain't him?" While he was speaking, he didn't take his eyes off Veda.

"You have a description of him, haven't you?" I said and laughed as if I thought he'd made a joke.

"Okay, so you're not Jackson," he returned. "So we ain't collecting the thirty grand reward, but we're having a lotta fun this night. You're the third guy with a dame we've stopped. You don't object if we have a little fun with your girlfriend, do you, pal?"

"I wouldn't start anything I couldn't finish if I were you," I said.

"Haw! Haw!" The fat guy slapped his thigh. "That's pretty good. You're the punk who'd better not start anything. If he makes a move, Tim, let him have both barrels."

"You bet," the weasel-faced man said and tittered.

The fat guy went up to Veda.

"Hello, sugar," he said. "You and me are going for a little walk."

Veda looked at him. Her eyes were steady.

"Why?" she said in a hard, flat voice.

"That's a secret," the fat guy said. "But you'll find out quick enough." He grabbed hold of her by her shirt.

She didn't try to get away, but continued to stare up at him, her eyes hardening.

"Come on," he said.

"Wait!" I shouted. "Leave her alone."

The shotgun barrel slammed into my chest, sending me staggering back.

The fat guy lifted Veda by her shirt and walked off with her into the bushes. She didn't struggle or cry out. The others turned to watch. The weasel-faced man began to shiver. He glared at me murderously, then suddenly as Veda gave a choking little scream he looked over his shoulder. That gave me the chance I'd been waiting for. I took a leap to one side, jumped forward as the shotgun exploded, smashed my fist into the thin, vicious face. I had the hand grenade out now and I drew the pin.

One of the men took a potshot at me with his rifle. I felt the slug fan my face. I lobbed the grenade into the darkness away from them and threw myself down behind

the car. The night was split open by a violent explosion.
The car rocked in the blast and the darkness was lit by a
blinding white flash. I was up on my feet again and
running toward where Veda had screamed. The grenade
had scared the daylights out of that bunch of toughs.
They went rushing into the darkness, yelling at each other
and falling over themselves to get away.

I found Veda and the fat guy in the bushes. He was
holding her against him, staring toward the car, his face
blank with surprise. He was so startled by the noise of
the grenade that he let me pull Veda out of his grip.

"What was that?" he mouthed at me. "Did you do
that?"

I hit him in the middle of his fat face and as he staggered back I snatched up his rifle and smashed it down
across his shoulders, beating him to the ground.

"No!" Veda screamed and caught my arm. "You
mustn't!"

I tried to push her away, but she clung to me. I struggled to free myself, a red curtain of rage before my eyes,
but she wouldn't let go. After a moment or so I got a grip
on myself.

"All right, kid," I said, and she let go of me.

The fat guy lay flat on his back. He was breathing, but
that was about all.

"Come on," Veda gasped. "Quickly, Floyd! Please…"

She pieced her clothing back together, hugging herself. I snatched her up and carried her to the car. The
whole business hadn't taken ten minutes.

"Are you all right?" I asked as I sent the car flying
forward.

"Don't talk to me for a bit," she said. "Just let me get
over it. What beasts men are!"

She was crying to herself. I didn't look at her but kept

driving, and I cursed softly. After a while she stopped crying and lit a cigarette.

"I'm all right now, Floyd. Why didn't you keep your head? What did it matter? We can't go through Pasadena now."

"What do you mean?"

"The bomb…they'll telephone to Pasadena to stop us. The police will want to have a look at a guy who carries bombs in his car."

I thought for a moment. She was right, of course.

"All right, it was a mistake to use it, but what else could I have done?"

"You could have kept your head. He wouldn't have killed me."

I knew she didn't mean it.

"All right, I should have kept my head. So we don't go through Pasadena."

She opened the map and studied it. Her hands were trembling.

"We'll have to take the long way round by Altadena and down into Monrovia."

"We'll do that." I put my arm round her and held her close.

"I'm glad you lost your head," she said in a small voice.

After driving the best part of a mile I said suddenly, "Put on the radio. Tune it to ten—that's K.G.P.L., police reports to radio cars. I want to hear how the boys are getting on."

Her hand was steady enough as she switched on and spun the tuning dial. The radio hummed, then buzzed into life.

We drove along as we listened to a lot of stuff about a street accident on Sunset Boulevard. A few minutes later we got another flash about a car bandit holding up a gas station.

"Nothing in it for us," I said. "That's Altadena right

ahead. No reception committee waiting by the look of things. We won't stop, though."

The mechanical voice coming from the radio suddenly barked, "K.G.P.L.—Los Angeles Police Department. Attention all cars. Repeat as of nine-ten Brett killing. Look out for black Roadmaster Buick believed to be Floyd Jackson's getaway car." Here followed the licence number and a detailed description. "The driver of this car may be Jackson, wanted for the murder of Lindsay Brett. With him is a slim, dark girl, wearing slacks and shirt. The car, when last seen, was heading for Pasadena. Stand by for more information now coming in."

Neither of us said anything. I kept driving. No one seemed to have heard of Floyd Jackson in Altadena. No one seemed to care. We went through the main street at a steady twenty-five miles an hour. The time was a little after ten-twenty, and only a few cars and a few men loitered under the streetlights. None of the men had guns. None of them even looked at us.

We sat very stiff and still while we waited. The radio crackled and hummed. I thought of all the dozens of prowl cops in their fast cars waiting, as we were waiting, for further information before they swung into action and converged on us. My hands ached as I gripped the steering wheel. I could see Veda's profile as we drove past the streetlamps. She was white and tense.

"Attention all cars...attention all cars. Brett killing. Persons wanted for questioning are number one: John Rux, thought to be Floyd Jackson. Description: six foot one, a hundred and eighty pounds, about thirty-three, dark hair, believed dyed, tanned complexion, powerfully built; wearing light gray suit, soft gray hat. Number two: Veda Rux. Description: five foot six, a hundred and twenty pounds, about twenty-four, dark hair, blue eyes, wearing black slacks and a dark red shirt. These people were heading for Pasadena, but are believed to have changed their route. Particular attention to all cars on Highways 2, 66, 70 and 99. Don't take any chances. When last stopped Rux broke through the cordon by using what is believed to be a hand grenade. Intercepting cars should arrest Rux for questioning. That is all."

I slammed on the brakes, threw out the gear and stopped the car.

"Well, that's it, Veda. That puts you right in the middle of this jam, too."

"They're clever, aren't they?" she said in a small, strained voice. "I didn't think they'd ever get on to us, did you? If only you hadn't dropped that bomb."

I was so rattled I couldn't keep my voice steady.

"We're going into the foothills. There's nothing else we can do." I put my hand on hers. "Don't get scared. I won't let them do anything to you."

They were empty words and they couldn't mean anything, but they seemed to please her.

"I'm not scared. Let's go into the foothills. They'll never think to look for us there."

I started the car again and we drove off the tarmac road onto a dirt road.

It was dark and silent and lonely when we reached the foothills, and as black as a Homburg hat. I had no idea where I was going or what I was going to do—no idea at all. I kept thinking of all those prowl cars converging on us, packed with tough coppers with guns. If they caught me, no amount of talking would get me out of this jam. It would be done legally, and it would take time, but they'd kill me in the end. If they caught me….

I put my arm around Veda.

"We'll beat them, kid," I said. "Maybe they are smart but we're smarter. You'll see. We'll beat them."

More empty words.

CHAPTER TWELVE

THE SMELL OF COFFEE WOKE ME. It was still dark, and as I sat up I felt the wind cold against my face.

Veda was squatting over the primus stove. The bluish flame showed a hard, bleak expression on her face, and she looked remote and withdrawn into herself. She was very neat in her canary-colored slacks and thick sweater. Her hair was looped back with a red ribbon.

"That smells good," I said, yawned and threw off the blanket. I looked at my watch. It was a few minutes after five. "Couldn't you sleep?"

She looked up and smiled. The hardness went away.

"I was cold. Want some coffee?"

"You bet."

While she poured the coffee into mugs, she said, "I've been listening to the radio. They think we're heading for the Mexican border."

"Do they? Well, that's smart of them."

She was smiling as she handed me a mug, but her eyes were alert and uneasy.

"They have barricades on all the main roads. They say we can't get away."

"Maybe we'd better give up the idea of Tijuana."

"Yes."

I drank the coffee slowly. I didn't know where we could go.

"We'll have to head north," she said as if reading my thoughts. "We can't have another night in the open."

"Maybe that's what they expect us to do. They may be bluffing about Mexico. Redfern's no fool." I stood up. "Let me bend my brains on this. I'm going to have a shave and wash. Give me a little time to work it out."

I collected my shaving kit and wandered away to the stream by which we had camped. The water was very cold and hard, and I had the worst shave in years. When I got back, she was cooking bacon on the primus stove.

"It might be an idea to stick right where we are," I said, squatting by her side. "In the old days, moonshiners used these hills. We might find a cabin or a shed or something if we look around. They may get tired of hunting us if we hole up here. Give them a week and they'll get careless. We could pick our time and make a break for it when things have cooled off. Besides, I want a little time to raise a mustache. I think we should stick here if we can."

She nodded. "Yes."

Now we had some kind of plan, she relaxed and the uneasy expression went out of her eyes. While we breakfasted I told her about the moonshiners and how they used to hide their stills out in these hills, and bring their rotgut down to the towns in horse-drawn carts.

"There are dozens of stills hidden around here. We're certain to find a place where we can hide up."

While we were washing the dishes in the stream I said, "I woke in the night and got thinking. It was the first chance I had of thinking about this business. I was too rattled to use my head before—I've never been so rattled in my life."

"What did you think?"

"I got to wondering who shot Brett."

"Why, you did, didn't you?" The words seemed to jump out of her before she could stop them. The moment she said them she put her hand to her mouth and went white.

"What do you mean?" I demanded, staring at her. "You don't think I shot him, do you? I told you what happened."

"Yes. I know. I don't know why I said that. I didn't mean it. I'm sorry, Floyd."

"What is this? What are you getting at?"

"Nothing. I said I didn't mean it. I'm sorry, Floyd. Please forget it."

She wouldn't look at me, and I suddenly went cold.

"So you do think I killed him! Out with it! That's what you think, isn't it?"

She caught my arms and clung to me.

"I don't care if you did!" she cried. "I don't care. I only want to be with you. Nothing else matters!"

"This is crazy, Veda. So you thought all along I shot him?"

"I don't care." She drew away. "All right then, you didn't shoot him. I tell you I don't care."

I held her at arm's length. She was crying.

"Now look, kid, you've got to believe me. He was shot as I was looking for the compact. I was on the pedestal when I heard the shot. I went up there. He was sitting at his desk. The gun was right there in front of him. That's how it happened. You've got to believe it!"

"Of course, darling." She bit back her tears. "Of course." It was as if she were speaking to a child who had said he'd seen a spook.

"This is madness. If *you* don't believe me—that shows the kind of jam I'm in."

"But I do believe you. Don't look like that, darling. Please…it's getting light. We must be moving."

"If you think I killed Brett, why the hell have you come with me?" I shouted at her.

"Nothing you do or have done will make any difference to me. I can't help it. I don't care. You're everything to me."

I ran my fingers through my hair.

"Okay, so I'm everything to you. That's fine. But I didn't kill Brett."

"All right, darling."

I watched her take the dishes to the car and begin to pack. The crazy thing was I knew she still didn't believe me. She thought I had gone up there and shot Brett, and that I lied to her when I told her how it happened. Maybe Mick thought I had lied, too.

I went over to her as she was getting into the car.

"Look, Veda, I'll give you one sound reason why I didn't kill him. I went up there to collect twenty-five thousand dollars—remember? Well, I didn't get it. Do you think I'd gyp myself out of all that dough just for the joy of shooting him?"

"He must have had the money there for you. No one has mentioned it. Don't you think it was stolen?"

I took a quick step back. It was like running into a punch in the face.

"That's it!" I exclaimed. "That's why he was shot! Someone knew he was going to give me the money, and laid for him!"

"Yes," she said, but she still didn't look at me.

For a moment I didn't get it, then I grabbed and shook her.

"So you think I took it? You think I went up there and shot Brett so I could have the dagger and the money? Is that it?"

"Please, darling…you're hurting me."

Then it came to me.

"Gorman!" I exclaimed. "He knew. I told him! He knew I was going out there. He knew Brett was going to pay me twenty-five grand. I told him, like the dope I am. He could have fixed it. He could have gone out there and shot Brett, knowing I'd be around to take the rap. It was Gorman!"

She suddenly became as excited as I, and caught hold of me.

"Oh, darling, tell me you didn't do it. No, don't! I can see now you didn't. What a fool I've been! I thought— but never mind what I thought. I've been so worried. Forgive me, darling. Please forgive me."

"There's nothing to forgive," I said and pulled her to me. "It was Gorman. It must have been Gorman."

"We'll talk as we go. We must get on, Floyd. Look, it's nearly light."

"Gorman!" I said half to myself as I drove up the road that wasn't much better than a cart track. "He fits. What do you know about him, Veda? Was he short of money?"

"Sometimes. He gambled. Boyd often used to help him."

"Let's try and work this out. We know Boyd paid him well to keep quiet about the dagger. Look, it might have happened like this—when I told Gorman to get the dagger back from Boyd, Boyd may have demanded his money back. He's a dangerous customer, and Gorman may not have been able to return the money. He may have spent it. He asked me to split the twenty-five grand Brett was paying me, but I wouldn't play. He may have been desperate, and seeing the chance to get the twenty-five grand and push Brett's killing on to me, went out there, shot Brett, collected the money before I appeared on the scene."

"He would have had to have been quick."

"It took me about three minutes to get down from the pedestal, run up the steps and along the terrace. He could have done it if the money was on the desk."

"Yes, but what's the use?" she said bitterly. "We can't do anything. No one would believe us."

"Once a dick, always a dick. This is right up my alley. If I can prove Gorman killed Brett I'm in the clear. And that's what I'm going to do."

"But how can you? You can't go back there."

"The heat will be off in a couple of weeks. Then I'll go back."

"But you can't make plans, Floyd. We don't know what's going to happen in a couple of weeks."

She was right, of course.

The sun was coming over the foothills when we saw the shack. If we hadn't been keeping a sharp lookout we should have missed it. It was hidden behind a clump of trees and was a good quarter of a mile from the road.

"That's it!" Veda said excitedly. "If there's no one there, it's perfect!"

I stopped the car and got out.

"You wait here. I'll take a look around."

"Take the gun, Floyd."

"What do you think I am—a gangster?" I said, but I took it.

The shack was empty and looked as if no one had been there for years. There was nothing the matter with it. It was weatherproof and dry, and only needed a good clean-out to be habitable. Around the back was a large shed in which were the remains of a still: a heating chamber, a hundred-gallon tank and a row of rotting tubs.

I waved to Veda and she brought the car over.

We examined the shack together.

"It's perfect," she said excitedly. "They'll never think of looking for us here. We're safe, darling. I'm sure we're safe now."

It took us a couple of days to settle in. Scrubbing floors, sweeping, repairing the bunks, fixing the stove and cutting firewood took our minds off Brett. We didn't even listen to the radio.

On our second night at the shack, while we were sitting in the twilight watching the sun go down behind the hills, Veda said abruptly, "Get the radio, Floyd. We've been living in a fool's paradise."

"It's been like a vacation. But you're right. It seems you're always right."

I went to the shed where we garaged the Buick, brought back the radio and set it up on a wooden box between us. I tuned in to K.G.P.L., and we spent a tense half hour listening to a lot of activity that had nothing to do with us. I tuned in to the San Luis Beach station, and we listened to hot dance music from the Casino for another half hour and still nothing about us.

"Well, keep it on," Veda said and got up. "I'll start supper."

I sat and listened while she moved about the shack. Every time the dance music stopped, I'd stiffen and think, This is it. This is where they'll interrupt their program. But they didn't. They continued to play hot dance music as if Floyd Jackson had never existed.

We had supper and still the radio ignored us.

"You see, they've forgotten us," I said. "They've lost interest like I said they would. I bet if we bought a newspaper it wouldn't even mention us."

"I wonder," she said, collected the plates and went into the shack again.

It got too dark to sit outside, so I brought the radio in

and shut up for the night. Veda had made up the fire. It was cold at night up at this height, and the wind nipped off the sea. She knelt before the fire and I sat behind her. It was snug in there, and watching her, the flames reflecting on her face, it suddenly crossed my mind that for the first time in my life I was at peace with myself.

It was an odd feeling, and it startled me. I'd been around, done most things—lied, cheated, acted smart, made and lost money, played hell. It'd been the same ever since I could remember. There were a lot of milestones over thirty years best forgotten. Milestones that marked the things I'd done, seen, loved and hated. More low spots than high spots. Faces in the past—forgotten faces that swam out of the darkness unexpectedly to remind me of a mean act, a shabby deal or a broken promise, like turning the pages of a forbidden book. Blackmail, easy money, too many drinks, punching my way out of trouble. The end justifying the means, no matter how shabby. Self first in a jungle of selfishness. Women, out of focus and only half remembered—a laugh; a trick with a cigarette; long, tapering legs; a torn dress; elusive perfume; a crescent-shaped birthmark; nails that dug into my shoulders; white flesh above a stocking; blondes; brunettes; redheads; silver wigs. "You were always a sucker for women." Nearer thirty than twenty, blonde, sickeningly eager. "There are things a man doesn't do. He doesn't take money from women." Wondering if she'd believe me. The hidden smirk when she didn't. Making it easier for me by putting the money in my pocket. Low spot.

"This is the last. You're not getting any more out of me, you stinking cheat!" The man in the pawnshop running grimy hands over the fur coat. "Thirty bucks…I'll be robbing myself." Sending her the pawn ticket. Poetic justice at the time—a despicable act in retrospect. Empty pockets. The uneasy ache for a smoke and a drink. Blackmail. "This letter…my expenses, of course. I can't work for nothing." And now murder. The steps go down, but never up. "Shoot him like a mad dog." Murder. "Attention all cars…wanted for questioning." The surprised look in the dead and empty eyes; the little blue hole in the center of his forehead. "If they catch you, they'll kill you." And Veda. "I don't care. You're everything to me." A high spot.

It was an odd feeling all right.

Veda said suddenly, "We're running short of food."

Her voice startled me, like turning on the light in a haunted room.

"What did you say?"

"We're running short of food."

I hadn't thought of that. I hadn't thought much about anything while we'd been alone together. But as soon as she spoke, I got the uneasy, hunted feeling again. Fool's paradise was what she had said. Fool's paradise was right.

"I'll go into Altadena tomorrow," she went on, and raised her hands to the fire.

"No," I said, "I'll go."

She looked over her shoulder to smile at me.

"Don't be difficult. They're not looking for me. I'm just the woman who's with you. On my own, they'll never give me a thought. You can drive me as far as the dirt road and I'll walk the rest of the way. It can't be more than three miles to the Altadena road. I'll get a lift from there."

"No," I said.

We argued back and forth, then she got up and said she was going to bed.

"You're not going to Altadena tomorrow," I told her. "I'm going to bed."

The next morning I asked her to make out a list of the things we needed.

"I'll go as soon as I've cut some wood. There's nothing to worry about."

When I came back with the logs she had gone. She had taken the Buick and had left a note on the table. It said she would be back as soon as she could, and not to worry, and that she loved me.

It was then I realized how much she meant to me, and I started after her. But after walking three miles down the cart track, I gave up. I knew it would only make things worse for her if we were seen together. I knew she stood a chance of getting to Altadena and back if she was alone. I returned to the shack and waited. It was the longest day I've ever spent, and when the sun began to dip behind the hills and there was still no sign of her, I was fit to climb a tree.

But she came back. As I was getting ready to go down and find her, I saw the wing lights of the car in the distance. As she slid out of the car, I grabbed and held her. I didn't have to say anything—she understood all right.

"I'm so sorry, Floyd. I meant to get back sooner, only I had to be sure no one was following me. I have everything."

"Was it all right?"

"Yes. I've brought cigarettes and whisky and enough food to last us a week, and the newspapers."

But there was something in the tone of her voice that made me nervous. She was casual—too casual—but I didn't say anything until we had unloaded the car and I had taken it around to the shed at the back.

I returned to the shack and closed the door. In the

harsh light of the acetylene lamp, she looked white and tense.

"They think we've slipped through the cordon," she said as she put the groceries away. "The papers are on the table. They think we're in Mexico."

I glanced at the newspapers without much interest. There had been a big airline disaster and that filled the front page. Brett's killing had been shifted onto page three. As she said, the newspapers seemed to think we were in Mexico. One paper said Brett had drawn twenty-five thousand dollars from his bank and no trace of the money could be found. They gave that as my motive for killing him.

While I was reading I still felt there was something wrong. Veda chatted away as she prepared supper, but there was a tautness about her that scared me.

"Did you run into trouble down there?" I asked abruptly. "What is it, Veda?"

She smiled, but the smile did not reach her eyes.

"No trouble, darling. It went off perfectly. No one even looked at me."

"Something's on your mind. What is it?"

"I saw Max Otis."

Silence hung in the room like smoke while we looked at each other.

"Gorman's chauffeur? In Altadena?"

She nodded.

"I was in a store buying the groceries. I saw him through the window. He went into a beer saloon. He didn't see me. I'm sure of that. But it gave me a fright. What's he doing in Altadena?"

"If he didn't see you, it doesn't matter. I don't think we need worry about Otis. If it had been Redfern..."

"He hates me."

"What makes you say that? I got on all right with him. He hated Gorman and Boyd, but why should he hate you?"

She made a little grimace.

"He was always prying. I caught him going through my things. I reported him to Boyd. He hates me all right."

"Well, if he didn't see you it doesn't matter. You're sure he didn't see you?"

"Yes."

We were a little jumpy for the next couple of days, and although we didn't say anything to each other, we both kept a sharp lookout, and any unexpected sound—a door creaking, the wind against the shutters, a rat gnawing in the shed—brought us to our feet. But we got over it. The manhunt that had started with such violence and enthusiasm had evaporated like fog before the wind. It seemed certain now, the radio told us, that we were in Mexico, and our escape was just one more black spot in O'Readen's incompetent administration.

My mustache was coming along, and in another week I decided it would be safe enough to return to San Luis Beach. I was determined to find Brett's killer, and the more I thought about it, the more convinced I was that Gorman was at the bottom of it.

I didn't say anything to Veda about what I had in mind. I knew she didn't want me to go back. I didn't know what I was going to do with her while I was in San Luis Beach. She couldn't go with me. That would be asking for trouble. I didn't want to leave her in this lonely shack. It was a problem, and it had to be solved before I could get after Brett's killer.

It was on the sixth night of our stay at the shack that it happened. We were sitting in front of the fire, listening to Bob Hope on the radio. Veda was mending a shirt of mine and I was whittling some clothes-pegs for her. It was a domestic scene—the kind of scene you'd expect to find in any home. I was laughing at a crack from Hope when I glanced up, and the laugh nipped off as if a hand had caught me around the throat.

Veda looked over her shoulder; a quick movement that froze to stillness.

He stood in the doorway, a sad look in his moist eyes, his nose a little more hooked, his mouth smirking.

"Pretty nice," he said. "Like home. I thought you'd be up here. I saw her watching me through the store window. I reckoned to give you a surprise."

"Hello, Max," I said.

"Does she still walk in her sleep?" he asked, came in and shut the door.

It was then I saw the .45 in his hand.

CHAPTER THIRTEEN

THE KETTLE BEGAN TO BOIL and steam rose from the spout in a thin and persistent jet. The kettle lid lifted and clacked back, lifted and clacked back again. Veda took the kettle off the stove, then sat back and picked up her sewing again. A muscle twitched in her cheek, pulling her mouth out of shape, but she gave no other sign that she was aware of Max. It was like someone seeing a ghost standing at the foot of the bed, and refusing to admit it is there.

"Better put that knife down," Max said. "You might cut yourself."

I hadn't realized I still had the knife in my hand. I suppose I could have thrown it at him, but I'm not good at that sort of thing. I dropped the knife on the floor.

"I don't expect you're pleased to see me," Max went on. "Two's company and three's a crowd."

"Yes." I still found it difficult to breathe evenly.

"I thought there was no harm in looking you up. It's not as if I was staying long."

"Well, we are a little cramped for space."

He eyed Veda and smirked.

"Don't suppose you mind that. A girl doesn't seem to get in the way like another man."

"That's right," I said.

"I could do with something to eat. Maybe Miss Rux

might put something together. Anything will do. I'm not fussy."

Veda laid down her sewing, got up and opened the store cupboard. The .45 pointed at the center of her spine. It was an odd feeling, sitting there, seeing the gun threatening her. If I'd held the knife in my hand now I would have thrown it.

"It's been a long day," Max said. "I've covered a lot of ground looking for you."

I didn't say anything.

He sat down at the table away from us and put the gun on the table within reach of his hand. While Veda cooked bacon, he smoked.

"You two have had some excitement, haven't you?" he said. He seemed friendly enough, apart from the gun. "They think you're in Mexico. I thought you were, too, until I saw Miss Rux. My home's in Altadena. After you took Gorman's ring, I quit. There didn't seem much work around so I went home. I live with my old lady and sister."

"That must be nice for them," I said.

"We get on. The trouble with my old lady is she drinks too much. It costs a lot to keep her in liquor."

I couldn't see much in that for me so I didn't say anything.

"When I was a kid I used to come out here with my old man," Max went on. He seemed to like the sound of his voice. "He had a still four, five miles from this one. When I saw Miss Rux I guessed you'd be out here somewhere. It took me a couple of days to find you. You'd be surprised how many stills are hidden around here."

"Is that right?" I said and shifted in my chair.

His hand hovered over the gun. In spite of the ingratiating smirk, he was nervous.

"If you have a couple of eggs to spare, miss, I can use them," he said to Veda. "And a drink, too. Kind of snug here, ain't it? You two've done all right for yourselves. Radio, too. That's useful. I bet you've kept abreast with the news. I bet you've had many a laugh at the cops. You've played it pretty smart."

Veda broke two eggs into the pan.

"Would it worry you if I got out my cigarettes?" I asked.

His hand dropped to the gun. "I shouldn't. I've seen that trick in the movies. It wouldn't be safe."

"Look, let's not fool around anymore. What do you want?"

Veda straightened and looked across at Max. There was a pause. The atmosphere became so taut you could hang a hat on it.

"Well, I reckoned you two would want to keep together," he said. "It seemed to me you wouldn't want to be separated. The way I see it is like this. Miss Rux is a nice-looking frail. You two have been alone together for some days. Well, a guy doesn't whittle clothes pegs all the time when a frail like Miss Rux is around. I reckoned you two wouldn't be tired of each other so soon."

"Suppose you cut out that stuff and get to the point."

"Sure, but I wanted you to know how I figured the thing. You know how the cops are—separate jails for males and females, no thought for lovers or husbands and wives. You know how it is."

"Keep talking," I said and there was a snap in my voice that made him grip the gun.

"Well, I read about you collecting twenty-five grand off Brett. That seemed to me to be an awful lot of dough."

We waited while he smirked. The writing was on the wall now, but I wasn't going to help him out.

"You see, my old lady needs money," he went on.

"She kills a bottle of gin a day. Sort of like medicine to her now. That's something I haven't got—money."

"That's all right," I said. "I can stake you if that's what you want. I'd be glad to. A hundred bucks would buy a lot of gin. More than she could handle."

He rubbed the tip of his hooked nose with a dirty finger.

"It would, but I wasn't thinking of a hundred bucks." He shifted forward on the edge of his chair. "It's like this. You two want to keep together. You don't want to be bothered by the cops. No one but me knows you're up here. It struck me you might want me to keep my mouth shut as well as giving the old lady some gin."

"If you put it like that, I guess you're right."

"That's the way I saw it." He stifled a nervous giggle. "No one—I don't give a damn who it is—wants to be tried for murder. It's a serious thing. I knew a guy who stood trial for murder. He got a good lawyer, and he spent a lot of money trying to convince the jury he didn't kill the guy. The trial lasted six days. He fought every inch of the way, but they stuck him in the gas chamber in the end. That's a horrible end. It takes three minutes to choke to death. No one wants to risk that."

The eggs hissed and spluttered in the boiling fat. It was the only sound in the room for a minute or so.

He went on. "So I reckoned you'd come across in a big way to avoid that kind of trouble."

"Did you get around to a figure?"

"Yeah—I thought twenty-five grand would be a fair price." His hand lifted the gun. "Look at it this way—"

"You're crazy!" I exclaimed, leaning forward to glare at him. "That's all the dough we've got. How do we get away if we haven't any dough?"

Again he rubbed the tip of his nose.

"I didn't reckon that was my funeral. I kept turning it over in my mind, and I couldn't see how I could go wrong." He stubbed out his cigarette and lit another. He didn't raise his eyes off us for a second. "Of course, I didn't expect you'd part easily, and I thought you might try a trick or two. So I fixed things up before I left. There's a note for my old lady telling her where I've gone and who I've gone to see in case I run into trouble. She may be a rum-dum, but she's no fool. She'll know what to do with that note. So don't let's have any trouble."

"You haven't anything to sell. Suppose I did give you the twenty-five, there's nothing to stop you turning us in when you've got it."

"I wouldn't do that," he said seriously. "I like you. There'd be no sense in double-crossing you. Give me the money and I'll forget you exist."

I began to understand how a rat feels when the door of the trap snaps shut.

"No, you wouldn't. You're forgetting the thirty-grand reward. You wouldn't pass that up, Otis."

He gave a little start and looked away. He hadn't forgotten.

"I've got to get back. You'd better part, Jackson. You haven't any alternative."

Veda dished up the eggs, flicked the bacon on the plate. She reached for the whisky, poured a liberal shot into a glass.

"Straight or water?" she asked. Her voice was as harsh as emery paper.

"Straight," he said, watching me. "What do you say, Jackson?"

"Give it to him," Veda said curtly.

I turned to stare at her. She gave me an awful little smile that just flickered at the corners of her mouth, then she walked across the room with the plate of food in one hand and the whisky in the other.

"Well, all right," I said as taut as a banjo string. That smile tipped me. She reached the table as I stood up. Max had the gun pointing at her, but as soon as I moved he shifted it to me. That movement gave her the chance. She threw the whisky in his face, dropped the plate and grabbed his gun hand. The gun went off. I crossed the room with two jumps and hit him on the point of his jaw. His head snapped back, and he fell out of the chair. I grabbed up the gun, but the punch had settled him. I forgot him when I looked at Veda. She was leaning against the table, very white, her hand pressed to her side. Blood trickled between her fingers.

"Veda!"

"It's all right. It's nothing. Tie him up!"

"Let me look."

"Tie him up!"

There was a ferocious expression in her eyes that shook me.

"Right," I said and went through his pockets. He had a .25 in his hip pocket, no money and a flabby wallet I tossed on the table. I took off his belt, twisted his hands behind him and tied them. I tied them so tightly that his flesh bulged over the belt. Then I went to Veda. She had pulled up her sweater and was looking at a shallow furrow along the top of her hip.

"It's nothing," she said. "Get me a wet cloth."

While I washed and strapped the wound, neither of us said anything. I poured her a drink and one for myself.

"That was nervy of you," I said. "You took a chance, but there was nothing else for it. He wouldn't have let me get that close."

"Do you think he left a note for his mother?"

"I don't know. Maybe he's bluffing. I don't know."

The muscle twitched in her face.

"We'll have to find out."

"What the hell are we going to do with him? It means we'll have to get out of here, Veda."

"Never mind that—it's the note that matters."

"Yes."

I went over to him and shook him. It took a little while to bring him around. I had hit him a lot harder than I intended. Finally he began to groan. After a minute or so he opened his eyes. When he saw me bending over him, he went the color of a dirty sheet.

"All right, Max," I said. "You've played your hand. It's our turn now. Where do you live?"

"I'm not talking!"

"Yes, you are. I don't want to beat you, but you're talking. We've got to get that note of yours. If we get that, we can keep you here for a week or so, then when the heat's off us we'll turn you loose."

"I'm not talking!"

I stood him up and began to hit him with my fists. Every so often I asked him where he lived and he told me to go to hell. He had a lot of pluck, and I didn't get any fun out of wading into him. He passed out after I'd clipped him a shade too hard, and I drew back, blew on my knuckles and glared down at him in disgust.

Veda stood against the wall, her face empty and as white as chalk.

"You're wasting time, Floyd."

I threw water into his face, shook him alive.

"Where do you live?" I got set to sock him again.

He mumbled curses at me.

"Wait!" Veda said.

I drew away from him, turned to look at her. She had

snatched up the poker, and as I watched she pushed it into the fire.

"We're wasting time," she said, and again that awful little smile flickered at the corners of her mouth.

We stood there staring at the poker until it turned red-hot, then she pulled it out.

"Hold him," she said.

"Look, Veda…"

"Hold him!"

I grabbed Max, and he screamed. She came slowly toward him, her lips off her teeth.

His head was rigid with horror. Looking over his shoulder, I had a sudden cold, empty feeling inside me.

"I'll talk," he said suddenly, and his knees sagged so I was holding his weight. He nearly pulled me over. "Don't touch me. It's the fourth house on the Altadena road on the left as you go in. The house with the white gate. The note is under my pillow."

She dropped the poker and turned away. I saw a shudder run through her. I shoved him into a chair, snatched up the poker as it began to burn a hole in the wooden floor.

"I'll go now," I said.

"Yes."

"Watch him. Don't take any chances with him."

"He'll be here when you get back. Hurry, Floyd."

I touched her shoulder, but she shrank away.

"I'll·hurry, kid. Don't go near him. Just watch him."

I picked up his .45 and shoved it into my hip pocket, put the .25 on the mantel. As I reached the door, I glanced back. Max was huddled up in his chair, staring at Veda, who stared back at him.

Then I remembered something, came back, opened the store cupboard and took out two bottles of whisky.

Max gave a strangled sob, but I went quickly to the door without looking at him.

Outside it was starlight and cold. The moon was only just coming up above the foothills. I stood for a moment, rubbing my aching knuckles. I thought about the expression on Veda's face. I hadn't any doubt that she would have burned him as she said she would. The thought sent a chill up my spine. I shrugged it off, and went quickly around the shack to the Buick.

I got onto the Altadena road after twenty minutes of fast driving. The clock on the dashboard showed ten-twenty as I drew up outside a house with a white gate. It wasn't much of a place, but then I didn't expect a palace. The moonlight lit up the burned patch of garden, the rickety gate and the fence that looked like a giant saw with half its teeth missing. I was scared the gate would fall to pieces if I touched it, so I stepped over it, and walked up the hard mud that made a path to the door. There was a light showing through tattered blinds that covered the downstairs window. I climbed the three wooden steps, fumbled for the bell and rang it.

The smell of garbage and wet clothes drifted from the yard in the rear and made me wrinkle my nose. I thought of Veda alone up there in the hills, and the cringing horror that had been in Max's face. I thought of the Buick cluttering up the road outside this house. If a prowl car passed they'd know I was in there and they'd surround the place silently and then yell for me to come out. There was nothing I could do about that. It was one of those things.

Shuffling feet came down the passage, the door opened. I couldn't see anyone, but guessed by the smell of stale gin that she was there somewhere in the dark.

"Is Max in?"

"Who wants him?" The thick, clogged voice came from a throat like oil from a bottle.

"The name's Dexter. Are you Mrs. Otis?"

"That's right."

"Max told me about you. I understand he's looking for work. I have something in his line."

"Well, he ain't in."

I tried to see her, but it was too dark. It was an odd feeling to lie to this voice and not see who owned it.

"That's too bad. I came late hoping he'd been in. When will he be back?"

"I dunno. Maybe soon. I dunno."

"I'm paying good money. He said if ever I had anything to let him know. Can I wait? I won't be this way again."

"I'm going to bed." There was a surly note in the voice now. "I dunno when he'll be back."

"I have a couple of bottles of Scotch in the car. It wouldn't be hard to pass the time."

"You have?" The voice became alive. "Well, think of that! You come in. There's nothing to drink in this damned house. Max's always promising to bring in a bottle, but he never does. You come in, mister."

"I'll get the Scotch."

I went down the steps, climbed over the gate, collected the two bottles and came back. She had opened the living room door and light from an oil lamp filtered into the passage. I walked into a smell of dirt, stale food, cats and unwashed clothes.

Ma Otis stood behind the oil lamp and stared at me with bright black eyes. She was short and fat and dirty. She had the same hooked nose as Max had, but there the resemblance ended. There was nothing sad about her eyes, although they were moist. A straggle of gray hair fell over one eye and she kept blowing it away. She could have pinned it back without much effort, but I guess she preferred to blow at it.

"Let's sit down," I said. "This is an aristocratic liquor. It must be—it says so on the label."

She giggled at that and licked her lips. Max had called her a rum-dum, and a rum-dum she was. She fetched a couple of dirty glasses and poured herself a drink that would have floated the hat off my head if I had drunk it. She didn't bother to be polite or make conversation, and as soon as I was sure she had no other interest except to empty the two bottles, I kept feeding her the stuff and waited for her to pass out.

When she had reached the halfway line of the second bottle, I began to wonder if I'd brought enough supplies. There was only one small drink left in the second bottle when she suddenly lost interest in things. It was only because she stopped lifting her glass that I knew she'd gone over the edge. She sat there, staring at me with blank eyes and blowing at the strand of hair.

I got up and moved around the room, but she didn't attempt to follow me with her eyes. I guessed it was safe enough, and went into the passage and up the stairs. There were only three rooms upstairs. One of them belonged to Ma Otis. I could tell by the pile of empty bottles in a corner.

The next room I went into was neat and clean, and by the blue serge suit hanging on the back of the door and the rubber slicker on the bed, I guessed Max slept there. Under the pillow I found an envelope. I sat on the bed and read what he had written. In a way, it was a pathetic letter. He said if she found it he would be dead or in trouble, and he gave a detailed description where he would be found. He kept repeating about the reward and how she must collect it. He knew he had to deal with a mind ruined by gin, and he made it as simple and clear as he could. He covered six pages driving it into her head what she had to do, and not to let Kate (who was the sister, I guessed) get her hands on the money.

I burned the letter as soon as I had read it. Then I went downstairs. Ma Otis was still in the chair, her blank eyes gazing at the opposite wall. She kept blowing at the strand of hair, otherwise she might have been dead. A big black cat stalked around her, sniffing at her as if whisky was a new kind of smell. Maybe it had gotten used to the smell of gin. I didn't know. It looked at me with reproachful eyes, and I felt like a heel.

I collected the two empties, looked around to make sure I hadn't left anything and went to the front door.

I stood for a moment looking at the Buick, my hand on the .45. A girl was standing at the gate. We looked at each other. I guessed she was Kate. I went down, walking slow, keeping the empties out of sight behind my back.

"Did you want anything, please?" she asked as I reached the gate. She was thin and pale and shabbily dressed, and her hooked nose spoiled whatever beauty she might have had.

"Why, no, I guess not," I said. My voice sounded like a rusty gate squeaking in the wind.

"Have you seen Mother?" She flinched as she said it. "Is it about Max?"

"That's right. I had a job for him, but he's out. Tell him Frank Dexter called. He knows what it's all about."

The cat came down the path and began to rub itself against the girl's thin legs. It still looked reproachfully at me.

"He's been away two days," she said, and laced and unlaced her fingers. "I'm worried. I don't know where he is."

"Your mother said he'd be back tonight, but I haven't time to wait."

"She—she's not very well. I don't think she really knows. Max went off two days ago, and we haven't seen him since. I was wondering if I should go to the police."

I opened the car door, slipped the bottles onto the seat without her seeing them.

"You do what you think best. I wouldn't know. I just wanted to give him a job." I got into the car. I wanted to be as far away as I could by the time she went into that room and found what I had done to her mother.

"Perhaps I'd better wait another day. Max is so wild. He might be in trouble. I don't want the police…" Her voice trailed away helplessly.

"That's right," I said. "You wait. He mightn't want you to talk to the police." I trod on the starter and engaged gear. "Well, so long."

I watched her in the rearview mirror. She stood in the moonlight, looking after me. The cat continued to twine itself around her thin legs. I thought of Max up there in the shack with a bloody face and Veda guarding him. He was in trouble all right. Just as I turned the corner, I looked again into the mirror. She was walking up the path leading to the house. I suddenly felt a little sick.

CHAPTER FOURTEEN

BLACK AND RAGGED CLOUDS were drifting across the face of the moon as I garaged the Buick and walked over the rough, scorched grass to the shack. All the way up from Altadena I had thought about Max, wondering what we were going to do with him. I was still thinking as I reached the shack.

The obvious thing to do was to keep him with us until we were ready to quit—we weren't ready yet, but in another week it should be safe enough to make a move. But it wouldn't be easy to keep him a prisoner for a week. I should have to be with him the whole time, unless I kept him tied, and that wasn't as simple as it seemed. The safest thing as far as we were concerned would be to take him somewhere and put a bullet through his head, but I wasn't going to do that. I drew a line at murder. Even if no one ever found out, and the betting was that they wouldn't, I still had to live with myself, and although I hadn't been very fussy the way I had acted in the past, I was changing my ideas now. I was going to walk upstairs instead of down for a change, and see if I liked myself any better for doing it. I thought I should.

No light showed from the shack, but that was to be expected. I had spent some time nailing old sacks across the window. A chink of light up here could be seen for miles. I made no sound as I walked to the door, and for a moment or so I stood to listen. Then I tapped on the door.

"Veda?"

There was a little pause while I wondered if Max had got loose and had tricked Veda off her guard and was waiting for me on the other side of the door with the .25 ready to drill a hole in me. Then the door opened and Veda stood outlined against the lamplight.

"All right," I said and went in, shutting the door behind me.

Max was sitting just where I left him. The blood had dried on his face. He looked like an emergency case in a casualty ward, waiting for attention; only he wasn't going to get any attention from me.

"Did you get it?" Veda asked. Her voice was as metallic as a sheet of tinfoil.

"I burned it. Any trouble?"

"No."

I went over to Max and stared at him, balancing myself on the balls of my feet, my hat at the back of my head, my hands in my trouser pockets.

"You had a fist full of aces but you fluffed your hand," I told him. "And that still makes you a damned nuisance."

He peered at me through puffy eyes. Fear as ugly as violent death sat on his face. "You didn't hurt her?"

"No. What do you think I am? We had a few drinks together. That's how it was."

He caught his breath sharply. "I guessed that's how you'd do it. I'm glad you didn't hurt her. She ain't a bad old lady."

I made a grimace, thinking of the dirt and the smells and the pile of empty bottles. Still, she was his mother; that made a difference.

"You'd better wash yourself. Don't try anything smart. I don't want to kill you, but I will if I have to."

I helped him out of the chair, undid the belt around his wrists. Veda moved over to the mantel and picked up the .25. She wasn't taking any chances with him. While he rubbed his wrists and groaned to himself, she watched him narrowly.

After he had washed the blood off his face and attended to his cuts and bruises, he came back with me into the outer room and waited awkwardly.

"We'd better have some food," I said to Veda. "Then we'll turn in." To Max I said, "Sit down."

He sat down and watched Veda as she served up. He seemed more scared of her than of me.

"You'll have to stick around for a few days," I told him. "It won't be pleasant for you, but you brought it on yourself. You're in the way and you're eating our food, but I don't know what else to do with you."

"I could go home," he said uneasily. "I wouldn't say anything. I swear I wouldn't."

"Don't be funny. I'm not in the mood for corny jokes."

We had supper. He didn't seem to be hungry, but having Veda sitting opposite him, staring at him with frozen blue eyes, would take the edge off anyone's appetite.

It was getting on to midnight by the time we had cleared up and were ready for bed. I threw a heap of sacks in a corner.

"You can sleep there. I'll have to tie you. Don't start anything. If I hear you trying to get away, I'll shoot and apologize after. We're in too big a jam to take chances with a rat like you."

He was very docile, and stood silent and still while I strapped his wrists again. I led him over to the sacks and he squatted down. I locked the shack door and took the key. The only way he could get out would be to tear down the sacking across the window, and I was sure I'd hear him if he did that.

Veda and I went into the inner room. We left the door ajar. I was tired. It had been a nervy evening, and I kept thinking of Ma Otis, blowing at her strand of hair, her eyes getting glassy and the reek of whisky on her breath.

"How's your side?"

"All right. It's a little stiff, but it's nothing."

I sat on the edge of the bunk while she undressed. She had a beautiful little figure, and even with Max on my mind, I got a buzz from her.

"What happened at his place?" she asked as she slipped her nightdress over her head. As the flimsy garment fell about her body, a lot of glamour went out of the room.

"There was nothing to it. The old girl was a rummy. I fed her Scotch and she passed out. The note was under his pillow. It was loaded with dynamite. I burned it."

"Would she know you again?"

"I don't know. She was pretty far gone. Maybe not."

She slid into the lower bunk.

"What are we going to do with him?"

We spoke in whispers so he couldn't hear. The atmosphere in the shack had changed now. It was no longer like home. With him out there, it was just another hideout.

"Keep him here. What else can we do?"

"He knows you're growing a mustache."

She stared at me, her eyes frozen, the muscle in her cheek twitched.

"We'll have to watch him all the time. He's spoiled everything, hasn't he?"

"Yes."

I began to undress.

"Mick would kill him if this was happening to him. He doesn't deserve anything better, coming up here, trying to blackmail us. He would have skinned us if it hadn't been for you."

She looked away.

"No one would know."

"That's right."

There was a silence until I climbed up into the top bunk, then as I leaned out to snuff the candle, she said, "It would be the safest thing for us. He frightens me, Floyd."

"Yeah, but we must get the idea out of our heads."

"Yes."

I reached down and took her hand. It felt dry and cold in mine. "Don't think about it. There's nothing we can do. It won't be long now—a week at the most. Then we'll go."

"He'll tell the police. They think we're in Mexico. As soon as he tells them we were here, they'll start after us again."

She was right, of course.

"Maybe we'd better take him with us. We might get to Mexico. Then we could turn him loose."

"You don't mean that, do you? You wouldn't ever be able to prove you didn't kill Brett."

I thought about that. If the police knew we were still in the state, there'd be no hope of going after Gorman.

"That's right." I suddenly wanted to have her close to me. "Would you like to come up here with me?"

"Not now. My side aches a little. Tomorrow night, darling."

"All right."

I stared into the darkness, feeling alone. It was as if we'd been walking along a path together and suddenly come up against an impassable barrier. We could hear

Max twisting and turning in the other room, trying to make himself comfortable. Once he groaned. I felt no pity for him.

"I wouldn't want to live in Mexico all my life," Veda said suddenly.

"You wouldn't have to. A year would do it."

"A year's too long. You'd never be able to pick up the threads again. If you waited as long as that you'd have no hope of proving Gorman killed Brett."

"We're in a nice jam, aren't we? I didn't kill Brett, but they think I did. By killing Max I could prove I didn't kill Brett, but where does that get me? I'm trying to prove I'm not a murderer. The only way I can do it is to become one. A sweet jam. All right, suppose I kill him. You and I will know, even if no one else does. We have to live with each other, and knowing I killed him would make a difference. We might not think so at first, but it would."

"Yes—you mustn't kill him."

That brought us to where we had come in. A full circle, and no solution.

"Maybe we'll think of a way."

"He might get ill and die."

"That's a pipe dream. He looks good for another forty years."

"Yes. Maybe he'll have an accident."

"Not him. He's the careful type. No, I guess we can't think along those lines."

Max began to snore.

"He's not worrying. He knows he's safe enough." Her voice was bitter.

"Try to sleep. We could go on like this all night."

"Yes."

I lay in the darkness and racked my brains for a way out of the mess, but there wasn't one. If we let him go, he'd betray us for the reward. If we kept him here, we should have to watch him the whole time, and any moment he might surprise us. If we packed up and left him here, it would only be a day or so before the police would be after us. The problem went on and on in my brain—a treadmill of despair. I heard Veda crying softly to herself, and I hadn't the heart to comfort her. The darkness was thick and airless. Max's uneasy snores tormented me, and when I did fall asleep I dreamed that Veda turned against me and was in league with Max. Every time I looked at them they were smirking at me, and it was I who lay on the sacks in the outer room, and Max and Veda were together in the inner room. And I lay in the darkness and heard them whispering to each other, and I knew they were planning to kill me.

I woke suddenly, cold and uneasy, and stared into the darkness. My heart was beating rapidly, and because I couldn't hear Max snoring I was scared. I put my hand down to touch Veda, but my fingers moved into the little hollow where her head had rested and felt the warmth of an empty pillow. I remained still, feeling blood moving through my body in a cold surging wave.

"Veda?" I called softly and sat up. "Are you there?"

As I listened, I heard a movement in the other room. I slipped out of the bunk, groped frantically for the flashlight I kept under my pillow. I turned the beam on the lower bunk—it was empty. A board creaked outside as I jumped for my gun. The door leading to the outer room was shut. It had been ajar when we had gone to bed. I stood listening, the gun in my fist, the beam of the flashlight on the door. I saw the latch lift, and the door began to open. As I thumbed back the safety catch, the hair on the nape of my neck bristled.

Veda came in.

"What's the matter? What are you doing?" My voice croaked.

She didn't say anything, and came slowly toward me, her arms hanging limply at her sides. She seemed to float rather than walk, and in her flimsy white nightdress she looked like a ghost.

She moved into the beam of the light and I saw her eyes were closed. She was walking in her sleep. The serene death-in-life of her face, the mystery of the sleeping body, moving in unconscious obedience to her dreaming mind, made me start back. I could hear her gentle breathing. She looked very beautiful—more beautiful than I'd ever seen her look before. She passed me, slipped into the bunk and lay down. For some moments I stood looking at her, then I went over to her and covered her gently. My hands were shaking and my heart banged against my ribs.

"It's all right now, darling," she said in a drowsy murmur. "We don't have to worry anymore."

If I had been cold before, I turned like ice now, and as I went to the door my legs buckled. There was no sound coming from the outer room. I stood listening, afraid to go in, hearing the wind against the shack and stirring the trees outside. Then with an unsteady hand I threw the beam of the flashlight across the room onto Max.

He lay on his back in a puddle of blood that welled up from a red stain above his heart. In the middle of the stain something short and black was growing.

As if breasting a gale, I struggled over to him. She had driven a knife through his heart. He looked serene and happy. He had gone in his sleep, and I knew by the look on his face that death had been quick and easy for him.

I don't know how long I stood staring at him, but it was some time. This was murder! If they ever found him there'd be no chance for me unless I told them Veda had done it in her sleep, and who would believe me? She and I were alone with him. If I didn't kill him, then she did. It was the kind of setup Redfern would love. But she hadn't murdered him! Even now she didn't know he was dead. Maybe her hand had struck the blow, but that didn't mean she had murdered him. It came to me then that I couldn't tell her what she had done. I loved her too much to make her suffer as she would suffer if she knew. There was a chance I could get him away and bury him before she woke. I could tell her he escaped. I could tell her anything so long as it wasn't the truth.

I leaned forward and pulled out the knife. More blood welled out of the wound.

I crept into the inner room and got my clothes. She slept peaceably now, a smile on her lips. I took my clothes into the other room and gently closed the door. Scared to light the lamp, I dressed hurriedly by the light of the flashlight, then I poured myself a drink. Not once while I was dressing did I look at Max. The thought of touching him gave me the horrors.

The drink helped me and I went over to the stack of tools that stood in a corner. As I picked up a spade, the whole damned stack came crashing to the floor.

I heard Veda call out, "Who is it?" Then the door jerked open and she stood there, her face white and her eyes startled, staring at me. I felt sweat running down my face and there was a tightness inside my head that bothered me.

"It's all right. Stay where you are."

"Floyd! What is it? What are you doing?"

"Keep out of this!" I couldn't keep the fear out of my voice. "Go back to bed and stay there. Keep out of this!"

"Why, Floyd..." She was looking at the spade I held

in my hand and her eyes widened. Then she turned swiftly to look at Max, but it was too dark to see him.

"What are you doing?"

"Keep out of this, Veda! Leave me alone."

"What have you done?"

"All right." I threw down the spade. "What else could I have done? Keep out of it. That's all I ask you. Keep out of it and leave it to me."

She walked to the lamp and lit it. Her hands were steady, but her face was as white as a fresh fall of snow. In the hard glare of the acetylene lamp, the blood on Max's shirt glistened like red paint.

I heard her stifle a scream. She stared at him for a long moment of time, then she said quietly, "We said no. Why did you do it?"

"Could you figure out any other way?"

"If they ever find him…"

"I know. You don't have to tell me. Go back to bed. You must keep out of this."

"No. I'm helping you."

My nerves recoiled at the determination in her voice.

"Leave me alone!" I shouted at her. "It's bad enough to handle him without you being here. Leave me alone!"

She ran into the bedroom and shut the door. I was shaking like a muscle dancer. Even another shot of Scotch didn't help much. Without looking at Max, I went out into the darkness, clutching the spade.

It was beginning to rain. We hadn't had any rain for weeks, and it had to pick this night. I looked around in the darkness. No lights showed, no sound came to me, but the rising wind. It was lonely and wild—the right spot for murder.

I went to the shed, put the spade in the backseat of the Buick, drove around to the shack door. It wouldn't do to bury him anywhere near the shack. His last trip had to be a long one.

I went into the shack. She was dressed and bending over Max as I entered.

"What are you doing? What the hell are you doing?"

"It's all right, Floyd. Don't be angry."

I went closer.

She had wrapped him in a blanket and had tied the ends together. He looked harmless now: a bundle of clothing going to the cleaners. She had done what I had been dreading to do.

"Veda!"

"Oh, stop it!" she said fiercely and stood away from me. "I can manage now. You mustn't have anything to do with this. I want you to keep clear of it."

"I'm not staying here alone. And what does it matter? Do you think they'd believe I had nothing to do with it?"

We looked at each other. The frozen look in her eyes worried me.

"All right."

I took his shoulders and she took his feet. As we carried him out of the shack I thought of his pale, thin, shabbily dressed sister. *Max is so wild. He might be in trouble.* Well, he wouldn't get into any more trouble after this.

We drove across the foothills, through the rain and into the darkness. We had put him in the boot on the rubber mat, and I kept thinking of him and the way he looked when I had found him. Veda waited in the car while I dug. I worked in the light of one of the headlamps and I felt her eyes on me all the time. We buried him deep. When he went into the hole the blanket slipped and in the light of the headlights we both looked into his dead face. I let go of him and stepped back. He thumped down in the wet soil and was gone, but that dead face was with me then as it is with me now.

We spent a lot of time in the pouring rain, replacing the turf and stamping it down. If the rain kept up all night it would wash away the traces of the digging by the morning. I didn't think they would find him.

We were wet and cold and very tired when we drove back. Neither of us could think of anything to say, so the drive back was in silence. There was blood on the floor to clear up and we both worked at it. We scrubbed the rubber mat in the boot, we looked carefully around for anything that belonged to him, and I found his limp wallet that had fallen under the table. There were some papers in it, but I didn't feel like going through them just then and I put the wallet in my hip pocket. Finally we were through. Looking around the room, there was no trace of Max anymore, yet the room was full of him. I could see him standing in the doorway, sitting at the table, smirking at us, lying back in the chair with his face bruised and bleeding, lying on the floor with the serene look in his eyes and the knife in his chest.

"I wish you hadn't done it." The words came out of her as if she could no longer keep them in. "I won't say any more about it, but I'd give everything I've ever had if you hadn't done it."

I could have told her then. I wanted to, but I didn't. I had made such a damned mess of my life, one thing worse didn't matter—anyway, that's the way I saw it then. With her it was different. She was going up; a thing like this could ruin her.

"We won't talk about it. Let's have some coffee, and you'd better change."

While she was putting the kettle on, she said, "Will they come out here to look for him?"

"I don't think so. No one knows he's out here. They'll look for him along the coast if they look at all. They won't take much notice of his mother. He's not Lindsay Brett."

"Should we stay on here?"

"We have to."

She gave a little shiver. "I wish we could go. I keep feeling he's still here."

"I know. So do I. But we have to stay. There's nowhere else to go. We've been safe here up to now."

The dawn was coming up over the hills as we finished the coffee. I thought of the long day before us. Both with our secret thoughts. It came to me suddenly that it couldn't be the same again. She thought I had killed him; I knew she had. No, it wasn't going to be the same again. Women are funny animals. You never know with them. Love between a man and a woman is a brittle thing. If ever she fell out of love with me, my life would be in her hands. Looking at her now, I wasn't sure if she had already fallen out of love with me. It worried me. It was another step down. Another low spot. It was down now all the time.

During the next three days everything we had built up between us crumpled away. It started with small things. We suddenly found we hadn't much to say to each other; talking was an effort, but we made the effort, and living the way we did there was nothing to talk about at the best of times, except the things two people talk about when they are in love. Well, we didn't talk about those things— we talked about the rain, and whether we had enough food, and would I get some more logs and would she fix a hole in my sock. She didn't come into my bunk anymore; and I didn't want her to. We didn't say anything about it, but that's how it was. She'd be undressed and in her bunk by the time I had made up the fire in the outer room. I didn't have to torment myself by watching her take off her clothes, knowing the way she felt; there was no point in that. Once or twice I touched her and she suppressed a shiver, so I quit touching her. Max was with us twenty-four hours of the day. Neither of us could get him out of our minds. During those three days a tension began to grow that only needed a spark to touch it off. But there was no spark. We were both very careful about that.

At night when I had snuffed out the candle, I kept thinking of her as she had seemed to float into the room with her eyes closed, looking beautiful. And below me, as she lay in the darkness, I knew she was thinking about me; imagining me sneaking out there to knife the little punk who had his hands tied behind him. I guessed the image kept growing the more she thought about it until I must have seemed to her to be some kind of monster.

I was turning all this over in my mind and feeling pretty low as I made up the fire for the night. She had already gone into the inner room and I could hear her as she undressed. I locked the front door, turned out the light and gave her a few more minutes before going in there. She was already curled up in her bunk, her back turned to me as I came in. That's the way it was now: she couldn't bring herself to look at me.

"Good night," I said and rolled into my bunk.

"Good night."

Going down all the time, I thought. All low spots now. Veda slipping away from me like water through my fingers. Max's dead face. Gorman jeering at me. Material for nightmares.

I didn't know how long I slept but I woke suddenly. Since Max's death I had slept badly and the slightest sound would bring me upright in bed. I woke now to hear someone moving in the room. It was dark. I couldn't see anything. The stealthy sound sent my heart racing and a chill up my spine. I thought of Max as I slid out of the bunk and I began to shake. More movements, the sound of even breathing, close—too close. I pressed the button on the flashlight.

I don't know how I missed her in the darkness. She was standing right by me. Her eyes were closed and her black hair framed her face that was peaceful in sleep, and she looked lovely. I moved away from her, my heart racing. She had a knife in her hand; the knife I had used to make clothes-pegs for her when Max had surprised us. I watched her touch the blankets in my bunk. I saw her raise her hand and bury the knife to the hilt in the blankets and mattress where but a second or so before I had lain.

"You'll be all right now, darling," she said, and a little smile flickered at the corners of her mouth. "You won't have to worry anymore."

She climbed back into her bunk, drew up the blankets and settled down. Her breathing was as undisturbed and as even as a child's in its first sleep.

I left her there and went into the outer room. The fire was dying down and I put on another log, careful not to make a sound. Then I sat before the fire and tried to stop shivering.

I didn't sleep any more that night.

CHAPTER FIFTEEN

WHEN THE SUN CAME UP behind the hills, I went into the inner room to get my clothes. She had been up, for the blind was drawn and the window was wide open. I looked quickly to see if she was awake, and she was. She lay in the bunk, the blanket pushed back. They say love and hate are separated by the thickness of a hair. After what had happened last night, my love for her had been badly shaken. I was scared of her, and that's not far off hate. As I looked at her she turned her head. Her eyes were feverish.

"I didn't hear you get up," she said in a flat voice.

"I didn't make much noise. I couldn't sleep."

She watched me as I picked up my clothes. I knew it wasn't far off now. I could feel it. We were sparring for an opening.

"You stay where you are," I went on. "It's early yet. I'll make some coffee."

"Don't be long. It's time we had a talk, isn't it?" She sounded as polite as a collector of alms, and as sincere.

There it was. I didn't let her know I had come to the same conclusion.

"I'll be back."

While the water boiled, I dressed and took my time over a shave. My hand was unsteady; I was lucky not to cut myself. When I made the coffee, I poured two fingers of Scotch into a glass and drank it. I might have been drinking fruit salts.

She had combed her hair and put on a silk wrap and was curled up in the bunk by the time I returned. She didn't look well: too fine-drawn and her color was bad. There was a brooding expression in her eyes I didn't like.

"The rain's stopped," I told her. "It's going to be fine." A brilliant remark considering the sun was shining through the open window, but I had to say something.

She took the mug of coffee and was careful not to look at me.

"Please sit down."

It didn't seem possible that a couple of days ago we had been lovers. Voices are funny things; they can tell you more than an expression on a face if you listen. And I was listening very attentively. There was no point in kidding myself any longer. This was it.

I sat away from her. The gap between us was about as great as the gap between our minds.

"Do you remember what you said when we were talking about Max?" she asked abruptly.

"I said a lot of things."

"About making a difference."

I sipped my coffee and frowned at the floor. So that was how she was going to handle it.

"I guess so. I made quite a speech. I said, 'Suppose I kill him. You and I will know, even if no one else does. We have to live with each other, and knowing I killed him will make a difference. We might not think so at first, but it will.' That's what I said."

"So you've been thinking about it, too?"

"That's right."

"It has made a difference, hasn't it?"

"I said it would. All right—it has."

There was a pause. I could feel her uneasiness as I could feel the cold draught from the open window.

"I had a dream last night. I dreamed I killed you." No regret—just a statement of fact.

"Well, you didn't," I said, but I couldn't look at her.

There was another pause.

"It's time we left here," she went on. "There doesn't seem much point in us keeping together any longer—not now, I mean. It would be easier and safer for you to get away if you were alone."

Well, it was nice of her to think of my safety, but I hadn't expected this. If it was to happen I should be the one to break it up. I was getting tired of being brushed off by my women. It was getting to be too much of a habit.

"If that's how you feel." I finished my coffee and lit a cigarette. My hands were still unsteady.

"Don't let's pretend. It's the way we both feel. You don't seem to realize the sense you talked when you said it would make a difference."

"I have prizes for talking sense. One day someone's going to collect my bright remarks and put them in a book."

"I guess I'll get dressed."

That was her way of saying there wasn't anything more to discuss. There wasn't.

"Right," I said and went out of the room.

Standing before the fire, watching the flames without actually seeing them, I wondered what it would be like without her. This was a stage I usually reached with a woman, only I had thought it would be different with Veda. I didn't expect it would come to this. I knew it would happen sooner or later with the blonde who had given me money, and the redhead who had dug her nails into my shoulders and the rest of them, but somehow—not Veda. I knew I was going to miss her. She had a place in my life and there'd be a gap when she had gone.

After a while she came in, carrying her bags. She was wearing her canary-colored slacks and sweater in which I had first seen her. It seemed a long time ago. In spite of the drawn look and her color, she was still lovely to look at.

"Where are you going?" I asked. "There's no point in rushing into trouble. They're still looking for us."

"You don't have to worry about me."

"Yes, I do. I'm going after Gorman. Until I've proved he killed Brett, I'm still in a jam. If the police pick you up, you might talk. That's how it is."

"They won't pick me up. I wasn't born yesterday."

"I'm sorry. Until I've fixed Gorman you must be somewhere where they can't find you. You're going to Mick's place."

"No."

"That's where you're going, Veda."

"I said no."

We stared at each other. The spark we had guarded against so carefully was now in the powder.

"When I've fixed Gorman, you'll be as free as the air. That's the way it's going to be, Veda, and you'd better make up your mind to it."

"You want to murder me as well, don't you?" Her voice was shrill.

That was something I hadn't expected. She was full of surprises this morning.

"What are you talking about?"

"You want to murder me as you murdered Brett and Max."

"Don't start that again…."

The table was between us, otherwise I would have

beaten her to the jump, but she got the .25 first. It was still on the mantel, and I'd forgotten about it. She snatched it up, whirled around and pointed it at me as I threw the table out of my way. The look on her face brought me to an abrupt stop. I was looking at a stranger—fierce, hard and dangerous.

"That's how you planned it, isn't it?" she cried. "First Brett, then Max, now me! You fooled me all right. I believed all that stuff about Gorman killing Brett until you killed Max. You cold-blooded brute! No one but a killer could have done what you did. He was defenceless. His hands were tied and he was asleep. How could you?" her voice shot up. "How could I ever trust you again? I'm in your way now, aren't I? I know too much! Your precious friend Casy would keep me until you were ready to kill me. But not this time."

"You're crazy! I didn't kill Brett!"

"Go on—say it! Tell me you didn't kill Max, either." Her jeering little laugh set me raging. Then I let her have it.

"That's right—I didn't kill him. It was you! You—in your sleep. How do you like that? You—walking in your sleep—did it! I saw you!"

Contempt and loathing showed in her eyes. "And to think I loved you! Boyd said you were a cheap crook, and you are. You're worse than that—you're despicable."

"All right, I'm despicable." I was shouting at her now. "But that's how it happened! I wasn't going to tell you, but you've asked for it! You went out there—"

"Do you think I believe it?" she screamed at me. "Do you think anyone would believe it? Only a dirty warped mind like yours could have thought up such an idea. You don't frighten me! I'm through with you! Do you hear? I'm through with you!"

I stared at her, and suddenly my rage went from me. She was right. No one would believe a yarn like that. I shouldn't have told her. I should have tried to have held on to what little respect and feeling she had had for me. It was too late now.

"Okay, forget it. Forget everything. You'll need money. We'll split what I got from Boyd. If you think you can look after yourself, go ahead and look after yourself."

"I wouldn't touch a nickel of yours. I despise you. Sit over there. If you make one suspicious move you'll get it."

"All right, if that's how you feel. Do you think I give a damn?"

"Sit over there and keep quiet."

I sat over there and kept quiet. Nothing seemed to matter at the moment. If the cops had walked in I'd have welcomed them.

She picked up the two bags in one hand. The .25 still covered me.

"I'm taking the car as far as the dirt road. If you want it, you'll find it there."

"Take it to hell and go with it!" I said, and turned my back on her.

The door slammed. I just sat there, feeling like hell. After a few minutes I heard the car start up. I ran to the door and looked out. The Buick was bumping over the grass toward the distant cart track. I could see her at the wheel. Her head was held high and there was a defiant tilt to her chin.

"Veda!"

She didn't look back. I don't know if she heard me, but I didn't call again. The Buick gathered speed. I watched it for a long time until it was a tiny moving speck against the slope of the hills. When it disappeared I returned to the shack.

It was still early, not yet seven o'clock, and there was no heat in the sun. I felt cold. My first move was to the whisky bottle. As I picked it up I remembered it had been like this with every woman I'd known. As soon as they had walked out on me, I'd fly to the bottle. Well, it wasn't going to be like that this time. I was through with making a dope of myself over a woman. I balanced the bottle in my hand. The label called it an aristocratic liquor, and it was, but that didn't stop me. I threw the bottle across the room. It smashed against the wall and whisky sprayed over the floor and glass flew around like shrapnel.

I told myself I was going to cut Veda out of my life; and I meant it. I had a job to do. I was going after Gorman. I had money and a lot of rude health. I was tired of being chased by the cops. I was going after Gorman and I'd get him, providing the cops didn't get Veda first. If they caught her, she'd talk. She wouldn't bother to shield me now. I was sure of that. There was no time to waste.

I went into the inner room, packed my bag and had a last look around. There was plenty of evidence that we'd stayed here, but I had no time to cover our tracks. If anyone found the shack they'd know right off that it had been used as a hideout, and it wouldn't take long to guess who'd used it. Well, no one had found it up to now; maybe no one would find it when I'd gone.

There was nothing belonging to Veda, except the faint smell of her perfume. I was sentimental enough to look carefully in the hope of finding a memento, but I didn't.

She had said she'd leave the Buick near the dirt road. The sooner I got down there the better. I'd have to risk driving the car to Mick's place. There was nothing else for it. With a little luck, and knowing how dumb the Santa Medina cops were, I'd get through without being spotted.

And that's how it worked out. I found the car a quarter of a mile from the dirt road, out of sight behind some trees. As I got in, I smelled her perfume. It gave me an odd, lonely feeling, but I nudged it out of my mind. She had left the ignition key in the glove compartment. I always thought she had a tidy mind. Driving along the Altadena road I caught myself staring at every woman I passed; none of them was Veda.

At Altadena I went into a drugstore and put through a call to Mick. No one looked at me. No one started running. When Mick came on the line he sounded as if he'd just woken up. I told him I was coming in, that I didn't think anyone would recognize me, and I was calling myself Frank Dexter.

"Can you get Lu to meet me with a car at the second crossroads? It'll be safer if he handled the Buick."

Mick said he'd fix it.

"I'll be waiting for you. Got the frail with you?"

"I'm on my own."

He grunted and hung up. He was never a guy to ask questions—action first and talk after. It was a good policy.

Lu was sitting in the Cadillac when I arrived at the crossroads. He waved and smiled and seemed glad to see me.

"Still tired of life?" he asked as he got into the Buick. "I thought you were in sunny Mexico by now. Where's the blue-eyed babe? Don't tell me you ditched her?"

"We parted," I said shortly. "You'd better get going. This car's hot."

I drove the Cadillac into Santa Medina and the first person I saw was O'Readen. He was climbing the steps to police headquarters. He looked old and stooped and wasn't smiling. He didn't see me. It was odd running into him like that, but I didn't bat an eyelid. I had taken a good look at myself in the mirror before leaving the shack. If I couldn't recognize myself, how could he?

"I'm looking for Casy," I said to the guard on the door when I arrived at Mick's place. "The name's Dexter."

"Go right in. He's waiting for you."

Mick wasn't taking any chances. The guard was new. I hadn't seen him before, and he took no interest in me.

It was too early for anyone to be around. A couple of cleaners were in the bar, but after a casual glance at me, they went on with their work. I pushed open Mick's door, glanced in. Mick was pacing up and down, his hands in his pockets, a dead cigar clamped between his teeth. He looked up, scowled at me.

"Beat it. Who told you to come in?"

"You did," I said, and closed the door behind me.

He came over and grabbed my hand.

"That damned mustache! You look like a Spaniard. Dammit, I'm glad to see you. Sit down. What the hell are you doing here? Why aren't you in Mexico?"

"I'm back to find Brett's killer. I think I know who he is. Look, Mick, I was crazy to run away. My place is here. I'm going to find Brett's killer and I'm going to collect the reward."

"You're crazy! Redfern's still looking for you. O'Readen has given up, but not Redfern. San Luis Beach is as hot as a stove. If you stick your nose in there you'll get burned."

"Give me a hand with this, Mick, and we'll split the reward. It's worth thirty grand. What do you say?"

"I'll help you for nothing. I have all the money I can use."

"No one has. You'll do it for fifteen grand or I'll count you out."

"We haven't got it yet. What do you want me to do?"

"I figure it's Gorman. He knew I was going out to Brett's place. I want to find out where he was when Brett was shot. If he hasn't a cast-iron alibi—and he won't have—I'll call on him and beat the truth out of him."

"Watch out. From what I hear that boy's tough."

"I'll take care of him."

"Well, all right." He paced up and down. "I'll turn Lu on to it. Okay?"

"Fine."

He telephoned for Lu, but he hadn't come in.

"He's ditching the car," I said.

"Tell him I want him as soon as he shows up," Mick said into the receiver and hung up.

"They didn't trace the gun that shot Brett, did they?"

"Yes…it was his."

"Brett's?"

"That's right."

I slid farther down in the chair. "Brett's? That's odd."

"Why odd?"

"Odd Brett's killer got hold of it. Almost looks as if Brett knew him. I wonder if Brett knew Gorman? You get what I'm driving at, don't you? If the gun was Brett's you can bet he was carrying it in case I started any tricks. He was expecting me, and he was taking care I didn't double-cross him. Maybe he had the gun lying on the desk where he could reach it if he wanted it. His killer must have known him to have got close enough to grab the gun. See what I mean?"

"Yeah."

"I'll have to find out if Gorman knew Brett. Gorman fixed up for Veda to do her act at Brett's house, but I doubt if he fixed it with Brett personally. He'd work through Brett's secretary." Then I remembered the fair girl who had burst into the room as I was making my getaway.

"Did they ever say who the girl was? The one who found Brett, and saw me? She was a blonde—a looker."

"Sheila—Sheila—I forget. She was to be the future Mrs. Brett."

"Was she? Can't you remember her name?"

"I've kept the cuttings. I'll turn it up."

While he was pawing through a mass of cuttings, I thought about the gun. I couldn't imagine Brett letting Gorman get close enough to grab it. This was a disturbing thought. Of course Brett might have been off his guard, but it didn't seem likely—not a smartie like Brett. The time factor was important, too. I reckoned it took about ten to fifteen minutes, no more, for the guard to escort me to the steps, for me to fool around looking for the compact, to the moment I'd heard the shot. In that time the murderer had to lull Brett's suspicions to let him grab the gun, shoot him, take the money and beat it. Fast work—unless… Suppose, I said to myself, Gorman didn't kill him. Suppose the future Mrs. Brett had done it. She could have gone into Brett's room and picked up the gun without giving him the jitters. But why would she? Unless they'd fallen out and she knew I was on my way and this was as good a way of picking up twenty-five grand as another?

"Sheila Kendrick," Mick said, and tossed the cutting over to me. "That's the name."

There was a photograph of her: she looked cute in a Jantzen swimsuit; not that she wouldn't have looked cuter without it. There wasn't much about her. She came from San Francisco, would have been the future Mrs. Brett had Brett lived, had been a dancer in the successful musical *I Spy Strangers* and had won a couple of beauty prizes.

I threw the cutting on the desk as Lu came in.

Mick told him what was wanted.

"Get after him, and if he has an alibi, check it, and when I say check it, I mean check it. There's five hundred bucks in this for you if you make a job of it."

Lu fluttered his eyelashes.

"And find out if he knew Brett personally. That's important," I said.

"Don't worry, dear," Lu said, and sniffed at his cornflower. "I can use five hundred. I'll make a job of this."

"He kills me," I said when he had gone.

"He kills most people, but he's smart."

"Well, there's nothing I can do now until he comes back. I don't want to get in your way, Mick. Shall I wait in your hideout?"

"No, stick around. No one comes here unless I say so. Make yourself at home. You're not in the way." He offered me a cigar, but I wasn't feeling festive enough. "What happened to the frail?" He had been wanting to ask that question ever since I had arrived. Now his curiosity got the better of him.

"We parted."

"You did? Well, that surprises me. I thought you and she—" He broke off and grinned. "But I guess I'm talking too much."

"That's all right. You know it is. We had a week together, but it didn't work out." I wasn't telling anyone about Max, not even Mick.

"You never know with women." He shook his head. "And she was a swell looker, too. Shows you, doesn't it? You can't tell by looks. I knew a twist once who was magazine cover stuff, but she was no good—colder than an iceberg. Then there was a dame who had a face like a hangover, and a figure like two planks nailed together." He rolled his eyes. "But was she hot!"

I groped in my hip pocket for my cigarette case and found Max's wallet instead. I'd forgotten about it, and while I listened to Mick talking about the women he'd known—always a favorite subject of his—I thumbed through the contents of the wallet. There was a five-dollar bill, a couple of bus tickets, a letter from his mother and three obscene photographs. I tossed the pictures over to Mick. On the back of the letter was a penciled scrawl that brought me to my feet.

I remembered the untidy handwriting of the letter Max had left under his pillow. This note was in the same fist.

It read:

For Alma from Verne: "A man's best friend is his wife."

I felt in my vest pocket and took out the card Brett had given me. The same words. I stood thinking. Two guys write the same dozen words and get themselves knocked off. Did it mean anything? Was I missing anything?

I felt Mick's eyes on my face.

"What's biting you?"

"I don't know…nothing, maybe."

I folded the letter and put it and the card in my pocket.

"Getting kind of cagey, aren't you?"

I grinned at him. "I guess so. Once a dick, always a dick. I'm sorry, Mick. I don't think it's anything."

He shrugged. "Play it the way you like. I'm here if you want me."

Lu got back late in the afternoon. I was jittery by that time, and when he came in I grabbed him.

"Well? How did you get on?"

He shook his head.

"He's in the clear. He didn't shoot Brett. He was at the

Casino all evening. There're a hundred witnesses who saw him. He didn't leave until two o'clock."

"Any chance that he sneaked out and came back again?"

"Not a chance. He was playing roulette and never left the table. I've checked until I'm dizzy. He didn't shoot Brett, and he didn't know Brett, either. He's never even spoken to him."

Well, that seemed to be that.

CHAPTER SIXTEEN

THE HOT EVENING SUNSHINE came through the slats in the venetian blinds and made a pattern on the carpet. The pattern, from where I was sitting, looked like the bars of a prison cell, and added an incentive to my thoughts. I was alone in Mick's office, and had been alone for the past hour. The office door was locked, and I had no fear of interruptions. I sat in the desk chair; a cigarette burned forgotten in my fingers, a glass of whisky stood neglected on the desk while I exercised my brain until it creaked.

Gorman hadn't shot Brett. Well, someone had, and it was up to me if I was to save my neck to find out who that someone was. I had already sent Lu out to check Boyd's alibi, but that was routine. I didn't believe Boyd was the killer. He had no motive. Whoever had killed Brett had wanted money. Well, if it wasn't Boyd, who else was there to suspect? Sheila Kendrick, the future Mrs. Brett? A possibility. One of Brett's servants? One of the guards? Or Mr. or Miss X, the unknown? I didn't know.

Already I had decided the quickest way to arrive at a solution was to begin at the beginning; to ignore anything that was a guess and to concentrate only on facts. If I didn't hurry and find the killer, the police would find me, and then that would be that.

What facts had I? Not many: Brett knew the killer, otherwise the killer wouldn't have got near Brett's gun. The motive for the killing was the twenty-five grand. Then there was the mysterious twelve words that had interested Max as well as Brett: *For Alma from Verne: "A man's best friend is his wife."* What did that mean? Did it play a part in Brett's death? Why had Max also scribbled the words down? Who were Verne and Alma?

Fingernails tapped on the door. Mick's voice called softly. I pushed back my chair, opened the door, let him in and locked the door again.

"How's it going?"

"It's not," I said. "My brain feels as if it's walked miles."

"What are you working on?"

"I'm waiting for Lu. He's digging into Boyd's alibi. It's a waste of time, but I'm checking everything. You never know. Here, take a look at this." I tossed over Brett's card. "Make anything of it?"

He frowned at the words, then shook his head.

"Means nothing to me. Some code, do you think? I wouldn't say a man's best friend's his wife, would you? I thought a man's best friend was his dog."

"Don't be such a damned cynic. It's the kind of sentiment a guy would have engraved on a wedding ring, isn't it?"

"I wouldn't."

"I'm not talking about you. I'm talking about a guy who is in love with his wife. That's something you wouldn't understand."

"I guess not." He ran stubby fingers through his hair, frowned again at the words. "How does this figure in the setup?"

"Brett gave me his card. He wanted me to telephone him. I found that on the back, and it's got me puzzled."

Mick shrugged. "What the hell? Why should it have anything to do with his death?"

"I have a hunch that it has. It must mean something, and I can't afford to pass anything up. If I could find out who Verne and Alma are it might help. But how do I do that?"

Mick thought, shook his head.

"Well, there are the Baillies of course, but it wouldn't be them. A guy like Brett wouldn't know the Baillies."

"You mean Verne Baillie, the bank bandit?"

"That's who I mean, but it's a shot in the dark. It couldn't be him."

"No." I reached for a cigarette, paused and frowned, then lit up. "He had a wife, Alma, didn't he?"

"That's right. That's why I thought of them."

"It couldn't be them. Brett wouldn't mix with bank bandits. That doesn't make sense. Besides, they're dead, aren't they?"

"Yeah. Verne was killed by the Feds a couple of years ago. Alma was killed in a car crash a year later."

I calmed down. "You know, for a moment I thought we had something. It's a coincidence though, isn't it? You're sure they're both dead?"

"I guess so. Anyway, Lu will tell you more about them. He was friendly with Verne."

"I don't think it matters. As you say, it can't be them. I wish I could question the future Mrs. Brett. She might tell me a lot if I could get at her."

"You can't do that. I'd forget it if I were you. It only complicates things. It's nothing to do with the killing, you can bet on that."

But then he didn't know Max had also been interested in those old words. But I wasn't going to talk to anyone about Max.

A tap sounded on the door. It was Lu.

"Any luck?"

He shook his head. "It wasn't Boyd. He was at his house all evening. Anything else I can do for you?"

"Well, it isn't Gorman and it isn't Boyd. Who else have we left? There's Sheila Kendrick. She was right on the spot. But we can't check what she was doing at the time Brett was shot unless we tip our hand, and we can't afford to do that. It could have been anyone. I mean someone we've never heard of. It's hell, isn't it?"

Lu smiled sympathetically.

"I know just how you feel. It keeps coming back to you, doesn't it?"

"Yeah." I got up and began to pace up and down. "You knew the Baillies, didn't you?"

"I knew Verne Baillie. Why bring him up?" He seemed startled.

"How well did you know him?"

"Pretty well. We kicked around together three or four years ago. When he married I didn't see much of him. But what's he got to do with this?"

"I don't know." I threw him Brett's card. "Make anything of that?"

Lu gaped at it.

"That's Verne all right. He was always saying Alma was his best friend. They were crazy about each other."

I began to get excited again.

"Are you sure, Lu? This is important."

"Of course I am. I know Verne used those words hundreds of times. All his pals were sick of hearing them. I was, too."

"Could he have known Brett?"

"Verne? Not a chance. Be your age. Verne wouldn't mix with millionaires."

"And yet Brett wrote those words on his card."

"Looks as if you have something there," Mick said. "But I don't know what you're going to do with it now you have it."

"Verne never knew Brett," Lu said with conviction. "He was never closer to the Pacific Coast than Kansas, and that's a long way from Brett's territory. I don't know what this means, but I do know Brett and Verne never hooked up."

"What happened to him, Lu?"

"He was shot. It was after the Tulsa bank robbery. Maybe you remember it. Verne got away with a hundred grand. It was a sweet job. He and Alma pulled it, but things went wrong. I think she lost her head. Verne had a machine gun with him. He knocked off a couple of tellers, wounded another, killed two bank guards and wounded a cop."

"Yeah, I remember now. It caused a hell of a sensation. That must be two years ago."

"It was. The Feds cracked down on Verne and they hunted him night and day. They finally traced him to a house in Dallas, surrounded the place and fought it out with him. When they got into the house they found he had twenty slugs in his body, and still he wasn't dead. He died on the way to hospital. Alma got away."

"What happened to her?"

"She had been out shopping when they trapped Verne. They found the hundred grand in suitcases in the house, so they knew she hadn't much money. They went after her, but she slipped through their net somehow. A year later they got a tip she'd been seen in Elk City, but she had gone by the time they got there. A couple of days after, the sheriff of Gallup spotted her and gave the alarm. She'd been hiding in

Albuquerque and was once more on the move, so they thought. They found her body a few miles from Gallup in a smashed car. She had hit a tree. The car had caught fire, and she was pretty well smashed and burned. But it was Alma all right. That happened about twelve months ago."

I did a little thinking, then shook my head. "It doesn't get me anywhere." After pacing the floor for a while and thinking some more, I asked, "There was no doubt the girl was Alma?"

"It might not have been," Lu said with a grin, "but the Feds said it was, and they don't make mistakes. It was her car. One of her bags had been thrown clear. It was full of her stuff. They couldn't identify the body. They had no record of her fingerprints, and the body was badly burned. If it wasn't her, who else could it have been?"

"No one missing at the time?"

"They didn't say so."

"No, I guess I'm trying to make too much of this. Do we know anything about Sheila Kendrick?"

"I don't."

"We'd better check up on her. Get after her, Lu. I want to know where she came from, what she's been doing for the past few years. She comes from San Francisco. You'll have to go out there and dig. It's important."

Lu looked enquiringly at Mick. "Do I do it?"

"Sure you do it."

"All right, but you're barking up the wrong tree."

"Maybe you're right, but it's the only lead I have. I'm going to do a little digging myself. I have to start from the beginning. Maybe I'll turn up something if I go back far enough. I'm going to work on the Baillies."

"I can't see how they figure in this," Mick said, shaking his head, "but you work it the way you think."

"Wait a second, Lu," I said, as he moved to the door. "Did you ever see Alma?"

"Once, but not to talk to. She was waiting in a car for Verne."

"Remember her?"

"Not really. She was fair, but that's all I can remember. I didn't get a good look at her."

"Okay, Lu." When he had gone I said to Mick, "Well, I'll move off first thing tomorrow morning. Take care of that twenty-five grand for me. If I come unstuck, you keep it."

Early the next morning I drove out of Santa Medina and headed for Albuquerque. On the way I stopped at Gallup and called in on the sheriff's office. He was an elderly, well-nourished party with a lot of spare time on his hands. He welcomed me when I explained I was a writer and wanted information about the Baillies.

"Not much I can tell you," he said, hoisting his feet onto the desk. "Sit down and make yourself at home. I ain't got any liquor to offer you, but maybe you can get along without it."

I said I thought I could, and started in to see what I could get out of him. He remembered the car smash all right. It had been the talk of Gallup for weeks.

"It happened like this," he told me, sucking at his pipe. "I was standing in the doorway, sunning myself, when she drove in. The description the Feds had put out wasn't much. I knew they were looking for a fair girl in a dark brown leather coat and driving a green coupe Chrysler. Well, the car this girl was driving was a green coupe Chrysler, but the licence plates didn't tally with the ones in the Feds' handbill, and she wasn't wearing a leather coat. I was interested, mind you, and I watched her, but I didn't think it was the girl. She bought groceries, and I kept wondering if she was Alma." He grinned boyishly at me. "If she was Alma, then she was dangerous and I'm too old to fool around with guns. I let her go. But I called up the local office and reported having seen her. Well, they found her a mile or so out of town, smashed up against a tree. That's all there's to it."

A nice efficient sheriff, I thought. The Feds must have loved him.

"They were sure the girl in the car was Alma Baillie?"

His mouth fell open. "Why, sure. There was a reward out for her, see? By rights I should have got it, but the federal officer claimed it. He was pretty decent about it and gave me a share. He didn't make a mistake. He had all the proof he wanted. The leather coat was found. It was burned, but it was easy to identify. And there was plenty of stuff in her bag to convince me it was Alma."

"How about fingerprints?"

"What are you getting at, young man? They didn't have her prints recorded. You want to take it easy. If you go through life being suspicious of people you'll be an old man before you know it."

I thanked him, gave him a cigar and went out into the sunshine again, far from satisfied. From Gallup I drove to Albuquerque and called in on the news editor of the local newspaper. I spun him the same yarn, and asked if he had any information regarding Alma Baillie that might be helpful.

The news editor was a smart little guy, with keen gray eyes that looked at me through a pair of heavy shell spectacles.

"Just what did you want to know, Mr. Dexter?"

"I'd like to see the house she stayed at, and I'd like to know if you believe she met her end in the car, or whether it was some other girl."

He blinked at that.

"Funny you should say that. At the time I had my doubts, but nothing came of it. The federal officer identified her. It was a lucky break for him. He earned the two-thousand-dollar reward."

"What happened to him?"

"He retired. He's chicken farming now."

"What made you have doubts it wasn't Alma?"

He grinned at me. "Well, you know how it is. We're suspicious people, Mr. Dexter. Someone in Gallup said there were two girls in the car, but the sheriff said he was a liar and maybe he was."

"Who was he?"

"I forget his name. He's left the district now."

"Know where he's gone?"

"Amarillo, but he's an unreliable witness. Half the time he's drunk and the other half he's trying to scrape up enough money to buy liquor. We decided he was talking out of the back of his neck."

"I'd take it as a favor if you could hunt up his name and address."

It took a little time, but he got it for me in the end.

"Jack Nesby," he told me after a clerk had dug through the records, and he gave me the address.

I went around to the house where Alma Baillie had lived, but the landlady wasn't helpful or couldn't tell me anything. I wasn't sure which, but I didn't get any information from her. From Albuquerque I went to Amarillo where I found Nesby propping up the bar in a beer saloon. He was old, and dim-witted and a little drunk, but he brightened up when I bought him a large whisky.

Yes, he remembered seeing Alma come into Gallup. He poked a grimy finger at me and wagged his head as he peered at me with dim eyes.

"It was a frame-up," he told me hoarsely. "That Fed

was after the reward. There were two girls in the car. I saw 'em as plain as I see you. There was the smart one and the shabby one. The sheriff saw 'em, too, but he kept his mouth shut because the Fed paid him off. When I spoke up they threatened to run me in for vagrancy."

I looked at him doubtfully. The news editor had been right when he said this guy as an unreliable witness. In a court of law he'd be hopeless, but this wasn't a court of law.

"What was she like...the shabby one?"

He brooded, struggled with a dying memory and gave up.

"I dunno," he admitted. "I didn't pay much attention. I've got beyond girls, mister. But there were two of them, and I'll swear it."

"Was she fair, too?"

"I don't reckon she was. I think she was dark, but I wouldn't know."

"What makes you say she was shabby?"

"By her clothes." He looked a little surprised at the question. "She had on a dirty old raincoat and no hat. The other was smart, real smart. You know how it is."

There was nothing else I could get out of him, so I bought him another Scotch and left him. I got in the car and sat for a while thinking. I took my time and I went over everything I'd seen and heard since I first met Gorman. It took more than an hour, and from time to time I jotted down on the back of an envelope an idea that came to me. I was still in the dark, but there was a glimmer of light ahead and I knew if I kept plugging away I'd get somewhere. I remembered what Veda had said about her past life. This road on which my car was parked was the road on which she had traveled from Waukomis to Hollywood: State Highway 66. Somewhere between here and Waukomis I should find the restaurant where she had worked. I decided I'd look that over just in case I might pick up something.

It took a little time, and I was two days on that road, asking questions, stopping at every road restaurant, pull-up and café, and finally I came to the place at Clinton. I knew it was the place because at the back was a big barn.

I parked the car outside, pushed open the screen door and marched in. It wasn't much of a place; a lunchroom with an S-shaped counter, stools and a few tables for those who wanted to eat in style. There were the usual jukebox coin slots and a display of sandwiches under glass.

A thin, surly-looking man in a soiled apron leaned against the counter and stared into space. He didn't bother to look in my direction as I came in and said, "What's yours?" as if he didn't care.

I ordered a coffee and a slice of apple pie. When he dumped the coffee before me and began sawing at the pie, I said, "Didn't a girl named Veda Rux once work here?"

"What of it?" He slapped down the pie and stared at me with hard eyes.

"I'm trying to trace her. She's come into a small slice of money. There's a ten-dollar reward for information."

"Is she in trouble?"

"No. Someone's left her two hundred bucks. I'm trying to find her." I took out two fives and let him have a good look at them.

"Well, she worked here," he said, thawing out. "I dunno where she is now. She was going to Hollywood, but I don't know if she ever got as far."

"You wouldn't have a photograph of her?"

"No."

"A good looker, wasn't she?"

He nodded. "A bitch. Never could leave the truckers

alone. Always taking them in the barn at the back when I wasn't looking." He scowled as his mind went into the past. "A no-good tramp."

"Dark, nice figure, blue eyes?" I said. "That her?"

"Not blue eyes...I'd say brown."

"Is that right? Left-handed, wasn't she?"

He nodded.

"When did she leave here?"

"About a year ago."

"Can you get closer? I want the date." I took out another five and added it to the notes already on the counter.

He stared at the money, thought for a moment, shook his head.

"Can't remember. But hang on. I'll find out. I keep a diary."

I had finished the pie and the coffee by the time he returned.

"July fifth of last year."

That was three days before Alma's car crash. I gave him the money, thanked him and went out. More light ahead, I thought, and after checking my map I drove out of town.

My next stop was Waukomis, Oklahoma. I arrived at dusk. It was a typical Midwestern farming town and I blew into the first beer saloon I came to.

"I'm looking for the Rux family," I told the barkeeper. "Any of them in town?"

He wrinkled his fat nose. He didn't seem to think much of the Rux family.

"There's a married sister who lives up on the hill. Martin's the name. The rest of them pulled out when the old man croaked, and a good thing, too. A damned wild family—always getting into trouble."

I grinned.

"Yeah, they were that. I'm trying to trace Veda Rux. Remember her?"

"What are you—a dick?"

"No. She's come into a little dough. I want to pay out. Remember her?"

"I remember her all right. She was the wildest of them all. Never could leave the men alone." He shook his head. "So she's come into money?"

"Where's this sister of hers live?"

He gave me directions and I drove up the hill to where a cluster of wooden shacks huddled together against the skyline.

Mrs. Martin looked no more like Veda than I did. She was big and fat and blowsy, but she was friendly as soon as I told her why I was looking for Veda.

"I ain't seen her in years," she said, wiping her red hands on a dirty towel. "Fancy! Who left her the money?"

"A fella she knew. I can't trace her. You wouldn't have a photograph of her?"

"Only when she was little."

She produced that and I stared for a long time at the thin, vicious little face.

"Anything on her that'd help to identify her?"

"She had a birthmark." She simpered. "But it's where it shouldn't show."

"What kind of birthmark?"

"A round red mark, the size of a dime." She told me where it was located. She was right about it not being on show.

"And she was left-handed, wasn't she?"

"Yes."

"And blue eyes?"

"Oh, no—brown."

I thanked her. That seemed to be that.

I wasn't wasting any more time. I had all the information I wanted. I had to find Veda.

I began the long drive back to the coast.

CHAPTER SEVENTEEN

I HAD A HUNCH THAT IF Veda learned I was looking for her, she'd look for me; and that's how it worked out.

Mick helped by passing the word around to the boys that we wanted Veda, and whoever found her would earn himself some folding money. We gave the boys her description; it was as complete as we could make it, down to the birthmark, and I knew, sooner or later, the news would reach her that I was after her.

It wasn't going to be easy to find her, but I was willing to bet she wasn't far away. My only hope was for her to come looking for me—it was a gamble and it came off. As soon as the hunt for her began I gave her every chance to find me. I drove around Santa Medina and the outskirts of San Luis Beach. I sat around in beer saloons and cafés and coffee shops. I took long walks. I was seldom off the street. It was hard work, but I kept at it.

After three or four days of this she walked into the trap. I was sauntering along Main Street when I became aware I was being tailed. I have had a lot of experience tailing people and shaking off guys who've tried to tail me. A dick working for a bonding agency has to be smart, and I've developed an instinct for knowing when someone's following me. It didn't take me long to spot her. She was a redhead now, but I'd have known her walk anywhere in spite of the sunglasses and the auburn hair. And I'd know that figure, too. I'd know it blindfolded.

She hadn't an idea how to tail anyone. For one thing she was dressed all wrong. You don't tail an ex-dick in a bright red shirt and a pair of sand-colored slacks unless you want him to know you're tailing him. Neither do you skip behind trees or into shop doorways or behind hedges the way she was doing it.

I waited long enough to be sure it was her, then I shook her off, made a quick circle around her and got on her tail. She didn't know it, and she didn't shake me off. I stuck to her like a burr and she never saw me.

She was bewildered and rattled by the way I had suddenly vanished, and for some time she kept prowling the streets trying to find me. I moved along in the rear, and she never thought to look behind her, so anxious was she to pick up my trail. After some time of this she stood on the edge of the curb and tried to make up her mind what to do. I stood about ten feet from her, reading a newspaper and holding it so it shielded my face.

She didn't expect me to be so close and therefore she didn't see me. Finally she gave an angry little shrug and set off toward the car park. I had my car handy and was ready for her when she drove out of Santa Medina in a brand-new Mercury.

I guessed after a while that she was heading for San Bernadino. There was no other town on this road, and San Bernadino was the first stop. I accelerated and got in front of her, and after a while I increased speed and soon lost her in a cloud of dust. By the time she arrived in San Bernadino, I had garaged my car and hired a two-seater coupe. It was the easiest thing in the world to drive straight after her and she didn't know me from Adam.

I wanted to know where she lived, and she took me

right to the door. It was like taking dimes from a blind man's cup. The house was up on a hill in a well-screened garden. I saw her stop the Mercury in front of the entrance and go inside. That was good enough for me.

I made enquiries in the town about her and learned she had rented the house furnished, then I drove back to Santa Medina, satisfied that the end was in sight.

I spent a little while with Mick explaining what I wanted him to do. At first, he was inclined to argue, but I persuaded him to see it my way, and in the end he agreed to play.

Early next morning I went out to San Bernadino, left the car at the garage and walked up to Veda's place. There was plenty of cover and I settled down behind a hedge in her garden and waited for her to show herself.

I had a long wait, but around noon she came out. For a moment or so she stood on the front step and looked around the garden. She looked right at me, but that didn't worry me. I was too well-hidden, and she would have needed X-ray eyes to have seen me. She was about fifty yards from me and I thought she looked ill. The red-dyed hair didn't suit her, her skin was pallid, and there were dark smudges under her eyes. She was dressed in a yellow-and-black flowered frock that showed off her superb little figure, and in her hand she carried a big sun hat. All new stuff. She was spending money all right.

I watched her drive away toward Santa Medina, and I guessed she was going to look for me again. I let her go. I was up there to look the house over. There'd be time to talk to her when I'd found what I was expecting to find.

When I was sure she was well out of the way, I walked up to the front door and rang the bell. No one answered. I took a quick look around before working on the lock. High flowering hedges screened the door from the road.

No one was likely to see me. After a minute or so I turned the lock and pushed open the front door.

The only thing that came to meet me as I walked in was the faint smell of her perfume. But I was cautious, and went from room to room with my gun in my fist. She had no one to look after her. The house was impersonal, clean and unfriendly. I felt sorry for her living like this. It couldn't have been much fun. Even the shack, primitive as it had been, was more homely than this place.

As soon as I satisfied myself that there was no one lurking in a cupboard or behind the curtains, I went to her bedroom. I thought it likely she wouldn't be back before nightfall, but I couldn't count on that. I had to work fast.

The wardrobe in the bedroom was locked, but I opened it without difficulty. On the floor of the wardrobe was her suitcase. This was also locked, and the lock resisted all my efforts to open it. Finally I cut the lock off by sawing through the leather.

There were only two things in the bag that interested me: a big wad of five- and twenty-dollar bills and a gold compact. I flicked through the notes. There must have been about twenty grand in that bundle—part of the money Brett had promised me for the dagger. I wasn't surprised. By now I had guessed who had killed Brett, and this confirmed it.

"Don't move," she said from the doorway.

I hadn't expected her, but I had known the risk. It was something I'd told Mick to take care of.

"Hello, Alma," I said, and smiled at her.

She was pointing a .38 at me, and there was an expression on her face that might have meant anything.

"Have you told anyone?" she asked. Her voice was low and controlled.

"The boot's on the other foot now, isn't it? Remember what you said, 'First Brett, then Max, now me.' It's my turn to say it to you."

"Have you told anyone?"

"Yeah. I'm sorry, kid, but I couldn't take any chances."

I was watching her knuckle turn white as she began to take in the slack of the trigger. It was an unpleasant moment. I thought she was going to give it to me before I was ready.

"Joe tipped you, didn't he?" I said. "I thought he would. The birthmark gave it away, didn't it, Alma? I knew the only way to find you was for you to come to me. As soon as Joe told you about the birthmark you knew I'd found out about Veda. It was Joe, wasn't it? It was Joe who let you out so you could kill Brett. You must have been very seductive to Joe, Alma."

"Don't call me that!"

"Why not? You're Alma Baillie, aren't you?"

"How long have I before they come?"

"Not long."

"How long, Floyd?"

The way she was looking at me now made my heart pound. I was always a sucker for women. If she had put down the gun I would have taken her in my arms.

"Not long. Listen, kid, why didn't you tell me? I would've looked after you. Why did you try to push Brett's killing onto me?"

"You were a natural for it, and I can't resist naturals. Have you told the police?"

"Redfern."

Her mouth set.

"All right, Floyd. At least you won't be at the trial."

"Shooting me won't get you anywhere. You can't get away, unless…"

"Unless...what?"

"Unless you clear me. I could fix it for you if you did that." All the time I was talking I was getting ready to jump her. I had pushed the suitcase out of my way, my muscles were tightening and I was judging the distance. It was going to be a pretty desperate jump.

"How?"

"Mick owns the police in this town. We could get you out of the country."

The awful little smile flickered at the corners of her mouth. I suddenly realized how Max must have felt when she was coming at him with the poker. I began to sweat.

"I don't trust you, Floyd. Once a cheap crook, always a cheap crook."

I was ready now. In another second she would see I was ready. It was now or never.

"Okay, Redfern," I shouted suddenly. "Come in and take her."

I had her rattled. She half turned to the door. I launched myself at her. I was a fraction late. The gun exploded in my face, and I felt a slug kick the top of my ear. Then I was on top of her, trying to grab her wrists. She was as quick and as slippery as a snake. She nearly rammed the gun in my side, but I knocked it away as she fired. I felt the slug rip through my coat. I could feel her hot breath against my cheek as I grabbed her gun hand and hung on. She hit and scratched at my face, twisted and kicked. But I had the gun now, wrenched it from her, threw her off and struggled to my feet.

As she came at me I yelled to her, but she didn't stop. She seemed to know I wouldn't shoot and she flung herself on me, snatching at the gun. I had to hit her. I didn't want to. Maybe you don't believe it, but I didn't.

"Stop it!" I yelled. I was scared by her ferocity. "Stop it, will you?"

Panting, she came at me again. I threw the gun away so I could grapple with her with both hands. Twice she nearly got my eyes with her fingernails. Blood was running down my face. As I got to my feet, she threw herself at the gun. I reached her as her hand closed around it, and I got hold of her dress. She kicked out at me, got up and jumped away. The dress ripped off her. She looked wild now with blood running down the side of her face from a cut over her eye. She was bringing up the gun as I grabbed her wrist. We fell on the bed. My hand was slippery with sweat and I couldn't hold her. She twisted away, fired at me. The slug chipped a bit out of my arm and as she fired again, I hit her wrist. The barrel swung toward her as the gun went off.

For a moment we lay staring at each other, then the gun dropped from her hand, and I got unsteadily to my feet.

"Veda!"

I scarcely heard the squeal of car tires on the gravel outside.

"Veda!"

"Satisfied?" There was a jeering note in her voice. She looked down at the hole in her side. Blood began to run down the blackened flesh where the gun flash had caught her. "Well, this is it, Floyd." Her voice was in a choked whisper. "I hope it makes you happy."

"You fool! Why did you fight? I could have got you away if only you had cleared me."

The door jerked open and Redfern came in. Behind him was Summers.

"Why didn't you come before?" I blurted out. "Why the hell didn't you come before?"

"It's Jackson!"

Summers threw a gun on me.

"Hold it!" he snarled. "One move and you get it."

"She's hurt. Do something! Get a doctor!"

Redfern went over to Veda. I heard him say, "Did he shoot you?"

She said, "Yes, and he shot Brett. He killed Max Otis, too. Make him show you where he buried Otis. Don't let him get away with it."

"Veda!" I went to her, pushing Redfern aside. "Don't bluff. I have all the evidence I want. Tell them the truth."

She laughed at me. "Poor cheap little crook. It's not coming right for you this time."

She was white and her eyes seemed to have sunk deep into their sockets.

"Veda—"

"All right, Jackson, leave her alone," Redfern said curtly. "Take him out of here," he went on to Summers. "Watch him."

"I'm not leaving her—" I began.

Summers hit me on the side of my jaw. His cameo ring and his fist knocked me silly. I went down on my hands and knees. She was laughing as he dragged me out.

It took me a minute or so to recover from that punch; by that time a couple of uniformed cops were in charge of me. I sat in the lounge and tried to stop the bleeding where the ring had ripped my cheek while Summers watched me and the two cops stood behind me.

"I want to see her—" I began, but Summers raised his fist.

"Shut up, you! If you want another poke in the puss, open your trap and you'll get it."

I waited. After a while an ambulance arrived. Minutes ticked past, then Redfern came in.

"I want to see her before she goes," I said.

He came over and stared down at me.

"She's dead, Jackson. Seeing her won't do you any good."

I felt a sudden emptiness inside me, but it was no good grieving. It was the best way out for her.

"Now, look, Redfern, I didn't kill her. I told Casy to call you up and let you know where I was and what I was doing. You were late, and she caught me. We fought. In the struggle the gun went off. It was an accident."

"All right," Redfern said, "it was an accident. Casy says you've cracked the case. You'd better start talking." He looked at the two cops. "Okay, boys, beat it. Stick around outside."

When they had gone, he sat down opposite me.

"So you know who killed Brett?"

"I know. I want to make a statement."

Summers pulled up a chair, took out a notebook and sat down at a table.

"Go ahead," he said.

"It starts back two years ago. Remember the Baillies? Verne was killed, but Alma got away. She went into hiding. A year later she was recognized and the hunt started all over again. She made for Hollywood. On the road she ran into a girl named Veda Rux, who was also going to Hollywood. Veda wanted a lift and Alma reckoned it would be safer for her to travel with another girl as the Feds were looking for only one girl. They traveled together, and Veda told Alma her life story and background. Alma hit on the idea of changing identities. She killed Veda, changed clothes with her, wrecked the car and set fire to it. The federal agent who found the car and the burned body wanted the reward. He knew there had been two girls in the car, so did the sheriff of Gallup, but they kept quiet about that, swore it was Alma's body and shared the reward. Veda was buried as Alma, and Alma was free to begin a new life."

Redfern lit a cigarette. "You're getting all this?" he asked Summers.

"I'm getting it," Summers said and sneered.

"Go on," Redfern said.

"If you know anything about the Baillies, you'll know Alma was crazy about her husband. He had given her a gold powder compact and she couldn't part with it. You might get it. It's in the suitcase on the bed."

Summers went out of the room and came back with the suitcase. I took the compact from him. I was aware both of them eyed the wad of money with more interest than the compact.

"Have a look at it," I said, and lifted the lid. "You'll see a photograph of Verne and Alma inside and across the photo the words 'For Alma from Verne: a man's best friend is his wife,' and if you'll study the photograph you'll recognize the girl who called herself Veda Rux."

Redfern took the compact and examined it, then with a little grunt slipped it into his pocket.

"Go on."

"Veda couldn't part with the compact although she knew it was dangerous, and that started the trouble." I went on to tell him how she had walked in her sleep, taken the Cellini dagger and left the compact in its place; how Boyd had bribed Gorman and her to let him have the dagger, and how Gorman had come to me to get the compact from Brett's safe.

"Neither Gorman nor Boyd knew how important the compact was to Veda. They thought it would connect her with the stealing of the dagger. She knew it would mean much more than that. It would reveal her true identity, and don't forget she was wanted for murder."

I went on to tell how I had played it and had hidden the compact, hoping to make money out of it, and how Veda, desperate to get it, had pretended to join forces with me. I showed Redfern Brett's card. "While we were in hiding, I showed the card to Veda. That told her Brett had seen inside the compact. I don't know how that happened, unless Brett had found the compact where I had hidden it and the inscription had puzzled him. He must have jotted the words down, meaning to make enquiries. Veda knew she had to kill him before he gave her away. I provided an alibi for her by keeping her locked up in Casy's penthouse under guard. But she persuaded the guard, a guy named Joe, to let her out, and she followed me to Brett's place. It was easy for her to walk in and get the gun. Brett knew her, and he may have thought she had changed her mind and was going to be nice to him. Anyway, she shot him. It's my guess the compact and the money were on the desk. All she had to do was to pick them up, get out of the way while I walked into trouble. Well, you know the rest of it. I've checked most of the facts, but the compact speaks for itself. You can see how it is."

"How about this guy Otis she talked about?" Redfern demanded.

"She killed him."

Redfern got up. "Let's go and find him."

"Now, wait a minute—"

"Come on."

We drove up in three cars. I went first with two cops. Redfern and Summers behind me and the prowl boys in the rear.

I showed them where we had buried Max, and they

dug him up. We stood around in silence while the prowl boys wrapped him in a rubber sheet and put him in one of the cars. Then we drove to the shack, and I showed them where he had died.

"I thought she had killed him in her sleep, but that was an act," I explained. "Max knew she was Alma Baillie. She told me she had caught him looking through her things. My guess is he found the compact and recognized the photograph. She realized she'd have to silence him before he told me. She had to kill him while I was there, and she hit on the idea of pretending to kill him in her sleep, and I was sucker enough to believe her. She pretended to try to kill me, too, to strengthen her act, and she got away with it. As soon as she was sure I didn't suspect her of either killing Brett or knowing she had killed Max, she left me. I found out Max knew about the inscription in the compact, and that put me on to her. Two men had known about the inscription, and both of them had died. I knew she had killed Max. It was easy to guess she had killed Brett. Then I remembered she had carried dark hair dye around with her. She was dark, and she wouldn't need it unless she was fair and was retouching her dyed hair.

"Do you get it? That put me on to the idea she wasn't Veda at all. I checked, made enquiries, found Veda had brown eyes, was left-handed and had a birthmark. The Veda I knew didn't have a birthmark—she had blue eyes and wasn't left-handed. I traced her here and before coming out here I told Casy to call you and get you out here, too. You were a little late. If you'd got here sooner she wouldn't have shot herself. That's about all."

"Okay, Jackson," Redfern said, getting to his feet. "We'll go down to headquarters now and get the statement typed, then we'll have another talk."

I didn't like the way he looked at me nor the cold edge

in his voice. We drove down to headquarters, and they left me in a room with a couple of cops while my statement was being typed. It was a long and uneasy wait. Neither of the cops said anything to me, and when I spoke to them they stared at me like a couple of deaf mutes. Finally, Summers came in.

"Come on," he said, and I didn't like the sneering grin he gave me.

We went down the passage and into Redfern's office. Summers closed the door and set his back against it. There was an odd atmosphere in the room. I couldn't make it out.

Redfern waved to a chair. "Sit down."

I sat down.

There was a pause while he glanced through a number of typewritten sheets that lay before him on the desk.

"I've been through all this," he said, and looked up. There was an amused expression in his eyes that startled me. "It reads like a hophead's nightmare, doesn't it?"

"I guess so, but that's how it happened."

"Oh, sure." He pushed the sheets away and folded his hands on the desk. "There's a lot of checking to be done. To make this story stand up, we'll have to get Boyd to admit he engineered the theft of the dagger, and that won't be easy. Boyd has a lot of money and influence. Then we'll have to get this guy Joe to admit he let the Rux girl out of the penthouse to murder Brett, and he may not want to put himself wrong with Casy. Then we'll have to get this federal agent to admit he lied when he identified the body as Alma's. It'll cost him his pension and he may think it safer to stick to his story. That goes for the sheriff of Gallup."

"I know all that, but that's what the police are for. You could make these guys talk. It only needs a little rough stuff," I said, staring at him.

"Sure, but I don't think I'm going to be bothered. It'll cost the state money and it'll take up a lot of time. Time and money are valuable, Jackson."

"If you don't do it, how the hell are you going to crack this case? You don't expect me to do it, do you?"

Redfern smiled.

"I'll let you into a secret, Jackson. I'm tired of being a copper. The political setup in this town is getting too tough. It's too hard to keep honest. I'm getting out and so is Summers."

"I don't get this. What's that to do with the case... with me?"

"Plenty." He lit a cigarette. "It has plenty to do with him, hasn't it, Summers?"

"It certainly has," Summers said, and showed his big yellow teeth in a grin.

"Suppose you tell me?" I said, and felt a chill run up my spine.

"The only thing that hooks this case together is the compact. That's right, isn't it?"

"Well, yes. It's important, but if you dig a little you'll get other evidence."

"The compact is the only link that proves Alma Baillie masqueraded as Veda Rux. No other evidence you or I could produce would do that, would it?"

"That's right."

"We have a big furnace down in the basement. Summers went down there an hour ago and dropped the compact right in the middle of it."

For a moment I could only stare at him, then I went cold.

"What the hell do you mean?" I shouted, and jumped to my feet.

"Sit down," Summers snarled and closed his fist. I remembered his cameo ring. I sat down.

"What is this?" I went on, but I knew all right.

"Look at it from our point of view," Redfern said quietly. "It doesn't matter a damn to us about the compact. We don't want it. It only complicates things. I'm satisfied you killed this girl, Rux or Baillie or whoever she was. I don't care who she was, nor does anyone else. I don't care if she killed Brett, or Otis, or if you did. Nor does anyone else—but you, and you don't count. I'm charging you with the murder of Veda Rux, and to save time and money I'm also charging you with the murder of Brett and Otis."

"You can't do it!" I cried. "It's murder, Redfern. You know I didn't kill her."

"That's the way it is, Jackson. I've had to wait a long time to get you where I want you. I've got you now. You've been very smooth and tricky and you've talked yourself out of a lot of grief in the past, but I don't think you'll talk yourself out of this this time. The compact's gone. Boyd won't talk. Joe won't talk. The federal dick won't talk. Summers and I are splitting the reward. There's also the twenty grand you say the Rux girl stole from Brett. We might as well have that. They'll think you've spent it. Do you get the idea now, Jackson?"

"If you think you're going to get away with this you're crazy," I said, but I had a hollow feeling inside me. He could get away with it.

"You watch and see. You're going up for trial, Jackson. You can trot out your story, but you won't make it stick. It's a hophead story. The jury will laugh at you. But my yarn will stick. She signed a statement before she died. It's the kind of statement a jury will love. I took care of that. Somehow I don't think she thought much of you. She played you for a sucker from the beginning." He nodded to Summers. "Okay, take him away." To me, he said with a grin, "So long, sucker."

Well, that's the way it is. I've written it all down from beginning to end so my lawyer has something to work on. And he's working on it, but I don't like the doubtful look in his eyes. He keeps talking about the past, and how the other side has raked up a lot of stuff about my record, the blackmail and women. He says without the compact he's helpless, and I don't think he knows what to do. It won't be long now. The trial begins tomorrow. The newspapers say it's a foregone conclusion. Redfern thinks it is. He tells me after they've finished me he's going to retire. He and Summers are buying a chicken farm. Odd how these dicks pin their faith on chickens. Casy comes to see me. He's not cheerful. The cops have put Joe under protective arrest so Mick can't get at him. But he swears he'll get me off. I don't know how he's going to do it—he doesn't either.

I keep thinking of Veda. I'm sure she loved me. If I hadn't tipped Redfern that she was in San Bernadino she wouldn't have signed that statement. But she reckoned I had double-crossed her, and she was right, of course. Well, it's too late now. I keep seeing her in my dreams. She's laughing at me. I hear her voice. "Poor cheap little crook. It's not coming right for you this time." It's getting on my nerves.

Why go on? The trial's tomorrow, and tomorrow is another day. I guess I'll get some sleep even if it does mean dreaming about Veda. I have a feeling she's not going to worry me much longer, but it's no good being pessimistic. I'll have to wait and see.

HARLEQUIN®
VINTAGE
COLLECTION™

KISS YOUR ELBOW

ALAN HANDLEY

In the theater reality and make-believe blend so intimately that Tim Briscoe was convinced he was playing the role of detective when he stumbled upon the lifeless form of Nellie Brant. But the corpse was real, even though everything else seemed fantastic.

There was the elusive man, the actress who chose sudden death for an audition, the onetime silent-film star, who stooged on quiz shows for his daily bottle, and Maggie, who loved him but didn't believe in the effect of too many Scotches.

Available now for a limited time only!

COLLECT ALL SIX ORIGINAL NOVELS FROM HARLEQUIN'S EARLIEST YEARS!

www.eHarlequin.com

VCKYE